MW00478922

USS POWDERKEG

Also by Max Allan Collins from Brash Books
The Perdition Saga
Road to Perdition
Road to Purgatory
Road to Paradise

Black Hats

USS POWDERKEG

MAX ALLAN COLLINS

BRASH
BOOKS

The characters and events portrayed in this book are fictitious. Any similarity to real persons, living or dead, is coincidental and not intended by the author.

Text copyright © 2008, 2018 Max Allan Collins All rights reserved.

Originally published under the title
Red Sky in Morning as by Patrick Culhane.

No part of this book may be reproduced, or stored in a retrieval system, or transmitted in any form or by any means, electronic, mechanical, photocopying, recording, or otherwise, without express written permission of the publisher.

ISBN: 1732065659
ISBN 13: 978-1732065659

Published by Brash Books, LLC 12120 State
Line #253, Leawood, Kansas 66209

www.brash-books.com

AUTHOR'S NOTE

This novel uses the historical setting of World War II, drawing upon experiences in the life of the author's father.

Nonetheless, liberties have been taken and certain known errors of fact have been included to suit the story.

The USS *Liberty Hill Victory* is a fictional ship based in part upon the real USS *Red Oak Victory*. With the exception of public figures mentioned in passing, the characters herein are fictional; and with the exception of the Port Chicago disaster and various major naval and military battles, the events in this novel are similarly fictional.

Readers are advised that the theme, time frame, and characterizations of this novel reflect offensive attitudes of the day, including unpleasant language in matters of race and sexual orientation.

USS Powderkeg was originally published in 2008 as *Red Sky in Morning* under the byline Patrick Culhane. Both the title and the byline were forced upon me, although *Red Sky in Morning* was a title I provided as a replacement for what had always been my intended title. The publisher had been pressured by someone at a major (and now defunct book chain) to publish two stand-alone thrillers of mine under a pseudonym, supposedly because I was typed as a writer of series fiction. I objected – the success of *Road to Perdition*, the Academy Award-winning 2002 film based on my graphic novel, had given my byline a higher profile and new credibility. But the publisher caved, and eventually – having little choice – so did I.

DALLAS MURPHY

Now, thanks to Brash Books, I have been able to revisit the novel, revising and tightening the text and correcting some errors (pointed out by keen-eyed readers), creating the definitive version of this novel – under its real name...and mine.

IN MEMORY OF MY FATHER,
WHO LIVED THE TALE

"Red sky at night, sailor's delight.
Red sky in morning, sailor take warning."
ITALIAN PROVERB

"I learned about machinery,
I learned how men behaved under pressure,
And I learned about Americans.
HERMAN WOUK
on his Navy service during World War II

ONE

JUNE 6, 1944

Ensign Peter Maxwell came slowly awake, teased by the expanse of ocean shimmering with morning sun out the bay window of the studio apartment. On a beachhead in Normandy, a battle had been raging for nine hours now; but this was San Diego, California, where Maxwell's war had been a quiet one so far.

The Murphy bed creaked as he turned onto his left side, away from the sun, to face Kay who, despite the creak of the bedsprings, had not stirred. His wife's easy, even breathing tried to lull him back to sleep and, though suddenly wide awake, he somehow couldn't manage to throw back the covers and climb out onto the cool wooden floor. Instead, he just lay there contentedly staring at her.

Like Pete, Kay was twenty-two, a brunette whose hair tickled the tops of her shoulders, with an oval face, wide-set blue eyes (concealed now behind long-lashed lids), a cute pug nose, and bee-stung lips. She was a petite five feet but curvy, possessed of the kind of Betty Grable figure that made a war worth fighting.

Kay had first come to Pete's attention when they were both sophomores in high school back in Liberty Hill, Iowa. A new girl in town (her father managed a chain grocery store out of Des Moines), she'd become instantly popular, thanks to her bubbly personality and fresh good looks. Soon she was head cheerleader to his captain of the football team, the couple well on their way to a King and Queen of the Senior Prom destiny.

But at first Kay had resisted that fate; at six foot, the brown-haired, dark-blue-eyed Pete towered over her, and she professed to find him obnoxious and pushy and just "too darn full of himself." Pete had persisted, teasing her in the high school hallways, and playing up to her girl friends, getting them on his side—always a key tactic in the battle of the sexes.

"You know," Kay said, in the sultry alto that didn't quite fit her all-American good girl looks, "we really can't go together. It's completely out of the question."

They were on their third date, seated in one of half a dozen jalopies parked out at Miller's Grove. Clouds were drifting across the full moon's face like wispy smoke, Kay looking pretty and pale in the ivory light, the bright red of her lipstick a dab of Technicolor in this black-and-white night.

Pete had his arm around her. "Why is going together out of the question?"

She put her head on his shoulder. "Because we are the complete cliché, you goofus."

"I *may* be a goofus—"

"No 'may' about it."

"Fine. Make it a complete goofus, far as I care. But we're *not* the complete cliché."

It should be noted that during their sophomore year at Liberty Hill High, everybody was using the words "complete" and "completely" a lot.

"Why *aren't* we the complete cliché, you big goof?"

He grinned. "Because I'm an end."

"What does that have to do with the price of beans?"

"If we *were* the complete cliché, I'd have to be the quarterback. And you'd have to be beautiful. Not just completely pretty."

She'd started laughing halfway through that, and now she slapped at his chest, and then she didn't stop him when he tried to kiss her. He got to second base that night, matter of fact.

The couple had been joined at the hip throughout the rest of high school. Their only brief separations came when Pete would travel one weekend a month to Des Moines for his training with the Navy Reserves.

Even then, war had been in the air and Pete (and his pop) had known that waiting for the inevitable draft meant Pete would wind up in the Army, which would put his future in the hands of Uncle Sam. And as much as he might love his country, Pete was prepared to keep his future in his own hands, thank you very much.

So, by joining the Navy Reserves, he'd managed some small part in choosing his own destiny; and to Pete, somebody taking potshots at a ship he was on was a better bet than the hellish trench warfare he'd heard about from his pop and his uncles, who'd fought in the last worldwide conflict, "The War to End All Wars."

Till this one.

He had been at the home of his Simpson College band professor, in Indianola, Iowa, Sunday morning, after church, rehearsing with the brass quartet, when they heard about Pearl Harbor.

They were playing along with Duke Ellington's "Take the A Train" on the radio when the song abruptly stopped and the quartet came to a ragged halt as a newscaster broke in.

"*This is Jonathan Manning with a WHO special news bulletin. The Japanese have attacked Pearl Harbor, Hawaii. Few details are available at this time. Stay tuned to WHO....*"

Pete was then in his second year at Simpson on a joint music and athletic scholarship, a rare jock (football, baseball, basketball) majoring in music (vocal and trumpet). Kay had followed him to Indianola but not as a coed: she was living with an aunt in nearby Des Moines and working for the phone company, saving up money for their marriage, after Pete graduated.

They'd gone together for over three years by then, and had done a lot of fooling around, heavy-duty smooching and petting; but that night of December 7, 1941, they'd taken a motel room in

3

Des Moines and gone all the way. Neither enjoyed it much, and a lot of crying had gone on, little of it having to do with the sex and a lot of it having to do with their certainty that Pete would soon be called up.

"Let's get married," Kay said.

They were under skimpy covers and December wind was howling out the motel-room windows, rattling glass and wood.

"Well of course we're getting married," Pete said.

"Right away, I mean. Run off somewhere. Elope."

"Can't. They won't allow it."

She frowned. "Who won't?"

"The Navy. I'm going after my commission and you can't get your commission if you're married."

"But afterwards...?"

"Right after. I promise."

The unkept promise of that commission dangled tauntingly before both Pete and Kay for what seemed an eternity. Pete started out an apprentice seaman, lowest rung on the Naval ladder. He was sent to Portsmouth, Virginia, by Norfolk, and on his first day he peeled potatoes until his hands were raw and then he peeled them some more; and on the second day, he cleaned latrines until his hands achieved a further rawness previously unknown to humankind.

That night Pete went to the chaplain's office, to seek some advice or solace or whatever he might find there that involved neither potato peeler nor toilet-bowl brush and noticed a sign on the bulletin board seeking members for the Norfolk Navy Center choir.

He went right over and signed up, and got in the choir, and a quartet to boot, and sang in both for several months—at churches and grade schools and junior highs and high schools and even on the radio for NBC and the BBC.

"That's wonderful," Kay had said over the long-distance telephone, when he reported his good luck.

"Beats the hell outa peeling potatoes and cleaning the can."

"What's next for you?"

"Columbia University."

"... What a wonderful opportunity!"

He knew, from her pause, that she was experiencing a pang of jealousy or envy or maybe worry, at not being with him. Or maybe the long-distance crackle was just lending a brittleness to her voice that couldn't be held against her.

In full support swing now, she was saying, "Studying in New York... I know it's rough sometimes, darling, but the Navy really *is* doing a lot for you."

That was true as far as it went; but the greater truth was that officers and ensigns were getting killed off with an alarming rapidity in this new war. And any guy like Pete, with some college under his belt, was a good bet for cannon fodder. ...

Yet even for that questionable privilege, a would-be Navy man had to struggle. Columbia had been a challenge for Pete, who as a music major had taken little math; piled with Navigation, Seamanship, Damage Control and all sorts of engineering courses, he'd faced a test at the beginning of class every day. And of the sixteen hundred in Pete's class, four hundred would not be there at the end.

Pete had not washed out. He divided his time equally between each class and did his best, staying right in the middle, grade-wise, knowing that if you were low in any one class on the weekend, you didn't get liberty—and Pete Maxwell never lost a liberty.

And once again, a notice on a bulletin board had come along, if not to his rescue, then to save his sanity: volunteers were being sought for the Midshipmen's Band. And Pete had broken the solemn Naval rule of never volunteering, and got right in.

"What does it mean?" Kay asked on the phone.

"Well, we practice twice a week, and play for the march in review, and everybody Navy in New York comes and watches on Saturdays."

"How exciting!"

But he could hear the longing in her voice.

So he tried to play it down. "It's not bad."

"Where do you play?"

"Oh, all around the New York area."

"And you looking so cute in your uniform. ... Don't let those New York girls get any ideas!"

"They can get all the ideas they want, 'cause ..." He crooned the finish: "... *I only have eyes for you.*"

She laughed. "You musical goof."

"And get this, honey—they're looking for a director. I'm one of seven who gets to try out. And if I make it, I'll be an officer. A two-striper."

"Oh, Pete, I know you can do it!"

And Pete had. After calling his pop for some advice, he'd gone to the music library and picked out a hard piece that he played in high school for the state music competition; he'd won in high school, and he won now. He got his two stripes and the punishment of the hard courses was eased by the joy of playing music.

Then, after graduation, newly minted Ensign Maxwell had gone back to Iowa for two weeks' leave, and he and Kay had had a big church wedding in Liberty Hill. Not many their age were there, just old people and little kids, but it had been nice to be home, even though Pete knew his lucky streak had run out: he'd been assigned to Amphibious Duty.

To get away from relatives, he and Kay shacked up in the Fort Des Moines Hotel and, after tears and lovemaking to last a lifetime (but still not enough), he'd left Kay in Des Moines and gone out to San Diego, or specifically Coronado.

He was assigned to an APA unit that would hit the beach on an invasion—each small boat would include a single ensign like Pete and a Navy coxswain and the troops they'd be taking ashore. During the thirteen weeks of training, an ominous statistic hung over the heads of all the ensigns in the program: to date, in that unit, 85 percent of their rank had been killed.

The day before Pete's training was set to end, at 8 a.m., another ensign came up to him and asked, "Are you Ensign Maxwell?"

"Yes."

"I'm relieving you of your duty."

"For how long?"

"Permanently. Report to Lieutenant Elder."

Wondering what he'd done, Pete reported to the lieutenant, a big good-looking Jewish guy, who said, "Ensign Maxwell, you're being assigned to Ship's Company for ten to twelve months."

Which meant Pete would stay on the base, that he wouldn't be going overseas, at least for now.

"Would you … mind if I called my wife and told her?"

The lieutenant had been amused by that, saying, "Go right ahead. But aren't you interested in why this change of duty?"

"I'm from Iowa, sir. We know all about gift horses."

Elder laughed again. "We need somebody to conduct the base choir. And your record speaks highly of your skills in that regard. How does that sound, Ensign?"

"Just fine, sir."

Afterward, strolling along past low-slung Ingram Plaza, he'd reflected with no little embarrassment on his youthful daydreams, back when he first joined the Naval Reserves—standing on deck, cannon fire raining all around him as he held valiantly to a lashed line with one hand while with the other wielding a cutlass, Tyrone Power-style, against a shadowy enemy, all the while, yelling, "Damn the torpedoes, full speed ahead!"

If the reality of his wartime service instead meant conducting the base choir at the U.S. Naval Training Station in San Diego, well, that was just fine with him—his hometown, Liberty Hill, had taken an ungodly number of casualties, including a dozen guys from Pete's senior class, making the various dire statistics hanging over Navy combat duty very real. Playing and directing music on dry sunny San Diego land wasn't the worst way to serve your country.

And he had been able to bring Kay out to join him and get a real good start on married life. After a few expensive weeks in a hotel near the El Cortez (its kitchen locked off so the couple could be charged hotel rates), the young couple had gotten these studio digs in the incongruously named I Have an Apartment Hotel.

The rent was steep, fifty bucks a month, but it had its own bathroom and that big window looking over the bay. Kay had taken a job at the nearby Western Union office as a teletype operator and that eased some of the burden on Pete's miniscule Navy pay.

The choir was why Pete had been spared an amphibious fate. They sang at Sunday services on the base, occasional appearances around San Diego, and even the odd bond rally now and then. Within the choir he created a quartet called the Fantail Four—three other officers assigned to base in various capacities—whose antics and mellow singing (their imitations of the Ink Spots and Mills Brothers were legend) found them playing opening act to USO shows coming through.

As to the choir itself, Pete took pride in the fact that the group of men he had inherited—some of whom, when he met them, couldn't carry a tune in a bucket—now sounded like a real honest-to-gosh choir. With personal appearances on and off base, building morale and spreading good public relations, this was a legitimate part of fighting the war on the home front. Or so Pete tried to convince himself.

Anyway, the choir was, officially, a sideline. His real job was under Captain Murray, a four-striper impressed with Pete's abilities to drill men. Pete worked with new trainees, getting their drilling up to snuff, and supervised night training, preparing these men to hit the beaches that Pete had been lucky enough to avoid, thanks to his musical skills.

But before long it had begun to nag at him, not guilty feelings exactly, but ... he wanted to do more. Here he was enjoying a life with Kay that included swimming in the ocean and afternoons at Mission Beach amusement park and the Balboa Park zoo—not to mention occasional weekends in Los Angeles, Grauman's Chinese for movies, and out dancing to big-name bands. And here he was directing a choir while preparing other guys to go do and die. ...

Studying Kay's face as she slept, he felt something that came over him on many a morning: he fell in love with her all over again, just as he had in high school, when she was calling him a goofus (she still did), and every time he experienced these feelings, again he wondered what the hell he was thinking, considering leaving her stateside to go and get his ass shot at in the Pacific.

Absentmindedly, like a painter applying a touch to a seemingly perfect portrait, he brushed a lock of dark hair from her face. Her eyes came open slowly and a smile blossomed. The pajama tops she wore were mostly unbuttoned and revealed the soft alabaster of her cleavage.

"Morning, glory," he said quietly.

"Is it? Morning?" She blinked and half-sat up and confirmed this opinion. Then she gave him a frowny smile. "Why so serious, silly?"

"I was just thinking."

She shook a finger at him. "You're in the Navy. You're not supposed to think. ... What *about* are you thinking?"

"Maybe ... about having my way with you."

She fiddled with his hair. "Having your way with me? ... Ensign Maxwell, is that any way for a Navy man to talk?"

He grinned and drew her to him. "No. I cleaned it up for you."

Kay started to laugh, but the sound was abruptly muffled as he covered her mouth with his.

She pushed him away. "I have morning breath! At least let me brush my teeth."

"Your breath is fine."

"Well, yours isn't!"

"I'm a man. I'm supposed to smell like this."

"Congratulations. Now go brush your teeth!"

Dutifully, a good little sailor, he obeyed his commanding officer; soon she padded in, the pajama tops barely covering up wonderfully indecent parts of her, to wait for him to finish, then brushed her teeth.

She was still in the foamy process when she asked, "Don't you need to get to work?"

"Yes, and we're wasting time."

She giggled, rinsed, and turned to him for the ritual unbuttoning of the pajama top. He was kissing the pink tips of her creamy pale breasts, right there in the cramped bathroom, when she said, "You're incorrigible."

"Then you shouldn't incorrige me," he said, and she groaned and laughed, and he picked her up in his arms and carried her like the naked bride she was from the bathroom threshold into the living room and the Murphy bed, depositing her there. Her perfect little bosomy twenty-two-year-old body was the most beautiful thing he had ever seen. He told her so, and kissed her in places he'd never dreamed of kissing a girl before he was married.

Fifteen minutes later, in a happy post-coital haze, he shaved, showered, and got into his crisp tan khaki uniform, then went over to tower above Kay, who still lay languorously in bed, sheet pulled to her pale throat.

Her husky alto purred, "Love 'em and leave 'em, huh, sailor?"

"Love you," he said, matching her kidding tone but dead serious. "Never leave you."

That got a smile out of her, but a funny one. "You *are* leaving, though."

Did she sense his inner struggle?

"Just for work," he said lightly. "And speaking of work, shouldn't you be getting ready, too?"

Kay shook her head. "Late shift tonight. I won't get off until nine."

"Want me to pick you up?"

"I appreciate the offer, but we both know what you want to do, with me working late, is haul your cornet down to one of those crummy jazz clubs and ..." She did a minstrel move, waving both hands. "... *wail!*"

"You think that's nice, making fun of an officer and a gentleman?"

She looked around. "I see the officer. Where's the gentleman?"

He leaned over, tugged at the sheet. "We could both take the day off. Sick call...."

She pulled the sheet up. "No, we can't. Somebody's gotta pay the rent."

"That's a low blow."

She heaved a pillow at him. "Get going! Go sing for your supper, Little Boy Blue, then go blow your horn. I'll get home just fine and be right here under this sheet for you."

"It's an incentive," he admitted.

Then from the closet he got the battered case that held his horn (the one his pop had played in a circus band years and years ago), and went off to war, which today meant drilling a bunch of hillbillies from the Deep South. When you took your eyes off of them, they'd peel off to try to skip class. It was like herding puppies. Or maybe hound dogs, in this case. Worse than colored boys.

The first thing he did when he got to the base, however, was look at the postings board. He'd made a daily ritual of this, since he'd done so well with bulletin boards in the past. But currently he wasn't looking for another musical opportunity.

He and the rest of his pals in the Fantail Four had vowed they'd do everything in their power to get off this darn base and into the war ... and together, on the same ship. The former would be easy, the latter tough—with the action in the Pacific intensifying, junior officers were being snapped up at an alarming rate, and it was only dumb luck thus far that had kept the choir's quartet together.

Usually, orders just came down and one day an officer would be there, the next he wouldn't. Ensigns and lieutenant j.g.'s were being shipped out fast and furious, and Pete knew that if they stood any chance of sticking together, it would be on one of the new vessels being cranked out up the coast.

Kaiser Shipyards in Richmond, California, were turning out Victory ships at the rate of one every eighty-five to ninety days; and although they were the ammo and cargo variety, not destroyers or battleships or even (if Pete dared dream big enough) an aircraft carrier, these were still ships, carrying men going off to war, not to sing off-key in the base choir.

So, every day, first thing, Pete looked at the postings board and hoped that an opportunity would come along. It wasn't as if there hadn't been any chances. Each guy in the quartet had a special skill that kept him on base and away from overseas duty, so this gave the four more leeway in making a choice. And if the four hadn't been so dead set on staying together, they could have left San Diego nearly a year earlier.

But along about then, Ensign Vince Rosetti's wife had left him. None of them had ever met the woman, about whom Rosetti (second tenor in the Fantail Four) had seemed loath to speak even before he got the Dear John letter.

A thick-set guy of average height and mixed heritage, Rosetti—an ex–L.A. cop who had earned a night-school engineering degree—had curly black hair, coal-black eyes that burned right through you, and muscles on his muscles. When Vince Rosetti had climbed into a bottle after the Dear John, the other three took the better part of six months pulling his ass back out.

And when Rosetti had said, "Fuck this candy-ass land duty— I'm going the fuck to sea," the others in the quartet had agreed the time had come, all right, but they'd still do everything they could to face that adventure together.

The other members of the Fantail Four were Lieutenant (junior grade) Richard Driscoll (first tenor) and Ensign Ben Connor (bass). Driscoll outranked the others.

"Fellas," the lieutenant (j.g.) had said early on in rehearsal, "please don't think anything as insignificant as military rank puts me above you."

"White of you," Connor had said.

Driscoll's grin was dazzling, one-hundred-watts, easy. "I'll let my social station take care of that."

"You prick," Rosetti said, laughing.

Driscoll—richer than God and better educated than Jesus ("Haah-vuhd")—was movie-star handsome with swept-back blond hair and sky-blue eyes. The son of a buck had it all and knew it...but Pete figured the guy didn't flaunt his superiority as much as he could have. Driscoll's snootiness, they'd decided, was mostly just an act—a small, kidding (if on the square) facet of what made Driscoll, well, Driscoll...who was, for the most part, a decent enough Joe.

Though the rest of the Fantail Four liked (or at least tolerated) Driscoll, many others on the base were less impressed by the lieutenant (j.g.). Ben Connor, on the other hand, everybody liked, despite the fact that he was Jewish and "Connor" was his show-biz name.

In fact, whenever Driscoll would inform people he was one of "the Newport Driscolls," Connor would chime in that he was one of "the Brighton Beach Cohns."

Ben had changed his last name to Connor when he got a job writing in radio—having a Jewish last name was no drawback in that world, but Ben held ambitions about performing. Even so, one look told the world the guy was Jewish—Ben's short, curly brown hair was a bird's nest above a wide forehead, narrow dark eyes, and a hawkish nose. And the comedy writer's perpetual frown belied his dry wit, his hangdog puss somehow working to make every woman he met want to mother him.

"Maybe you got the money and the looks," Ben liked to tell Driscoll, "but the Jewboy gets the girls."

Everybody, even Driscoll, routinely roared at this, one of those running jokes that could always elicit a howl.

And Ben was a master joke smith, running or otherwise. In three short years, before the war, Ben had gone from writing news copy and commercials to a berth on the hugely popular *Jack Benny Show*, making Connor one of the highest paid writers in radio. Responsible for many of Eddie "Rochester" Anderson's best lines, Connor wasn't above slipping a gravelly "Oh, Mr. Benny" into a conversation every now and then.

Pete was about to turn away from the board and trot off to choir rehearsal when his eye was caught by a slip of paper in the lower right-hand corner, just under the BUY BONDS and war-effort posters, a single thumbtack keeping the wind from getting it. He crouched to take in the posting and his eyes widened as he read.

Officers were being sought for a new Victory ship coming out of Kaiser Shipyard #1. Not just any Victory ship, either—this one had taken on a full cargo of coincidence with a significance that immediately magnified itself in the young ensign's mind.

The new ship had been christened Liberty Hill Victory *in honor of Pete Maxwell's tiny hometown.*

Not even bothering to look around to see if anyone was watching, Pete pulled off the posting and stood as straight as if at attention, mind whirling as he read it again. Four officers and four petty officers were being sought to lead the crew.

Now Pete knew providence was on his side. For all the church choirs he'd been in, and even had led, he didn't consider himself particularly religious; but this, *this,* had to be a sign from above.

A letter from his mother, months ago, had unwittingly explained why a Navy cargo ship was being named after a small town in southeast Iowa: most of Liberty Hill's sons had ended up in Company M of the Iowa National Guard, their unit at Kasserine Pass in Africa when Rommel counterattacked the Allies. Twenty-seven of Liberty Hill's young men went missing in that one battle. Another eighty were declared missing at some time during the war, and fifty had been declared Killed in Action.

The town only had five thousand or so souls to begin with. The battle of Kasserine Pass helped elevate Liberty Hill, Iowa, from an inconsequential hamlet to the town in the USA with the greatest wartime loss per capita.

Pete folded the sheet carefully and put it in his shirt pocket, then practically skipped to the chapel, so like a happy little kid did he feel. The two-hour morning rehearsal dragged by, but that didn't keep Pete from being thorough—this was Tuesday, and they had a bond rally coming up on Friday.

He didn't have a chance to share his news with the rest of the Fantail Four after rehearsal, but he made a point of telling them to save him a seat at lunchtime. They all gave him a what-the-hell look—they *always* sat together at lunch—while he settled in to go over some new music with his accompanist.

When lunch finally rolled around, Pete sprinted over to the mess hall, which was in one of the wealth of two-story red-roofed stucco buildings making up much of the base. Driscoll and Connor already occupied a table near the far corner. Rosetti was halfway through the cafeteria line, his tray piled with food. Though the shortest of the quartet, Rosetti ate like (and had the metabolism of) a man half-again his size.

Pete ran his tray along the steel bars, taking a small bowl of peaches, a slice of yellow cake, and filling a heavy ceramic mug with coffee before he got to the main food tubs manned by three enlisted men who doled out generous portions of food nobody was wild about getting a serving of in the first place.

For example, the chipped beef on toast, which Pete skipped in favor of an egg salad sandwich and a soggy-looking dill pickle.

At the end of the line, he picked up something even the Navy cookies couldn't screw up: two fresh oranges, one for now, one for later.

Normally, the rule was get it in the mess, eat it in the mess; but in Southern California, nobody ever bitched if you took an extra orange. The running joke was always, "So many goddamn oranges around here, it's like they grow on trees." Pete had heard the stupid joke again and again, and hadn't laughed the first time—partly because, truth be told, the casual profanity of the Navy still bothered him.

Pete approached the long wooden table. The other three of the Fantail Four were dressed as he (and virtually every other patron in the officer's mess) was: khaki day uniform, open at the collar, white t-shirt peeking out, black socks, black shoes mirror-polished. The only difference was Pete, Rosetti, and Connor each had single gold bars on their collars, whereas Driscoll's were silver.

Shortish Rosetti plopped down next to lanky Driscoll; Connor, taller than the former and shorter than the latter, occupied a seat opposite. Fairly bursting with his news, Pete strode over to join them, almost spilling his tray in a near collision with another ensign in the aisle.

Connor, who had seen that, nodded as Pete approached. The writer's mouth was full, but his eyes indicated the chair beside him he'd saved.

"Maxie, my boy," Driscoll said, "how is the world treating you?"

"The world doesn't give two hoots about me," Pete said good-naturedly.

Driscoll raised both palms. "Language, Maxie, language! There are children present." He nodded toward Connor and Rosetti.

Pete set the tray next to Connor and settled into a creaking wooden chair. Connor watched him suspiciously as Pete put a paper napkin on his lap and smoothed it in a way that would make a mother proud.

"Why the shit-eating grin?" Connor asked Pete.

"What?" Pete asked innocently, but he was grinning. And, truth be told, it *was* probably shit-eating.

Speaking of which, Rosetti was studying his tray as if it were a great big lab slide crawling with germs, specifically the chipped beef on toast. "Fucking shit on a shingle again," he growled.

Driscoll just shook his head. "You had other choices, Rosie— of main course *and* of words... Maxie, how can a clean-cut child such as yourself bear to be around such a vulgarian?"

"I ain't Vulgarian," Rosetti said. "I'm half-Mexican, and half-Italian, I'll have you know."

They all looked at him, wondering if their friend could be this big an idiot.

Then Rosetti grinned, said, "Got ya, ya bastards," and the ex-cop dug into his chipped beef with the same enthusiasm he'd brought to cursing it.

"Droll," Driscoll said. "Very droll, Rosie. But you're still a vulgarian."

"Not sure what that means, exactly, Dick," Rosetti said through a big bitefull, "but comin' from a fourteen-karat tight-ass like you, I'll mark it a compliment."

Before tackling his sandwich, Pete withdrew the sheet of paper from his pocket, unfolded it, and passed it wordlessly to Connor.

The writer slipped into his growly Rochester impression. "Don't tell me I'm finally gettin' the *pink* slip? You do know, don't you, Mr. Benny, that me goin' on relief means a raise!"

Everybody laughed at that, even Pete, but he didn't respond to the wisecrack, pretending to be engrossed in his sandwich as Connor read the posting.

Finally, Connor said, "What the hell is the USS *Liberty Hill Victory*? It sounds like a bunch of words fallin' down the stairs."

"It's our *ship,* fellas," Pete said, chewing egg salad. "Our ship that has finally come in."

"Our ship *would* be called something that inelegant," Driscoll said, between bites of his own shit-on-a-shingle.

"Our ship?" Rosetti asked.

"If we want it to be," Pete said.

The comedy writer's dark eyes left the page and went to his friends, one at a time. "A new ammo ship," Connor said. "In need of four officers and four petty officers."

"Ammo ship," Driscoll said slowly, as if the words made a bad taste on his tongue. "As in ammunition? The variety that can blow up under one's keister, ammunition?"

"Liberty Hill..." Rosetti said, frowning. "Pete, isn't that the name of that piece-of-shit bump in the road you grew up in?"

Pete took a drink of his coffee, swallowed, then said, "It's not a bump in the road. It's a town of five thousand."

"I don't think five thousand qualifies as a town," Driscoll said, "except perhaps in the Philippines."

"Don't be a dick, Dick," Rosetti said. It was not the first time he'd said it and would not be the last.

"Why *not* an ammo ship?" Connor asked.

Driscoll's eyebrows rose and his nose twitched. *"We're all willing to lay our lives on the line in this war.* There's no question of that. But setting sail on a floating powder keg? We can do better."

"Can we?" Connor asked.

Driscoll, openly irritated now, said, "Boys and girls, didn't we agree at the last student council meeting that we'd go after a *war*ship?"

Connor's eyes trained on Driscoll like twin gun barrels. "What kind of war can anybody fight without ammo, Dick?"

Driscoll threw a hand in the air. "Jesus Christ on a goddamn crutch—you're as bad as the farm boy."

"I didn't grow up on a farm," Pete said tightly.

"No offense meant," Driscoll said smoothly. "We admire you, Maxie, one and all—we only rib you because we love you."

Rosetti farted with his lips. "You're as full of shit as a Christmas goose, Dickie boy."

"Yet another rural reference, and from a *city* boy, of all people!"

Pete was used to getting ribbed about his corn-country background, and not just by Driscoll. His pop had been a rural mail carrier, which meant young Pete had actually been pretty well off during the Depression, his father's government job secure when the paychecks of so many others had vanished. Pete hadn't been rich like Driscoll, but the Iowan had been able to stay in school, which was more than could be said for a lot of young men in his hometown.

So Pete said to Driscoll, "Fuck you, Dick."

Six amazed eyes fell on Pete, who'd never before uttered that forbidden word—a word he'd never heard prior to joining the Navy.

This outburst from Pete seemed to tell Driscoll he'd gone too far with the chiding; and, as ranking officer, the lieutenant led the discussion throughout lunch, without any notable prejudice toward either ammo ships or country boys. The Fantail Four simply weighed the pros and cons of trying to position themselves aboard the *Liberty Hill Victory*.

Pete barely noticed his lunch as he wolfed it down. He stabbed a last morsel of dry cake, swallowed it, and followed with a long pull on his coffee. Around him, the parley seemed to be winding down, a decision in the offing.

"I say it's a good opportunity," Rosetti said. "It's a brand-new ship, not one of these refurbished shit buckets. What more can we ask?"

Driscoll gave him a sideways look. "We could ask for a destroyer, or even a cruiser."

Connor said, "But what answer would we get? And how are we going to find a cruiser or destroyer that needs all four of us at the same time?" Leaning forward, Connor said, "Or are we just flappin' our gums when we say we wanna play a bigger part in winning this war? Just hearing ourselves talk, and then comin' up with excuses not to follow through?"

Shrugging, Driscoll said, "Maybe we shouldn't stick together. Maybe we should go after separate posts. Easier to manage."

"Yeah," Connor admitted, "but we have this posting in our hands *right now*.... Dick, do you feel like you're winning the war decoding messages in Crypto? Or you, Vince, is the base motor pool how you want to tell your grandkids you fought the war, playing grease monkey in San Diego? I've certainly had enough pushing papers and typing ten kinds of horseshit in the C.O.'s office. Personally, I think Pete's right. We should grab this chance—we may not get another."

Driscoll said nothing.

"I vote yes," Rosetti said.

"You *know* I'm in," Pete said.

"Me, too," Connor said. "Dick?"

All eyes turned to Driscoll. Looking like a tall Alan Ladd, he pushed back from the table, lighted up a cigarette with excruciating ceremony, and finally grinned at them.

"I was just testing you girls," he said. He exhaled smoke through his nose, a grinning dragon. "There are no other sons of bitches on land or sea I'd rather get blown to holy hell with. Where do I sign?"

TWO

JUNE 6, 1944

To Seaman Ulysses Grant Washington (Sarge to his friends), San Diego was a piece-of-shit city, sunshine be damned. Not that the South Side of Chicago was paradise, more like a ramshackle collection of wooden-frame houses; hell, when the wind came in off the lake, trash blew around like an ugly damn hail storm. But even at its worst, the South Side was big city, alive and full of itself.

You could stand on the corner of Forty-seventh and South Park, smack dab in the middle of the Black Belt, and see nothing but shades of humanity: black, brown, yellow, olive, even white (store owners mostly). Bronzeville was a Chicago within Chicago, with colored lawyers and doctors and dentists and even coppers (like Sarge had been). From that corner you could see theater marquees with Lena Horne, Eddie "Rochester" Anderson, and Hattie McDaniel headlining. And sooner or later, if you hung around long enough, every damn Negro in Illinois would pass along by.

San Diego, on the other hand, was a goddamn retirement village—seemed like the only people on the street who weren't sailors were elderly white folk. The downtown was tiny for a burg this big, despite some tall modern buildings, and the pace was slow, maybe a hangover from the old Spanish days. Of course, on the periphery, all sorts of nasty joints pandered to the Navy boys, tattoo parlors and shooting galleries and hamburger stands and chicken shacks and taverns. And taverns. And more taverns.

Not that Sarge was welcome in any of them.

Back in Chicago, when you left Bronzeville, you could time to time feel a chill in the air, sure; but nothing as outright bigoted as the signs posted all around downtown San Diego telling Sarge and his kind to keep out.

Of course, you didn't necessarily have to be a Negro to find prejudice on these sun-splashed streets—one restaurant advised NO SAILORS, DOGS, OR COLORED ALLOWED. Sarge qualified for two out of three, but what really galled his ass was dogs getting better billing than blacks. Mother-*fucker*!

Back in Bronzeville, Sarge had been a man of respect, a police officer. And not just some lowly beat cop, hell no—he had risen to the rank of sergeant (he wasn't called Sarge because of his Navy rank, that was damn sure!) and soon made plainclothes detective. He wore a suit and tie to work, a genuine professional man. Out here, even wearing one of Uncle Sam's uniforms, he was in line behind the goddamn dogs.

Six months ago, when he'd first arrived at the base, Sarge had asked other Negro sailors about the city, and they had told him it wasn't much.

Orville Monroe, a short, delicate-featured cream-in-your-coffee complexioned seaman from New Orleans, had effeminately said, "This is no place for a God-fearing colored man, Sarge. You think it's by chance they call it 'Little Georgia'? I'll say it ain't!"

Several other Negro sailors had warned Sarge the long-lashed little man was "queer as a three-dollar bill."

But Sarge didn't give a damn about such things. In his experience as a copper, he'd come to feel pity for homosexuals like little Orville—they were high-strung, emotional types who got made victims by fifty-seven varieties of motherfucker. Long as Monroe didn't try to mount his ass, Sarge couldn't care less where the little man stuck it or got stuck.

Orville's kind was no different than nobody else: relations with other humans, sexual or otherwise, got frequently screwed up—all cops knew this. Black or white, homo or otherwise, relationships were hard; and no matter whose heart got broke, it usually boiled down to one or more of four things: drugs, money, sex, or love (love and sex weren't always the same thing).

Anyway, with the shit colored people faced, why should one Negro hate another over something as goddamn trivial as who the other wanted to bump bones with? Long as it wasn't some other guy's wife or other wife's husband, who the hell cared? That was almost as stupid as displaying prejudice to another Negro because they were blacker or lighter than you were, though plenty of that went on, too.

Like most cops (and even in Navy blues he remained at heart a plainclothes dick), Sarge had developed a world-weary acceptance of such absurdities, otherwise he'd have long ago gone Section 8 himself.

Continuing on down the street as afternoon eased into dusk, Sarge—in an undertaker's black suit and white shirt and black tie—gazed through the windows of shops and restaurants that brandished the usual signs warning him not to enter. He was just strolling along, getting the fish eye from white people, taking his time and waiting for his only real friend on the base, Willie Wilson, to catch up with him.

He and Willie had met at Great Lakes Training Center, the sprawling facility near Lake Michigan, forty miles from Chicago. The two city boys (Willie was from St. Louis) were bunkmates at blacks-only Camp Robert Smalls, where they'd spent three months. Both had been struck by the strict segregation at chow time—whites in one line, blacks in the other, eating on separate floors of the mess hall—and also by the way the clothing of the colored recruits tipped off where they came from.

Deep South boys arrived in coveralls; fellas from the West, sports clothes; and big city east-of-the-Mississippi types like Sarge and Willie wore suits.

At first, their shared love of music had given Sarge and Willie something to talk about, and they'd spent rare liberties taking the bus into Chicago, where Sarge introduced Willie to the really hopping South Side jazz joints. Then in San Diego, after they'd learned their way around that city, they'd gone to the Logan Heights colored section, where the barbecue cooked in big ovens rivaled Willie's hometown's BBQ and little three-piece jazz combos cooked even better. Finally, it had gone beyond talking about music and enjoying other people's playing to where they could make their own noise—like tonight at the Silver Slipper, the only club outside of the Heights that catered to the Negro crowd.

Soon Sarge glommed Willie coming out of a drugstore up on the corner, a small paper bag in one hand, a battered saxophone case in the other. As he stepped onto the sidewalk, Willie eased the paper bag into the side pocket of his charcoal suit coat.

Willie stood maybe four inches shorter than Sarge's own six foot three and weighed in at around one fifty, maybe one fifty-five, a good fifty pounds shy of Sarge. Willie's white shirt contrasted with the dark brown of his complexion as well as the multi-colored tie that to Sarge looked like a big wide rag somebody used to wipe up several cans of spilled paint.

The sax man's hair was cut short to his scalp, making his high forehead seem even higher, his mustache of the pencil variety. Even though Willie had held only two jobs in his life— horn player and (now) steward's mate—his face was as somberly knowing as a country preacher's.

Sarge wasn't much of a smiler, himself; part of it was his copper's mask—if the people he encountered, from victims to villains, could read him, he was a dead man.

Between growing up on the South Side and being a cop most of his adult life, Sarge had seen enough shit in twenty-eight years to fertilize motherfucking Kansas. The scars on his cheeks, ghosts of the knife used on him by a pimp named Abraham Hines, were not the only scars that Sarge carried; and he seldom spoke about any of them, visible or not. Some of the people involved, Abraham Hines in particular, weren't talkative on the subject, either—Hines being dead.

Willie caught sight of Sarge and waved.

Sarge waved back and gave up a grin.

Willie ambled over, a smile tickling his somber mug. "And how is Sarge doin' on this beautiful evening?"

"Fine, Willie," Sarge said. "Just fine." He began walking and Willie fell in alongside. "Go on—tell me how good you was with that woman. Let's get that shit out of the way."

Willie swung his blank face toward Sarge. "What woman?"

Sarge's eyes narrowed in a sideways glance. "One above that drugstore. Big ol' mama only a blind fool would even bother with."

"Man, you must got me confused with some other Willie Wilson. It's a common damn name, you know."

"Ease up on the b.s., Willie. I'm a copper from way back. You know you can't lie to me, son."

"Well, first of all she ain't that old. Also, she ain't that big, except in the places where I prefers them that way."

They walked some more.

Then Sarge asked, "That all you got to say about it?"

"You want me to kiss and tell? Doesn't I look like a gentleman?"

"Yes," Sarge said, "and no."

They stopped at a light.

Willie shrugged. "Truth? God's honest truth? Man, she was great."

"Was she."

"Only…" Willie cackled, an infectious laugh that belied his somber mask. "…I was *better.*"

Shaking his head, laughing despite himself, Sarge said, "You gonna be better, son, right up till her man comes home and catches you on Nookie Patrol."

"He ain't gonna catch us," Willie said, shrugging that off. "Fool's on some damn island in the middle of the South Pacific."

Sarge slapped his friend lightly on the back of the skull. "You think you the only motherfucker ever get liberty?"

"What's he gonna do, swim home?" Willie asked with a sneer. "Anyways, you just jealous, Sarge. Probably ain't had any quiff since you left Chicago."

"Not since yo mama," Sarge said, slipping into the street game of "the dozens," which dated back to when the least desirable slaves on the auction block were sold by the dozen.

Willie took the bait. "Oh yeah? Yo mama's so fat that when she jumped in the air, she got stuck."

"That so? Well, yo mama so poor? When I see her kickin' a can down the street and ask her what she doin'? She say, 'Movin'.'"

Willie said, "Yo mama's so dumb when she jump off the Empire State Building, she ask for directions on the way down. ..."

They kept up the verbal jousting as they ambled along, heading for a restaurant that would actually serve them.

Of course, Maybelle's was a restaurant only by the loosest of definitions. In the middle of a colored neighborhood, Maybelle's was nothing more than a frame house where the furniture had been removed and replaced by mismatched tables and chairs in every room except the kitchen and bathroom. Butcher-paper tablecloths were simply torn away and discarded after customers finished. Nobody cared about the lack of niceties, because the food was downhome heaven—better than anything Sarge had eaten since his Grams had passed on in '39.

Fried chicken, mashed potatoes and gravy, biscuits, and greens. Big bosomy Maybelle herself (or one of her girls) brought the food to the tables in huge bowls that you passed around. Maybelle didn't bother with menus—you ate what they brought you or you went elsewhere.

As usual, Willie seemed more hungry for one of the waitresses than he did the food she was serving—a high yellow gal of seventeen, maybe eighteen, name of Pearl. Willie spent more time chewing the fat with her than anything on his plate.

When Pearl left to get them each a piece of pie, Sarge said, "One o' these times, one of these girls is gonna have a boyfriend who is just gonna up and kill your sorry ass."

Preacher-man sober again, Willie said, "Better one of them than some damn Jap. Least I'll have it comin'."

Sarge let out a laugh, and Pearl brought them their slabs of pie and they dug in. As evenings went, Sarge was having a pretty fair time...and they weren't even to the good part yet—best thing about snagging a liberty on Tuesday night was they could play at the Silver Slipper.

He and Willie had been at the Slipper half a dozen times and were both known as solid cats. Right off, they'd fallen in with a local rhythm section, a bass player named Roscoe Gregg and a kid drummer name of Marvin Hannah, who they had to smuggle in. Mostly, teenage Marvin hung close to Sarge in this rough company. Everybody knew that Sarge had been a cop in Chicago and the umbrella of his reputation seemed enough for all of them to stand under.

Well, all but that first night, anyway....

Few months ago, not long after Sarge arrived at the base, Willie brought him to the Slipper to listen to the Nat "King" Cole Trio, whose "Straighten Up and Fly Right" had just got them a recording contract. He and Willie were in the middle of having a fine old time when Sarge saw a guy on the dance floor just haul off and punch a woman in the face. A young girl it was, and she went down, mouth a bloody smear. The music stopped, and the bastard bent over to grab her arm and jerk her up so he could maybe give her another one.

Problem was, at least for the woman-slugger, the arm he latched on to belonged to Sarge, who had parted the crowd and bounded onto the dance floor and got himself between the bastard and his battered date.

"What the fuck you think you doin', boy?" the guy had said, through his teeth, the words like steam escaping.

"I ain't doin' nothin', friend," Sarge said, removing the hand from his arm like a leaf that had drifted and clung. "Just makin' my way across the dance floor in this free country."

The guy's upper lip curled back. "I ain't your friend, Scarface."

Sarge's eyes tightened but his voice stayed loose. "Man, that ain't polite. Like hitting ladies ain't polite. Your manners leave something to be desired."

"Does they?" The bastard brought out a switchblade from nowhere, like Bugs Bunny producing a carrot; he flicked it open with a nasty click. "Maybe you'd like to give me a lesson?"

"Put that away," Sarge said calmly, "and there be no need...."

The bastard lunged at Sarge, thin blade making a bee-line for Sarge's left ribcage.

But Sarge elbowed his attacker's arm, driving it (and the blade) down, coming around with a forearm that smashed into the wide-eyed, teeth-bared face, producing a satisfying crunch as the bastard's nose busted.

Sarge's opponent yelped like a kicked dog, and the knife clattered to the hard floor. A wounded beast now, flailing, the guy swung a wild left that Sarge easily blocked to send a left of his own into the bastard's belly, air *whooshing* out, doubling him over as if bowing to Sarge, who swung a hard right fist that caught the guy's chin, lifting him off his feet and dropping him like a feed sack onto the dance floor.

Of course, the girl the guy had punched was soon hovering over her fallen escort, glaring up at her savior with ingratitude, blood mingling with lipstick. "You hurt my Enos! You a bad man, mister!"

Still, it worked out. The punched Judy's beau turned out to have his own rep as a real bad ass... till that night, anyway. After that, nobody at the Slipper ever messed with Sarge, his friends, or anyone else in the place when Sarge was around. Even the bartenders seemed happy to see Sarge come in—like having a free extra bouncer—and Enos and his girl had not been seen on the premises since.

Night was settling over the city cool and breezy, riding a light wind that would've barely rated notice back in Bronzeville. But even so, Sarge felt a homesick pang. Still, he had Willie and he had his music and, for tonight anyway, that would have to do.

They split the bottle of bourbon on the walk to the Silver Slipper. Wasn't a big bottle and, especially after the big meal, got neither of them anywheres near drunk.

The booze did give Sarge a nice warm feeling in his belly and, despite his confidence in every other part of his life, a little liquor was the boost he needed to give him the courage to take the stage. Once he got up there and the music started in, he felt fine, at home even; but until they got going, sailing along on a song, he'd rather face a hopped-up razor-wielding stickup artist.

The quartet had gotten good, fast, in part because they found time to rehearse in the basement of the Baptist Church Marvin attended out here. Sarge didn't spend a lot of time in church anymore—he'd lost his faith six years ago, after a little girl got raped and killed and dumped in Washington Park—but this church had a piano in the basement, so Sarge enjoyed his time there more than he did in most houses of God.

Once they had started to improve, the fellas had talked about adding a trumpet or cornet player, but so far hadn't had any luck. They tried two guys out, and one couldn't play by ear and the other played in the key of Q, so fuck that. They made do without a horn.

Sarge and Willie ambled up to the white-bulb-framed entry of the Silver Slipper and both shook hands with the big bouncer/doorman—a very dark-skinned Negro called Booger, who grinned as wide as a piano keyboard (with just as many black keys). Booger was dressed almost identically to Sarge—black suit, white shirt, black tie—only this boy used up enough cloth to outfit a planeload of paratroopers.

They hung around and talked to Booger, who was a 4-F from L.A., and finally Roscoe and Marvin showed up, the kid carrying his sticks, Roscoe hauling the huge stand-up bass without a case, like it was something he'd found on the street.

Once inside the ballroom-like club, they didn't have to wait long for their turn on stage, the girl singer ahead of them meeting a tepid response to her pale Ella Fitzgerald imitation, and rushing through her second number just to get off.

Soon they'd set up (the house band's drum set and piano were made available to other acts) and were ready to go, the emcee strolling out onto the stage. The crowd had heard these boys before, and the band wasn't the only ones that were ready: the crowd was, too.

Even as the emcee—a tall skinny Negro in a tuxedo who claimed he was Cuban (not black and from a truck farm in Oklahoma), said into his fat microphone on its skinny stand, *"Ladies and gentlemen..."*

Marvin clicked his sticks, counting off the opening to "Cow Cow Boogie," a nice barrelhouse piano song that let Sarge show off a little. "...three, four."

"...the Sarge Washington Quartet!"

The crowd clapped and hooted, and the music began.

Pete Maxwell kept a set of civvies in the metal music cabinet downstairs in his choir director's office. Off duty for the day, he had returned to the chapel to change out of his uniform into a lightweight brown suit. He only owned two: a black woolen job for winter and funerals, and this one, bought for his June wedding to Kay three years ago. Under the suit, he wore a white shirt and a snazzy red tie with splashes of white and yellow.

He was still riding high on the lunchtime vote and the Fantail Four's subsequent bidding on the posting for the *Liberty*

Hill Victory. The fine print had said volunteers with some college and sports background would be preferred—"good-sized men" only. Now, Rosetti wasn't tall but he was good-sized by any yardstick, and both Pete and Driscoll had sports experience, and all four were college men.

So the prospects seemed good.

As the dying sun set fire to the ocean, Pete left the base, his battered horn case swinging easily in his left hand. He walked to a nearby corner, found a newsstand, bought a paper, and kept walking for another two blocks until he got to his favorite diner, LORETTO's glowing in blue neon over the door. Inside, the place was clean, quiet, with only a dozen or so other patrons.

Pete put the horn case down on one side of a booth near the counter and dropped gratefully into the other. A short, blonde waitress with a cherubic face and a ready smile hustled over with a glass of water.

"Usual?" she asked.

"Yes, Janey, please," he said, and she flounced off, but he hadn't even gotten his paper unfolded before she was back, setting the coffee on the table along with silverware.

He thanked her, but she was already gone again. He glanced down at the two-inch black letters of the headline: ALLIES INVADE FRANCE.

Eisenhower was taking the fight to the Nazis, banging on Hitler's door at Fortress Europe and hoping to march all the way to Berlin. A little shiver ran up Pete's spine—if this was how things were going in Europe, how long until the Allies pushed to march into Tokyo? And if a push was coming, Pete wanted to be a part of it. The Fantail Four may have made their move at exactly the right moment. ...

Just as he folded up the front section of the paper, the waitress returned with a huge platter that contained his burger, french-fried potatoes, and an ice-cream-scoop-sized mound of coleslaw on the side. She set down the plate and refilled his coffee.

"Anything else?" she asked cheerfully.

"This is enough. Jeez, Janey, there's a war going on, y'know."

"Yeah," she said, heading off, "and you're helping fight it."

Was he?

Reading the baseball scores while he ate was probably the only thing Pete missed from his life as a bachelor. He would never read the paper at the table while he was with Kay, so these few evenings when she worked late and he stopped at this diner were the only times he got to actually study the standings and box scores.

Pete had been a lifelong fan of the St. Louis Cardinals; his pop had taken him to a number of games at Sportsman's Park, and this year the Cards were in first place. Sure, it was only June, but his team was bucking for their third straight National League crown, having lost to the hated Yankees in the World Series last year and getting bounced by the Bronx Bombers in five the year before. Felt good to be rooting for a winner.

When he exited Loretto's, dusk was darkening to night, still a little early to hit the jazz clubs, so he walked his supper off, enjoying the mildly breezy San Diego weather, smoking a Chesterfield. He'd been a smoker since sixteen, but stayed at a pack a day, because he didn't want his singer's throat to get too rough.

As Pete strolled past shops displaying colorful dresses, skirts, and blouses, his thoughts turned to Kay. The invasion in France was good news for him, but he knew it would upset her.

They'd had the conversation more than once.

"Come on, baby. Don't you think Hitler's got to be stopped?"

"Of course I do. I just think that can happen without the intervention of my husband."

Then he would have to tell her about the Liberty ship posting, and how he and the others had put in for it. There would be tears, possibly anger, but finally she would support him. She always did.

San Diego was a sleepy place for a big city, and the people— a lot of them his folks' age or older—were friendly enough. But he remained surprised, even shocked, by the signs in restaurant and shop windows saying WHITES ONLY or NO COLOREDS. Growing up in a small Iowa town, Pete hadn't come into contact with many colored people, or prejudice against them, either, besides "Sambo" jokes. His parents and Sunday school had taught him that all men were created equal, but maybe that was an easy tenet to believe when everyone in town was the same color.

He had occasionally seen Negroes on his trips to Des Moines for Reserves training, but he had never interacted with any of them. The same was true of his short time at Simpson College, except for Tyrone Green, the son of a school janitor, who sometimes bussed tables in the cafeteria.

To Pete, Tyrone Green—who was saving up to go to a Negro college down south—had been as nice a guy as any on campus; and some casual conversation revealed their mutual appreciation for music, particularly jazz and big band. Tyrone had loaned Pete some Louis Armstrong sides that were out of this world, and Pete had shared Benny Goodman with Tyrone. Still, Pete had taken some guff from a few other students for making a friendly acquaintance out of Green; nothing he couldn't handle.

Some colored sailors were housed on the far side of the base, but they'd never auditioned for the choir, so Pete had no dealings with them. Maybe he should have sought them out, because there sure were some great Negro singers in the world—like Paul Robeson, or Mahaliah Jackson. And President Roosevelt had called for the integration of the armed forces; but truth was, the presidential proclamation had been more window dressing than actual policy. Pete knew if he'd recruited colored singers, he might lose some or all of his white choir members—this was one base with two different navies.

Pete had met a really interesting colored fella off the base—a saxophone player named Willie Wilson from St. Louis, a steward's mate, lowest of the low in the Navy, a glorified busboy and all but invisible. Willie had this sober-as-a-judge expression all the time, but a dry sense of humor that could blindside a guy.

The two Navy men had found themselves walking out of the base one night, in civvies, and each noticed the other was carrying a horn case. They exchanged a polite hello and walked together for a while, finally starting to talk some music—Duke Ellington, Billy Eckstine, Louis Jordan.

Wilson had asked him that night, "Sir... if you don't mind my askin'... what's a white boy like you doin' listenin' to race music?"

Pete blinked and thought about it and then grinned. "I never thought of it as race music. I mean, I dig Artie Shaw and there's a place for Glenn Miller, too."

"Yeah, but we might not *agree* on the place."

Pete laughed. "Come on, it's a nice sound. Even if it's kind of..."

"White bread?"

"Are you telling me you don't sop up the gravy with white bread like us Iowa boys?"

Willie smiled slyly. "I been known to."

"Anyway, race has nothing to do with it. Good music is good music."

Pretty soon Willie had then told Pete about the Silver Slipper, a jazz club frequented by Negroes, where the music was "red hot."

As he walked, the traffic thinned, the lights dimmed and before long he found himself in a neighborhood he might not ordinarily have ventured into, the red and white and blue of neon signs on bars and joints not seeming particularly patriotic.

Finally, he saw the glowing white neon and white-bulb-framed entrance of the Silver Slipper, the only "genuine night-club in this shithole city" (as Willie put it) that catered to colored.

Two house bands alternated nights, a trio headed by a smooth-voiced young singer named Nat "King" Cole, who was starting to get some radio air play, and a wild outfit led by saxophonist

Illinois Jacquet. Tonight, like every Tuesday, was amateur night, which was what drew Pete and his horn to the Silver Slipper.

A large Negro stood near the door. He wore a black suit with a white shirt and black tie, like a bus boy, only this guy looked more likely to bust a table in two than clear it. Three inches taller than Pete's six feet, the doorman was a yard wide, blacker than the inside of your fist, with a short, nappy haircut and an expression that registered instant dislike. This guardian at the Slipper's gate had dark little eyes that managed to burn right through Pete and yet stay ice cold.

"Evening," Pete said, not giving the guy a chance to say no, not even slowing down as he yanked open the door and slipped inside. His eyes adjusting to the dim light, Pete checked over his shoulder to see if the doorman was following him. So far so good. . . .

The colored hatcheck girl gave him a surprised but not unfriendly look, but Pete had neither hat nor coat to check, and he just moved on into the club. Bigger inside than the outside suggested, the Slipper reminded Pete of the Col Ballroom, which a combo of his had played a few times in Davenport, a bigger town upriver from Liberty Hill. Like that room, this one was deep and high-ceilinged, with bars at both left and right, and tables crowded together to form a U around an endless gleaming dance floor.

Music from a quartet on the classic proscenium-style stage washed over him: Duke's "Take the A Train," a nice job on a big band sound from a handful of players. He was smiling, enjoying the tune, as his eyes slowly scanned the room and told him, quickly, that he was the only white person here.

The joint was jumping, couples filling the dance floor doing gyrating, gymnastic variations on the jitterbug, and a cloud of smoke hung so thick you could have sliced it for bacon—he could barely make out the band up on stage.

Still, Pete could feel the sea of eyes on him. He felt a queasy sort of nervousness, as if he had just set foot on a strange yet eerily familiar planet. No one said a word to him as he slowly made his way to the bar on the right, but the unspoken question—*"What the hell is a white boy like you doing here?"*—rang out as if the hall were empty and not a note was being played. ...

The wait at the bar was two deep, but as Pete approached a space opened—somehow simultaneously respectful and threatening. The bartender, a tall, thin Negro with pressed hair and a pencil-thin mustache, said nothing, and his half-lidded eyes appraised Pete like a cockroach crawling across a kitchen counter.

"Beer," Pete said.

"Tap or bottle?"

"Tap."

"Pabst or Miller."

"Pabst."

The bartender drifted sullenly away.

Ignoring glares all around him, Pete turned his attention to the quartet on the stage. The drummer was a small man who looked like a teenager and who played without a suit coat, his sinuous arms moving smoothly, like fluid shadows extending from the rolled-up sleeves of his white shirt. The bass player was a rangy man in a black suit, his hair cropped short, eyes closed, lost in a private smile as he played.

The sax player was Willie Wilson, the steward's mate who'd told Pete about the club. Willie was soloing now, his eyes shut as he snake-charmer swayed, his fingers dancing over the keys, jitterbug couples on the floor showing their appreciation by pausing to watch and whoop and applaud.

As Willie's solo wound down, Pete joined in the clapping. Man, these colored players could riff like *crazy*. ...

The surly bartender returned with half a glass of beer. "Buck," he said.

"A buck? For half a glass?"

The bartender just stared at him.

Pete knew damn well that a full glass of beer should cost him no more than a dime. But he flipped a dollar onto the bar and returned his attention to the band. He was here for the music.

The piano player had taken over the solo. His skin shone under the lights, giving him an almost blue cast. Eight-ball bald, the pianist watched the audience shimmy to the notes he played, but he didn't smile, serious as a surgeon, operating on this crowd through the music. Pete could make out scars riding high on the man's left cheekbone like two black caterpillars clinging on to dark skin.

The solo wound round and round and finally found its way back to the melody, where the quartet played through another chorus, no riffing, and ended it.

The crowd went wild, and Pete was right with them. They were good for an amateur-night band, darn good. He caught Willie's eye, gave him a smile and a wave.

Willie stuck out his fingers and wiggled them, like he was playing another riff on a sax that was no longer there.

Pete frowned.

Willie widened his eyes and swung his head in a "come here" fashion. For a split second, Pete wondered if he really should accept the invitation. He'd brought his horn, obviously in hopes of getting on that stage; but he hadn't considered just how white he was and how black the Slipper would be....

Finally he sighed, heard his pop saying *Nothing ventured,* and guzzled down the warm beer—if only it had been as cold as the bartender—and as the applause started to die down, Pete headed across the dance floor toward the stage. The crowd parted, but not like Moses and the Red Sea, more like a bunch of Romans getting out of a leper's way. As he neared the stage, Pete realized the rest of the quartet seemed pointedly less enthusiastic about his presence than Willie.

Nonetheless, Pete climbed the stairs at one corner of the stage, and Willie came over and reached out a hand and shook with him. Though couples thronged the dance floor, the room had turned quieter than the Liberty Hill cemetery at midnight. The jitters he was feeling weren't simple stage fright—he never got that—but fear, sweaty-palmed fright, as countless whites of eyes in dark faces fixed on him, the stage lights turning Pete paler, making a ghost of him.

The silence took on a leaden heaviness, and everybody but Pete stood frozen in place. He pretended not to notice as he set his case down and knelt to withdraw his cornet from its velvet berth. He stuck in a mouthpiece, ran his fingers over the three keys and used the spit valve, then swung his eyes over to Willie Wilson, who seemed pretty nervous himself about now.

Finally, the bass player broke the silence. "You expect me to play with some goddamn cracker?"

Willie gave the big guy a look that would have boiled an egg. "Did you say somethin'? I thought for a second I hear you say somethin'."

The bass player was slowly shaking his head. "I don't play with no candy-ass white motherfuckers."

With his sax in one hand and the other on the hip of his navy blue suit, Willie regarded the bass player with the expression of a disappointed parent. "Oh you don't? Who the hell been raggin' me to pick up a horn player? Who the hell turned down the two colored boys we tried out? Wasn't that you, Roscoe? Or am I imaginin' things again, like when I imagined you could play your way out of a motherfuckin' paper bag?"

Roscoe's forehead was wrinkled, his expression that of a hurt child. "I never said we needed no *white* horn player."

The piano player with the shaved head and the nasty scars spoke up. "Roscoe, put a damn lid on it." His tone was easy but carried a hint of menace.

"*Do* that, Roscoe," Willie echoed.

Swiveling toward the sax player, the piano player said, "You put a lid on, too, Willie."

"What? What'd *I* say, Sarge?"

A sharp glance from the piano player silenced Willie. Turning his attention back to the bass player, Sarge said, "You wanna be treated equal?"

Roscoe said nothing.

"Well, then, how're you any better than some nigger-hating redneck if you ain't gonna give this white boy a chance?"

Pete sneaked a peek out at the audience. They were bobbing around now, getting restless, and he wondered if it might not be the better part of valor to just pack his horn up and get the hell out before this really turned ugly.

"Maybe so," Roscoe said, "but Willie shoulda axed us first. He shoulda brung this clown's white ass to practice, and—"

Sarge cut him off with a look. "Since when do we stand on goddamn ceremony? I say we give the white boy a chance…" A big friendly smile blossomed. "… and if he stinks up the joint, we can kick the shit out of him, after."

Pete goggled at the piano player as the other band members laughed heartily at that. Some joke.

"White Boy," Sarge said, "you know 'Caravan'?"

Pete said, "Just tell me the key."

"C," Sarge said. "And that ain't Spanish." Then he counted it off: "One, two…"

And they were playing.

Pete came in, taking the lead, playing the melody while the young drummer banged out a jungle beat like a kid Krupa. Despite never having seen any of these guys but Willie before, Pete felt at home with them, and for all the yammering about him being white, the five musicians fell in together, sounding good from the starting gun. Tapping his foot in time, Pete started into his solo and he let it rip, riffing like Bix.

Slowly, just a few couples at first, the audience began to dance. Nobody applauded after Pete's solo, but nobody threw a tomato, either. Then Willie took a solo, after which there was a little dueling bit between Sarge and Pete, piano player taking over for the clarinet solo on the original recording. By the time the song wound down, the dance floor was full; and when they ended, admittedly a little ragged but together, the audience responded with applause ... on the grudging side, but applause.

Keeping it going, Sarge said, "You know 'I'm Not Rough,' kid?"

Pete nodded. "Louie."

"Mr. Armstrong indeed." Turning to the drummer, Sarge said, "Count it off, Marvin."

The little man behind the drums said, "And a one ..."

Sarge nailed the piano opening, then Pete joined in and they were flying again, this time Willie using the upper register of the sax to supplant the original clarinet. Pete was really having fun now—man, these guys knew how to wail. The song allowed plenty of room for Pete and Willie to trade choruses, then Sarge played the guitar solo on his piano, and when they got to the vocal part, Willie leaned over to a microphone next to him, like a lover whispering in his girl's shell-like ear.

"Now, I ain't rough and I don't fight, but the woman that get me got to treat me right. 'Cause I'm crazy 'bout my lovin' and I must have it all the time. It takes a brown-skin woman to satisfy my mind ... to satisfy my mind."

That got some whoops out of the crowd, as the band careened toward the end of the song.

As applause rolled over him, Pete's eyes went to the bar where the bartender who'd overcharged him was trying to get the band's attention, holding up one finger.

Willie nodded to the guy, then said to the band, "Hey, fellas, whadaya know, we get an encore."

They were all grinning at Pete now, Roscoe included.

"What should we play?" Marvin asked.

Willie said, "How 'bout that new Louis Jordan song?"

Sarge said, "What about it, White Boy? 'Is You Is Or Is You Ain't My Baby'?"

"That's a loaded question," Pete said, and shrugged. "Never played it, but heard it a few times. Why not?"

Before anybody could say anything else, Marvin counted it off. The drums, piano, and bass started, then Pete joined in and Willie took the vocal.

"*I got a gal who's always late, any time we have a date...*"

The steward's mate sang pretty well, Pete thought. Too bad he couldn't get Willie into the base choir—could always use another good tenor. Willie certainly was getting the audience's vote of confidence—they were boogying their behinds off, and Pete was digging every second of it.

"*Is you is or is you ain't my baby,*" Willie sang, Marvin the drummer doing the harmonies. The drummer wasn't as good a singer as Willie, but he was on key.

When the last note from Pete's cornet died away, the crowd went Section 8—Willie and Pete shaking hands at the front of the stage as the crowd cheered.

As Pete removed the mouthpiece from his horn and started to pack the axe back into its case, Sarge ambled over with his hand outstretched.

"Damn, son!" he said. "Guess we can't beat the shit out of you, after all. You know, you don't play half bad for a white boy."

Rising, Pete took the proffered hand. "Pete Maxwell," he said, returning the firm handshake.

"What, tired of 'White Boy' already?"

"That kinda thing does get old fast."

"That right?"

Pete, caught, could only grin, and the piano player chuckled dryly. Now that they were closer and the light better, Pete got a real look at those scars. Knife scars, by the look of them. Nasty.

Sarge gestured vaguely toward the club and said, "Let's go take a load off. Buy you a beer and we all get to know each other."

"Fine by me."

They packed up. The piano and drums belonged to the house, so Marvin and Sarge already had a table when Pete trailed Willie over. Roscoe sat behind Pete, the stand-up bass unwieldy between the crowded tables. Even though the band had been well-received, Pete could again feel eyes burrowing into his back.

Each Negro took one side of the small, square table, with Pete's chair at the corner between Willie and Sarge. Pete passed his Chesterfields around and everybody smoked. The piano player set a beer—a full, frosty glass—in front of Pete and shot Willie a look.

"Our drummer boy," Willie said, with an open-hand gesture, "Mr. Marvin Hannah."

The young man nodded to Pete. In the dim light over here, he seemed even younger.

"Our bass player, and head of our welcoming committee, is Roscoe Gregg."

The big man, vaguely embarrassed, managed a small nod toward Pete.

"What about Sarge?" Pete asked. "Does he have any more name than that?"

"You are in the presence of Seaman Ulysses Grant Washington," Willie said.

"Seaman?" Pete asked.

Sarge hiked an eyebrow. "Why, you think we all steward's mates, son?"

Pete held up a hand. "Whoa, no. I just thought with a name like Sarge … had you pegged for a soldier, maybe a marine."

Everybody laughed, including Roscoe.

Willie said, "No, no, Sarge was a copper. A real-life detective, back in Chicago. Puts the spade in Sam Spade."

"Chicago, huh?" Pete said.

"Bridgeport neighborhood," Sarge said. "Thirty-fourth Street. Been there?"

"No. Like to, though—lot of great music comes out of that town."

A small smile tickled the corners of Sarge's mouth. "Ever hear of Comiskey Park?"

"White Sox? Sure."

"Two blocks west of there, my stompin' grounds."

Pete looked around at them. "What about the rest of you fellas?"

"Right here in San Diego," Roscoe said.

"You in the service, Roscoe?"

The bass player shook his head glumly.

"Bum ticker, man," Willie piped in.

"Goddamn motherfucker," Roscoe said, tapping his broad chest. "I mean, man, I was *ready*. Kick me some Heinie heinie. Slap me some Jap. But the docs caught it in the physical. I begged the bastards, but they wouldn't let me pass."

Sarge nudged Pete. "Marvin ain't in neither, on account of he's only seventeen, and they don't let guys in service who ain't busted their cherries yet."

"Aw, come on!" Marvin said.

Sarge went on: "Boy ain't even supposed to be in *here,* but ..."

"But," Pete said, "he sure can play."

Marvin beamed. "Thanks, man."

With a flourish, Willie said to his friends, "And this is my buddy, Ensign Peter Maxwell."

"Ensign!" Sarge said. "What, we got an officer slummin' tonight?"

Feeling the beer a little now, Pete said, "Can't *all* be steward's mates."

Sarge just stared at him, but the other three cracked up.

Turning his attention to Wilson, Pete said, "Willie, what would you think about joining the base choir? You've got a good voice, and—"

"Ain't for us," Sarge said.

"What do you mean?"

"I know all about ol' FDR integratin' the services," Willie said sarcastically. "But how many of us colored boys you seen on your side of the base?"

Pete sighed. "Maybe you're right, least for now."

Shaking his head, Willie said, "I appreciate your interest, Mr. Maxwell, but I ain't holdin' my breath waitin' for things to change, neither. And if you did recruit me, you know you'd be courtin' a world of shit from the brass, right?"

"Well..."

"Right? And half your white boys would quit."

"...Right." After a final gulp of beer, Pete said, "This has been great, fellas. But I better hit the road. I got a wife at home." He started to get up, but stopped midway when Sarge caught his elbow.

"Wait, Pete," Sarge said. "I mean, it is okay to call you 'Pete' when we're in civvies?"

"Hell yes." He must have been drinking, to use language like that.

Sarge was saying, "Pete, we best all leave here together. You play a mean horn, but some of the hardasses around here won't give two shits about that, when you walk out that door."

"Oh. Well. Yeah."

Suddenly Sarge grinned at Pete; the guy didn't do much grinning, and it carried weight when he did. "Man, we sounded damn good tonight, and you know it. Wanna come back next week?"

"I'd love it," Pete said, then added, "If I'm still here."

"Yeah?"

"Me and some buddies put in for a ship. I don't know when or if I'll get my orders, but... if I'm still here next Tuesday, hell yeah, I'd like to play again."

Sarge's expression turned serious. "Then you better meet up with Willie and me before you get to this neighborhood. You got lucky tonight, son—you don't wanna have to learn how to walk with that coronet stuck in your white ass, do you?"

"Not really. Know a diner called Loretto's?"

"I know it," Sarge said, his voice cool. "They don't serve us there, but I walked by."

"Okay, somewhere else, then. Where *can* we grab a bite together?"

Willie's laugh had a bitter edge. "Mr. Maxwell, we can't eat together in the mess hall at the damn base. Where'n the hell you think they gonna let us eat together out here in Little Georgia?"

The fellas were nodding all around. And Pete knew they were right.

But he didn't have to like it.

THREE

JUNE 20, 1944

The orders had come through yesterday: the Fantail Four had all been assigned to the USS *Liberty Hill Victory*.

And yet here it was, eleven on Tuesday morning, and Pete Maxwell had yet to tell his wife Kay that on Friday he'd be transferred to Treasure Island, a Naval base in San Francisco Bay that had nothing to do with Long John Silver or Robert Louis Stevenson. From there, Pete and his three buddies would be deployed to their ship, currently being built across the bay in Richmond.

He needed to tell Kay, he wanted to tell her; but last night something had stopped him. He just hadn't been able to get the words out, and he'd felt lousy about it ever since.

This morning's rehearsal, his last as choir director, had gone well—they'd be fine at service Sunday morning; he'd told his men about his transfer and was given a resounding cheer and even an impromptu round of "Auld Lang Syne" that made Pete tear up, just a little.

This afternoon, he would pack up his gear and clear out his office at the chapel. Tomorrow he would show his replacement around, then Thursday he'd have a day off to spend with Kay. Time had slowed and become slightly unreal as he spent these final days at the base, drifting in the knowledge that he and the rest of the Fantail Four were about to get a lot closer to the real war.

Knowing Kay, however, he figured his first major battle might start here at home. . . .

At lunch, Pete had taken some ribbing from the rest of the guys about "chickening out" and not telling his wife about his new orders.

"How can you expect to be a leader of men, Maxie," Driscoll said, eyelids at half-mast, "when you're still under the thumb of the little woman?"

Rosetti pointed with his spoon and said, "Who wears the pants, Pete? Do you wear the pants or don't you?"

"Oh, Maxie wears the pants, all right," Driscoll said, not giving Pete a chance to get a word in edgewise. "Cute little lace pants, right, Maxie?"

"Screw you, Dick," Pete said good-naturedly.

"You *are* getting salty," Driscoll said. "Speaking of which, pass it—the salt, I mean. If this macaroni and cheese had any less flavor, I'd write the President."

Pete, who was suffering through chipped beef on toast for the umpteenth time, said, "She'll back me up, push comes to shove. I just know it's gonna hit her hard, is all."

Connor fell into his sandpaper-voiced Rochester impression: "If you afraid of your wife, Mr. Benny, I'll give you my razor—only it's a Gillette, and I'm outa *blades!*"

That made everybody laugh, then Pete said, "Go ahead and razz, you guys—you're bachelors. Your time will come."

Square-shouldered Rosetti said, "Maybe we *should* cut Pete a little slack, here. I worked the toughest streets in L.A., and the roughest customers I ever run across were wives who caught hubby cheating."

Languidly forking macaroni, Driscoll drawled, "Few sights are more frightening than a woman in a house robe and hair curlers with a frying pan at the ready ... and I don't mean to cook anything, except maybe her husband's goose."

"That's why Dick and me stick with the bachelor life," the curly-haired, hawk-nosed comedy writer said. "Even though my Gable-like countenance attracts all the *real* honey."

Handsome Driscoll merely smiled. "Maybe I just have higher standards, Connie. I prefer them with all their limbs and most of their teeth."

Connor shrugged. "Don't know what you're missing."

Pete and Rosetti were just grinning and shaking their heads; neither could keep up when these two got going.

Typically of Tuesday, Kay was working late at the Western Union office. Pete had dinner at Loretto's again, then went to the corner where he and Sarge Washington and his boys had agreed to meet before returning to the Silver Slipper for an encore performance. Roscoe and Marvin were already in the spotlight of a streetlamp, though the former lacked his bass and the latter his drumsticks.

"Where are Willie and Sarge?" Pete asked.

"Shipped out," Roscoe said with a fatalistic shrug.

"Where to?"

"I ain't Navy, man. How the hell would I know?"

"Sorry. Dumb question."

"S'okay. Anyways, Marvin and me just showed up to tell you, probably ain't safe for you over at the Slipper without Sarge to back you up."

Marvin asked, "No horn?"

Pete shook his head. "No, I just came around to say 'bye to you fellas—I'm shipping out this week, too." He shifted on his feet, tried to find the words. Then he said, "Listen, thanks for the chance, last week. I thought we really swung."

Roscoe stuck out a big mitt for Pete to shake. "Man, we blew the roof off that dump. You all right, Mr. Maxwell. Try not to take no shrapnel in that lip of yours, 'cause you can blow up a storm."

"Thanks, Roscoe."

Marvin stepped forward and shook hands with Pete, too. "You know, I turn eighteen next week, Mr. Maxwell. Keep an eye peeled, 'cause I'll be right behind you. 'Fore you know it, I'll be mowin' down some damn Nips."

Clapping the young man on the shoulder, Pete said, "We'll hold down the fort till you bring up the rear, Marvin. Meantime, just keep beating on those skins. One of these days, Buddy Rich'll be sweating."

They said their goodbyes and went in opposite directions, Pete wondering if he'd been, in his own way, as naive about the war as that kid Marvin. Would Kay see him as just another gung ho numbskull, trading in easy, safe duty for an assignment so dangerous nobody but Pete and his Fantail pals even signed up for it?

Just a block from home now, Pete felt a wave of fear go through him like nausea at the sight of a tub of chipped beef. But his fear was not out of what lay ahead, nor the duty in the Pacific, not even the indignant tears that Kay would surely unleash on him.

What made him afraid was *Kay's* fear—the pain and mental torture he'd be visiting on the person he cared most about in this world; the days and nights she'd face, where every knock on the door, every ring of the phone, could mean tragedy was calling. He knew damn good and well that she would be more scared waiting at home for him than he'd ever be in combat.

Combat moved fast, tragedies happened in a hurry, and her slow-motion war would be, in its way, much harder than his.

Framed by the picture window on a sea orange with sunset, Kay was sitting primly on the side of the lowered Murphy bed, hands in her lap, waiting for him when he unlocked the door and came in; she had on a cute little two-piece outfit called a Sailor Made—white blouse and skirt with nautical touches in blue, and open-toed sandals with her toenails bright red.

His expression must have given it all away, because he never got a chance to say anything. Like a condemned man walking the last mile, he went over to her and stood before her; he squinted a little, sun reflecting off water through the window.

Kay gazed up at him, her big blue eyes moist but her voice strong as she said, "When are you going?"

"You know?"

"I know. I know you. I know what you want. When?"

"Friday."

She swallowed and patted the bed for him to sit beside her. He did. She took his hands in hers and looked at him searchingly. "I should hate you for this."

"I know."

"Not for doing it. But for not talking to me about it. For knowing since yesterday and not saying anything, for not making this decision something I was in on."

"I know. I'm a dope."

"Well, you're my dope."

"I always will be, baby. And, anyway, you know this is the right thing for me to do."

She didn't raise her voice, but she did squeeze his hands just a bit harder. "You think I care about that? You really think I want anything but you and me and our family?"

"We … we don't have a family yet."

"Yes we do. We have you and me and our folks and, maybe, if we get lucky before you go away Friday, we can add to it."

He'd been wondering why the Murphy bed was down.

"You're going to take me to bed right now," she said. "You're going to drop your drawers and pull up my skirt and have your way with me, Pete Maxwell."

"I am?"

"You are. And then you're taking me out for a nice dinner, and we're coming back here, and you're making love to me again, like a nice respectable married lady."

He kissed her, a sweet small thing that grew into something passionate, but by the end she was crying and had wrapped herself in his arms, her face in his shoulder.

He said, "Baby, nothing means more to me than you. But if guys like me don't stand up and do something about this war, then the world'll go straight to hell, and where will we be? Where will our ... family be?"

She was sniffling and snuffling. "Shut-up and drop your drawers, sailor. That's an order. ..."

Soon his pants were down, her dress was up, and he was inside her and her legs were wrapped around him and she was crying and he was crying and right before they both climaxed she said, her eyes big, her cheeks scarlet, "You ... you ... better ... goddamn ... come ... *home* ... to ... me ... Pete Maxwell ..."

"I will," he gulped, and he came so hard, he thought he might die of it.

They went out for that nice meal—at Hob Nob Hill restaurant, a bit of a splurge—and spoke not at all of the war, just talked about home and old times, and generally behaved like sweethearts. They returned to the Murphy bed and the lovemaking was slow and romantic.

Wednesday and Thursday evening were repeats, with different restaurants substituted (she allowed him Loretto's on the last night) and, though it was essentially unspoken, their mission was for Kay to conceive a child. That this child might not have a father, if the war took Pete, was not a topic of discussion.

On these last two days, they spent every moment together. Kay was the dream companion, no moping, no crying, all upbeat, ever hopeful. They made plans for what they'd do after he got back. Pete liked the Navy well enough, but it wasn't the life for him, and frankly neither was playing his cornet in smoky joints, however much fun that was.

He loved music nearly as much as he loved Kay, but a life on the road was not in the cards, not when you were a married man getting ready to start a family. Vocal music, on the other hand, like leading the choir, that was a path that appealed—music teacher, church choir on the side, meant a stable life and a modest but acceptable income.

They had also decided that she would stay in the apartment only until the end of the month. Her Western Union manager here had helped her swing a job at the office back in Des Moines. She would live with her aunt again and take the streetcar to work.

"While you're away," Kay said, "I'll be building our nest egg. Then when you're home, home for good, we'll start looking for a house."

He had known better than to argue that with her, ambitious as that sounded. And she was right, a one-room apartment was not enough for a family. A house. Yes. He'd do his part for this war and come home to that picket fence everybody talked about.

Friday morning dawned cold and cloudy, but Kay insisted on walking him to the base, which she did, arm in arm, his sea bag thrown over the opposite shoulder. At the gate, in the Sailor Made again, she kissed him hard and hugged him fiercely.

"Don't forget your promise," she said. "You come back to me."

"I have every intention of doing just that, baby."

"I don't mind you doing your bit, but don't you go out of your way getting all brave and heroic. You keep your head down, Ensign Maxwell."

He kissed her lightly, then held her hard against him. "You are hugging the biggest coward in the Pacific Theater, lady. I promise."

She drew away. "Don't start lying to me now, mister. I know you better than that. You always try for first chair."

"Well…"

"All I ask is, no risks. Nothing silly. Just be safe."

"I will. I promise."

They shared one last kiss, sweet and soft and yearning, then he was through the gate. He looked back twice, but the second time, she'd turned and started away, walking with a determined gait that indicated she was off to fight the home-front war.

The bus was scheduled to leave at seven and he didn't want to miss it. When he got to the administration office, the other

Fantailers were already there, clutching large manila envelopes with their orders. Rosetti and Connor lurked behind the blond frat boy Driscoll, their eyes darting to his neck, then at Pete.

He finally took the hint and glanced at Driscoll's collar. The silver lieutenant j.g.'s bars had been replaced by the double silver bars of a full lieutenant.

"Jesus Christ, Dick," Pete said. "You got a promotion! Haven't they heard about what a prick you are?"

Driscoll grinned. "Maxie, Maxie ... such language in front of a superior officer."

Pete stuck out his hand. "Congratulations, pal."

Smiling, they shook firmly.

"I appreciate that, Maxie," Driscoll said. "As you might imagine, these other two scoundrels did not react as generously as a well-bred farm boy like yourself."

"Think about it, Pete," Rosetti blurted, only half-kidding. "That promotion makes Dick the damned XO! There's no end to the shit he'll put us through now."

"Yes," Connor said, "have Kay send you some knee pads, toot sweet—there will be regular ass-kissing on the hour."

"I was thinking more," Driscoll said, "of springing such sessions like surprise inspections."

Connor rolled his eyes. "You missed him already ordering us to alternate mornings, Pete, bringing him breakfast."

"I said no such thing," Driscoll uttered with a mock-wounded grin. "Of course, we'll include Maxie, meaning it's only every *third* day. ..."

The XO or executive officer was second in command to the captain and would take charge if anything happened to said captain.

"If you're the exec, Dick," Pete said, "who's the skipper?"

"Lieutenant Commander John Jacob Egan."

"Never heard of him. Any of you guys ...?"

Rosetti and Connor shook their heads.

"Captain Henderson didn't know much about him," Driscoll was saying, referring to the base commander who'd given them their orders. "Just that Egan's Old Navy. Went into the Merchant Marine in the thirties, got called back when the war started."

"Just what a bunch of fakes like us need," Connor said with a smirk. "A *real* Navy man."

Driscoll said, "We'll meet him at Treasure Island. We'll find out then if he's Captain Bligh or Commander Hornblower."

"You're confused already," Connor said. "Pete's the horn-blower."

Pete held up his hands, saying, "All right, all right, you clowns. Which one of you has my orders?"

They were all stupid smiles now.

Pete pressed: "My *orders*?"

Driscoll held out his palms. "Who knows? The old man wouldn't give them to us. He said to send you in as soon as you got here. Said he wanted to give it to you—personally."

Pete blinked. "Why, what did *I* do wrong?"

Connor shrugged. "Maybe the cookies overheard you complaining about the chow. I heard you call that stuff shit-on-a-shingle. You can get court-martialed for less in this man's Navy."

Something was up, but Pete had no clue what. He had just the length of the hallway to think about it as he strode with forced confidence toward the door with the pebbled-glass window that said CAPTAIN T. HENDERSON, BASE COMMANDER in black stencil letters.

The other three Fantailers trailed in his wake. He could feel their eyes on him, rubberneckers at a car crash. He dropped his sea bag on the floor and knocked firmly (but not *too* firmly) on the wood part of the mostly glass door.

From the other side a steady baritone voice said, "Come in."

Pete entered, shut himself in.

The office was sparsely furnished in the military fashion, metal desk in the center, two visitor chairs, coat rack behind the door, water cooler in one corner. The far wall was mostly divided windows with Venetian blinds slanting wide, today letting in not sunshine but overcast gray.

Behind the desk, ramrod straight, rail-thin, sat a man of perhaps fifty, his grooming as immaculate as his uniform. Captain Thomas Henderson had salt-and-pepper hair, a high forehead, a pointed chin and dark wide-set eyes; he was wearing wire-rim glasses, probably only for reading, which he was doing as Pete entered.

"Ensign Maxwell reporting," Pete said, standing at attention and saluting.

Henderson's return salute was lackadaisical. "At ease, Mr. Maxwell. I'll be with you shortly."

Pete stood quietly while the captain finished reading the page in front of him.

Finally, Henderson looked up and locked eyes with his visitor. "Your fitness reports are exemplary, Maxwell."

"Thank you, sir."

"You've been a leader, not just with the choir, but on the base as a whole."

"Thank you, sir."

"I suppose they told you."

"*They*, sir?"

"Your cohorts in the corridor. The Fantail Four minus one? I thought you boys were very entertaining, by the way, that Ink Spots routine you did at the Christmas party."

"Thank you, sir."

"So then they didn't? Tell you."

"Tell me what, sir?"

Henderson allowed himself a small half-smile.

"It's my honor," he said, rising, "to be the first to shake the hand of Lieutenant Junior Grade Peter Maxwell."

As they shook hands, the shell-shocked Pete managed, "A promotion, sir?"

"You've earned it, Maxwell." The captain sat back down. "You've earned your place on that ship, too. Stateside can be thankless duty. Let me say that I'm happy for all four of you men."

"Thank you, sir."

"This makes you second officer on the *Liberty Hill Victory*."

Since the captain was considered an absolute commander by the Navy, the first officer—Driscoll in this case—was second in command; and that put Pete in third position. "I will do my best, sir."

"I know you will." The captain's smile seemed almost human. "Now, get your tail moving or you'll miss your bus."

Pete turned to leave, but Henderson said, "One moment, Maxwell."

"Yes, sir?"

"Don't forget your silver bars—and your orders."

"Aye aye, sir," Pete said, tucking under his arm the envelope the captain handed him, and looking down somewhat dazed at the two shiny silver bars in the captain's outstretched palm, one for each side of his collar.

"Be proud of those," Henderson said. "I have a feeling this is just the beginning for you, Lieutenant."

Then Henderson shooed Pete out where his buddies were waiting in the hallway. The building wasn't very busy at this hour, but they still managed to make a few heads crane as they whooped and hollered and clapped the new lieutenant (j.g.) on the back as they headed outside.

By the time the bus pulled out, Pete realized with a blush of shame that he hadn't thought to take time to telephone Kay and tell her the good news. He'd correct that the first chance he got.

The drive up the coast was tortuous, and they felt every curve and bump in the cramped seats of the bus, the vehicle crammed with sailors headed for Treasure Island. They sat two to a seat, Pete with Rosetti, Driscoll with Connor just ahead. Pete couldn't help but go from face to face all around him, wondering if any of these guys would be part of their crew.

The bus stopped once for gas and lunch outside a little town called Cambria. Pete got change for a dollar and made the long-distance call to Kay, at work.

"I'm so proud of you," she said.

He was in a booth outside the roadside diner. "I'm still in California but I already feel a world away."

"No. Don't. I'm always right with you. If you need to talk to me, even if you're on some stupid island in the middle of nowhere... you *talk* to me. I'll be there to listen."

"... I love you, baby."

"I love you. And I'm with you, Lieutenant Maxwell, every step of the way."

Soon all of the sailors were loaded back aboard the bus, which took off again. A thick cloud of smoke hung in the coach and Pete joined in, firing up a Chesterfield; in this hurry-up-and-wait military world, smoking a fag was about all a guy had to do, half the time. His legs were cramped, his back ached, and it seemed to him the driver was working for Hitler or maybe Tojo, intentionally aiming his wheels at every possible pothole. In the next seat, Rosetti snored away like a '37 Ford with a bum muffler.

Out the window, Pete watched the sun set over the hilly landscape and, as they rolled along, saw in the distance lights coming on in San Jose, then Menlo Park, Half Moon Bay, and Pacifica. They rumbled north, entering San Francisco from the south, driving through the city until they got onto the Bay Bridge with its view, breathtaking even after dark. Halfway across, they took an exit ramp and the bus wound down a steep hill.

When they finally pulled up to the gate at Treasure Island, Pete wondered if he could get his legs and for that matter his ass working enough to get himself off the darn bus. He nudged Rosetti, who snorted like a bull and came awake all at once.

"What?" Rosetti asked. "More crappy diner food?"

As if the ex-cop wouldn't have gobbled it down.

"No," Pete said. "We're here."

In the seat in front of them, Driscoll turned around. "Who kissed Sleeping Beauty awake?"

"What the hell's that supposed to mean?" Rosetti asked, lighting a Chesterfield he'd begged off Pete.

"It means, my dear Rosie," Driscoll said, "that you've been snoring like a rhino with a deviated septum for this whole journey."

"Deviate this, Dick," Rosetti said, and grabbed his crotch.

"Very droll," Dick said.

Pete, who had seen this gesture often from Rosetti, was still not quite used to it. Not a lot of that sort of thing had gone on back in Iowa.

One of the gate guards came onto the bus like an irritated invader.

"Welcome to Treasure Island Naval Base," he said, in a tone more appropriate had he said, *Who the hell stole my wallet?* "The Admin building is shut down for the evening. We'll give the driver directions to the mess hall, then you sons of bitches can get a bite. After that, somebody'll show you where to bunk the night. Any officers aboard?"

The Fantail Four raised their hands.

The guard's voice took on a grudgingly respectful timber. "Driver'll drop you at the officers' mess, sirs, then someone there will show you where to bunk."

Without waiting for a response, the guard leaned over, spoke to the driver, then exited the bus.

"I could eat a horse," Rosetti said, sending blue smoke out his nostrils.

Connor said, "So could I, but if that's what they're serving, I may request Worcestershire. I'm just that fussy."

Driscoll turned back to Connor and said, "Your rabbi won't let you eat pork, but horse is kosher?"

"As we say in synagogue," Connor said, "fuck you and the horse you rode in on."

Driscoll tapped his collar with its new bars. "Fuck you and the horse you rode in on, *sir.*"

"What you said," Connor replied with a half-smile, "sir."

"Whoever rides it in," Rosetti said, "I'm eating the damn nag."

The bus lurched into motion. Momentarily, on their right, just visible in the gathering darkness, sat a semi-circular, art moderne, three-story building with a glass turret.

Somebody up front said, "Base HQ."

"*That's* the base headquarters?" Connor asked. "It looks like Lana Turner's dressing room."

California-boy Rosetti said, "This island was home to the Golden Gate International Expo, back in '39? That was the administration building."

"No shit," Connor said.

Driscoll was in the know, as well. "Pan Am used to own that building; it was earmarked for the terminal and tower of the new San Francisco International Airport, after the Exposition."

"That obviously didn't happen," Pete said.

"No," Driscoll said. "When the war broke out, the Navy came in, and Pan Am lit out for Mills Field across the bay."

"Still looks like Lana Turner's dressing room to me," Connor insisted, as they passed two palm trees standing sentry at the entry into the building's parking lot.

San Francisco Bay was on their left as they rode down a long blacktop lined by palm trees. Various buildings, most of them darkened for the night, loomed on the right. Five minutes later, having circled half the island, the bus drew up in front of a long, low-slung white building, its doors and trim painted blue: the officers' mess. The four friends clambered off, and the bus groaned away as they stood there on the blacktop, sea bags at their feet.

"Why don't we see a man about a horse?" Driscoll asked.

This was Dick's way of saying, *Who's hungry?*

They all headed for the door, brushing shoulders. Pete held it open while the others rushed inside, and he followed, surprised by how empty the large hall was. The only other inhabitants were two black steward's mates behind the steam table, a tall thin one with a short thin partner, both dressed in white, neither looking as if he'd sampled the food here (or anywhere else) for quite some time.

As the quartet got up to the counter and picked up trays, Driscoll asked, "Where in *Green Pastures* is everybody, boys?"

"They ate early, sir," the tall one said. "The CO wants a complete blackout after nine, and the base just got a new movie. They all hustled down there to see it before nine. It's a Humphrey Bogart."

"With that good-lookin' skinny gal from that other movie," the short one said. "Who said if you want me, jus' whistle?"

"Ah, Miss Bacall," Connor said, in reverie. "Sounds like a good one."

But the food didn't smell as good as the movie sounded.

Rosetti was looking down at the steam table. "I don't believe it," he moaned. "Put a target on my goddamn back and send the Japs around—shit on a shingle again!"

Normally they would have laughed at the muscular ensign's fate, but tonight, with nothing else to pick from, they shared it; and even though they hadn't eaten since midday, each man took serious stock of how hungry he actually was before facing the infamous dish.

"I wish it *was* fuckin' horse," Rosetti said.

But they ate it. They ate it in near silence, like kids forced by their parents to go to church, and by the time they finished, they were all ready to find their billets and surrender to exhaustion.

One steward's mate led the quartet to the officers' transit barracks, where they each found empty bunks and made up the cots. A couple of other bunks were already made up, but whether their owners were at the movie or somewhere else, who could say? Treasure Island served mainly as a layover stop for officers and enlisted men alike, on their way to new assignments.

Many of the ships being built these days were constructed in the nearby Kaiser Shipyards, where up to four ships could be assembled at once. The *Liberty Hill Victory* should be done by now. Its launch could well be in the next couple of days, and as Pete prepared for bed, he felt excitement seep through his tiredness as he realized how close he was to actually going to sea.

What would it be like? Back in Iowa they had the Mississippi, but mighty as the Missisip was, it was no ocean; at sea, no land in sight, he, his shipmates, and their ship would face not just the Japanese but the elements. Would it change him? Would it kill him? Would he come back more of a man, or would he not come back at all?

They were about to hit the rack when two young ensigns strolled in. The first was as blond as Driscoll, wiry, and with an easygoing smile. He introduced himself around as, "Larry Benson, Greenfield, Indiana," displaying a firm handshake, and Pete took an instant liking to him.

The other guy was a narrow-shouldered, mean-looking little guy with tiny dark eyes crowding a sharp beak-like nose. "Billy Cotton, from Tupelo, Mississippi," he said. He shook hands with all of them, but his grip was limp and moist, and the ritual seemed a chore to him.

"Where you headed?" Driscoll asked the Southerner.

Cotton said, "We got two more nights' shore leave, then come Monday, we're on a ship to Pearl. We're both scheduled to be replacements. Benson's got a cruiser, I caught a sardine can. What about y'all?"

"We've got an ammo ship," Pete said.

"Attached to the *Liberty Hill Victory*," Rosetti said.

The temperature in the barracks seemed to drop faster than the Cards' Emil Verban and Marty Marion could turn a double play.

"You guys are from *that* ship?" Cotton said, his upper lip curled back, his tone oozing distaste.

The Fantail Four exchanged confused glances.

"What about it?" Connor asked.

Cotton made a face like something smelled. "Benson, let's get the hell out of here," he said. "I ain't spendin' the night in these foul barracks."

"What?" Benson asked.

"Didn't you catch that?" Cotton asked. "They're from the *Liberty Hill Victory*."

Benson's face sagged and went pale.

"What the hell are you guys *talking* about?" Pete asked.

"Yeah," Rosetti said, chest out, "what the hell's wrong with you birds?"

"What's wrong with *us*?" Cotton said, his voice rising. "You got your fuckin' nerve."

Not knowing what to say, Pete stood there dumbfounded.

Rosetti might've mixed it up with the beady-eyed little S.O.B., but Cotton was already on the move, rushing across the barracks to a bunk where he stuffed a couple of loose items in his sea bag, then hefted it over his shoulder.

"Benson, come *on*," the jerk said. "Last chance. *I* ain't stayin' here tonight."

The easygoing blond sailor shrugged at the guys, but he followed Cotton and soon the pair was out the door without another word.

Rosetti started after them, but Driscoll caught his arm. "Rosie! Whatever crawled up their ass and died, you're not gonna go in after it. That's an undignified expedition for a man of your fine qualities."

Pete was at Rosetti's side. "Dick's right. Let it go. Maybe it's some kind of initiation or something."

Driscoll was gazing across at where the two sailors had exited, his eyes narrow. "Why the hell would they badmouth a spanking new ship like *Liberty Hill?*"

"Mr. Benny," Connor said, in gravel-voiced Rochester mode, "please tell me you didn't buy your *ship* down at the army surplus like you did the *Maxwell!*"

The Maxwell referred to was not Pete, rather the ancient wheezing automobile in which Rochester chauffeured the cheap-skate Jack Benny on the radio show.

And this was enough to get a laugh out of everybody, and they shrugged off this bizarre stupidity and headed for the sack.

Still, in the darkness, before drifting to sleep, each man pondered the same puzzler: what could possibly be wrong with a brand-new ship and a brand-new crew?

FOUR

JUNE 21, 1944

Not long after reveille, the Fantail Four learned why Ensigns Cotton and Benson had given them such a bizarre welcome.

Pete Maxwell and his buddies still hadn't met their skipper, but a trip to the headquarters building, after breakfast, got them a step closer: seemed their crew was doing calisthenics at the far end of the island, behind the last barracks.

Rosetti procured a Jeep from the motor pool, and they drove the same route as the bus last night, only under blue skies in California sun. Soon they'd exhausted that route, however, going farther and farther, past the movie theater, the bowling alley, the fire station, the power plant. ...

Pete was starting to wonder if the calisthenics their crew were undertaking might not be a swim in the bay.

Finally, behind two dingy ancient barracks that had been painted upon completion but never again, Pete saw sixty or so colored boys in dungarees and light blue work shirts, the regular outfit of a seaman. Under the perfect blue sky with its scattering of water-color white clouds, the black men were doing pushups, some with more effort than others. Two Negroes, their feet toward the Jeep, were down on the ground as well, but in an obvious leadership position.

And off to one side, bored out of their gourds, bewildered beyond their mental capacities, sat four white non-coms at a nearby picnic table, playing cards.

"Shit," Rosetti said, slowing, "we're lost."

"Are we?" Driscoll said. His voice rang hollow.

Rosetti leaned on the wheel. "I must've took a left turn to Africa."

Pete frowned. "You didn't turn at all."

"Don't you get it, gents?" Driscoll asked with a forced lightness. "Like they say in Connie's business, dis must be da place."

But Connor had no Rochester wisecrack for this occasion. Though (with the exception of Pete) the comedy writer tended to swear less than the others, he nonetheless summed up their situation with profane simplicity: "Oh, fuck."

"This *can't* be right," Rosetti said. "Gotta be some SNAFU...."

All Pete could think of was the fine print on that posting asking for "good-sized" volunteers. Sports background a plus. He felt sick to his stomach. And it wasn't the powdered eggs.

One non-com put down his hand of cards and abandoned the picnic table to approach the four officers who'd rolled up in the Jeep. He had an eager yet sickly smile.

"Begging your pardon, sirs," he said, his voice flat and Midwestern, "we seem to have some sort of a foul-up."

Pete didn't look at the guy; his eyes were on the field where Negroes were doing their push-ups; the whole situation had become obviously, horribly clear to him. He was the one who'd got his friends into this mess, and already he knew there was no way out.

To the non-com, Pete said, "You've been assigned to the *Liberty Hill Victory,* sailor. Isn't that right?"

"Yes, sir, but ... how did *you* know?"

Jumping down from the Jeep, Pete didn't respond. His attention was on the two colored sailors with their backs to him. He felt sure he recognized the one nearest to him; he hoped so, anyway—or did they really all look alike?

As Pete neared the Negroes doing push-ups, the two nearest (and facing) him popped up, yelling together, "Ten-*hut!*"

The pair supervising, their backs to Pete, jumped up and stood at attention without turning his way. Pete didn't need them to—that all-look-alike stuff was baloney. He did indeed know the man closest to him, and he felt a sudden small twinge of relief.

Falling in line next to the man, he said, "Seaman Washington, how are the men this morning?"

Gradually the push-ups had stopped and the colored sailors were getting to their feet and straightening to attention.

Sarge Washington was so stunned, he barely remembered to salute. "Men is fine … sir."

Pete nodded. He gazed out at the assembly of sailors, more black faces in one place than he'd ever seen, including the Silver Slipper.

"*Stand easy!*" he told them.

They did.

Pete turned to Sarge. "I take it you've all been assigned to one ship."

"Yes, sir. The—"

"*Liberty Hill Victory*," Pete finished.

Sarge's eyes narrowed. "That's right, sir. Looks like we finally gonna get in this war, as somethin' more than bus-boys."

Pete gave him a look.

"Beggin' your pardon, sir."

Pete's smile was so faint only the Negro could make it out; under his breath he said, "I dig you, Sarge."

Sarge's smile was similarly hard to see.

Gazing out over the vast complement of Negroes, Pete remembered something his mother used to say: "Be careful what you wish for, son." He'd wished for a ship, he'd wished for a crew, and it had all come true, hadn't it?

He'd wanted to get into this war, and it looked like he might be fighting the rest of it without ever needing to encounter a German or Jap to do so. In front of him were sixty, maybe seventy colored boys. This must have been how Custer felt, right before his last haircut.

In the third row, steward's mate Willie Wilson gave Pete a small discreet wave, which the new lieutenant (j.g.) acknowledged with a barely discernible nod.

To Sarge, he said, "Our four white non-coms don't seem very interested in joining the rest of the crew for the morning calisthenics."

Sarge shrugged and raised an eyebrow till it practically touched the white of his dogfood-bowl cap. "It never came up, sir."

"I see. How about your men, Sarge? They in shape?"

"Shipshape, sir," Sarge said, standing a little straighter himself. "Every man jack."

Pete nodded and unbuttoned his jacket. He lay it carefully on the ground as the rest of the Fantail Four came walking up, as if navigating a mine field; behind them, similarly cautious, ambled the card players.

"Maaaaxie," Driscoll said. He looked like a patient whose doctor had just delivered a grave diagnosis. "What in the name of Jesus, Mary, and Joseph are you up to?"

"Getting to know the crew. We're doing some exercises."

"That so?" Rosetti said, hands on his hips, something feisty in his tone. "Where the hell's the skipper? He might have an opinion."

"Skipper's not here. That puts you in charge, Dick. Okay with you if I lead the men in some jumping jacks?"

Driscoll's long face lengthened; his eyes disappeared into slits of skin. Then he took Pete by the sleeve and off to one side.

"Just what sort of minstrel show do you have in mind, Maxie?" Driscoll asked, his tone light but demanding.

"You figured it out before the rest of us, Dick. This is our crew. We're stuck with them, and they're stuck with us. Sooner we treat them like crew, sooner they'll treat us like officers. Any objection, Lieutenant?"

Driscoll squinted; the sun had something to do with it, but not everything.

Then the exec said, "None. It's a good idea. Well-reasoned, Maxie. Mind if I sit this out?"

"It's your plantation."

That caught Driscoll off guard, and he grinned and shook his head. "Fuck you, Lieutenant."

"Language, sir. Language."

Pete went over and stood next to Sarge, facing the rows of colored sailors; then Pete glanced behind him, shot a look at Rosetti, who, getting it, nodded and came jogging up and fell in beside the Negro standing next to Sarge. Now two whites and two coloreds were leading the exercises, side by side.

Finally Connor, who had been taking all of this in, shaking his head and laughing to himself, ran past the four leaders over to the front row of sailors and tagged himself on at the end.

Lighting up a Lucky Strike with his Zippo, Driscoll was sitting in the Jeep, cap back on his head, while the four white non-coms hovered nearby, wondering where they fit into this Alice-in-Wonderland scheme of things.

"*Jumping jacks!*" Pete called.

He started in, then Sarge and Rosetti, the other Negro, too, and so did Connor and the rest of the group.

"*Count off,*" Pete yelled, and a chorus of counting sailors did jumping jacks in a morning sun whose rays could not really compete with the cool bay breeze.

One non-com, a skinny, pockmarked character, said, "I ain't jumpin' around with a bunch of fuckin' monkeys."

The other non-coms winced, because this had been a declaration of sorts, loud enough to be heard by just about everybody.

Several black sailors ceased their exercising, and their expressions turned stony as they started forward.

Pete yelled, "*Halt,*" and they all froze, including those who had broken rank.

Now Driscoll came down out of the Jeep, sending his Lucky sailing in a sparking trajectory, and planted himself in front of the skinny non-com, leaning in till his nose was six inches from the man's. "And what's your name, sailor?"

"Griffin," the non-com said in a thick, Southern drawl. He was a sandy-blond blue-eyed kid, lean as a snake but with the pointed face of a rodent.

"What did you say?"

Griffin remained defiant. "I said I ain't jumpin' 'round with no monkeys."

His voice rising only slightly, Driscoll said, "I don't remember ordering you to. Did I do that, sailor?"

"No, sir."

"But I do admire your enthusiasm. Your spirit. So I tell you what, sailor. Get your ass over there and join in."

"Why should I? I don't see you doin' it."

Driscoll's smile was pleasant but his eyes weren't. "That's because I'm the ranking officer. It's that privilege of rank you've been hearing so much about. You, however, are an insignificant fly speck spoiling my view of these colorful sailors on this beautiful sunshiny day."

Griffin was getting scared now, shaking as he stood there with this strange exec lashing him with words.

"When you grow up to be an officer," Driscoll was saying, "you'll have such privileges. As of now, it's my privilege to tell you to get your goddamn ass in ranks and join in, or the only sunshine you'll be seeing on this lovely day is through the fucking bars of your cell window. In the brig."

For a moment, Pete thought that Griffin, whose lower lip had extended in trembling defiance, was about to take a poke at Driscoll. That, Pete knew, would have been a mistake. Not only was Driscoll taller and more muscular, he'd been on the boxing team at Harvard and, Pete knew from their training together, the new lieutenant had a lethal right hand.

Another non-com clapped Griffin on the shoulder. "C'mon, Griff. Bunch of niggers ain't worth goin' to the brig for."

Driscoll beamed. "Good. Another volunteer. All four of you, in fact—fall in over there, and impress me."

And the four non-coms joined the formation, each one falling in behind Connor, putting one white man on the end of the first four black rows. Their efforts were, at best, lackadaisical, but Driscoll pushed it no further as they were in line and part of the crew, however peripherally.

After the jumping jacks, Pete outlined a course using the buildings, and told Sarge to lead the men around them, double-time. Rosetti went with them.

Good, Pete thought. *Nice to have a cop along to maintain law and order.*

When the runners were a hundred yards away, Driscoll and Connor turned on Pete. They were not angry, exactly.

Exactly.

Driscoll was grinning like a skull, his hands on his hips. "What in the name of Eleanor Roosevelt did you get us into, Maxie boy?"

"Now we know why the posting wanted big guys," Pete said, "with athletic backgrounds."

As Rochester, Connor began, "Mr. Benny…"

Driscoll cut him off. "Rochester better stay in the wardroom from now on, eh, Connie?"

Connor laughed humorlessly. "Doesn't quite seem so damn funny, at that, under the circumstances.… They're gonna love our Ink Spots impression."

"A colored crew," Driscoll said, shaking his head. "Tell me you didn't know, Maxie. Just convince me you weren't so desperate to get on a warship that—"

"Give me a break, Dick!" Pete threw up his hands. "You think I had a clue about this? You think I wanted to spend the rest of the war babysitting a bunch of blacks?"

"They prefer 'colored'," Driscoll said, "and 'Negro.' That may help you avoid getting knifed in your sleep."

"Give it a rest, Dick," Connor said. "There's been talk of integrating this man's Navy for years."

"I just didn't think it would kick in *today*," Driscoll said dryly. "Much less on the ship we were all so eager to get posted on. ... Christ, fellas, the Japs are bad enough. You saw how our non-coms took it. Pete's gone and dropped us in the middle of a goddamn race war!"

"You're overstating," Connor said, "and you're overreacting."

"Am I? We were just maybe thirty seconds from a full-scale melee. If that Neanderthal Griffin hadn't backed down, we'd all've been fighting, probably for our goddamn lives."

Pete touched the lieutenant's arm and locked eyes with him. "Dick—we all of us said we wanted to do more in this war."

"Fighting the Japs! Not fighting Amos and Andy and the goddamn Kingfish. ... Christ, we'll end up fighting *all* of them, white *and* colored."

"And how," Pete said, "do you propose we get out of this? Go to the skipper and tell him, sorry, we don't like this assignment? We'd rather go out to sea with white sailors. Do you mind?"

Driscoll said nothing. He knew they were screwed.

Pete tried to put the best slant on it. "Look, we all know the Navy's going to integrate—deeper we get in this war, the more we need every able-bodied man. We just have an opportunity to—"

"Oh Christ," Driscoll muttered. "Muzzle him, somebody."

Pete pressed on: "With this duty, we can make a bigger impact than we ever dreamed of. Prove ourselves as men and as officers."

Pete might have been a roadside accident, the way Driscoll looked at him. "Has it occurred to you, Maxie—to *any* of you— that we're about to serve on the fucking USS *Powderkeg*? An ammunition ship run by colored boys who despise our lily-white asses?"

"I am lily-white," Pete admitted. "I'm a kid from Iowa where the closest thing to seeing anybody colored is when you get a suntan detassling corn. But I never knew a Jew before I met this crazy asshole Connor from Brooklyn. And I sure never ran into any Italian-Mexican mongrels like Rosetti. As for you, Dick, why you're whiter than the Hitler Youth. So who's better suited to take this on than us?"

"You're serious," Driscoll said.

"Well, I'm not asking for a transfer, first day on the job. Put it that way."

Turning to Connor, Driscoll asked, "Are you buyin' this load of holier-than-thou horseshit?"

"Calling me a crazy asshole does seem a little harsh," Connor said. "Otherwise, yeah. I'm with Pete."

Driscoll fell silent and so did Pete and Connor.

Soon Sarge Washington was leading the runners back around the last building. The big scarred seaman had barely worked up a sweat, although Rosetti, next to him, was drenched with the stuff. Bringing up the rear were the four white non-coms, Griffin the only one who seemed to be keeping up the pace, probably on sheer anger, the others lagging.

Pete made a circle with his index finger in the air. "Once more around, Seaman Washington."

Sarge smiled at him. "Aye aye, Lieutenant. We just gettin' warmed up."

Rosetti jogged to a stop as the rest of the runners went on by. He bent and put his hands on his knees and breathed deep. "Well? We stuck with this duty or what?"

With a sour smile, Driscoll said, "Seems we're doing this for history or mankind or some such flopdoodle. You'll have to check with Maxie to get the full details. What do *I* know? I'm only the XO."

Shaking his head, Rosetti said, "I figured it wasn't good news."

And he jogged back off, falling in behind the stragglers and encouraging them to pick up the pace.

The crew had just turned the first corner and out of sight when a Jeep pulled up next to the three Fantailers. A tall, sturdily built officer in sunglasses, his hat down nearly to his eyebrows, climbed out like he was taking a beachhead; on his collar, he wore the gold oak leaf of a lieutenant commander. The California sunshine had done nothing for his pasty complexion.

"Ten-*hut*," Driscoll said, and all three came to attention.

As he approached, the lieutenant commander removed his glasses and studied them. Pushing fifty, he had brown eyes with thick, shaggy brows, and a nose that had been broken at least once in a well-grooved face that included a chiseled chin. His mouth was a thin-lipped line.

All three men saluted and held it until he returned the gesture.

"Names and assignments," the commander said in a gruff baritone that would not have prompted Pete to offer the man an audition for the choir.

"Lieutenant Richard Driscoll, executive officer, *Liberty Hill Victory*."

"Lieutenant (j.g.) Peter Maxwell, second officer, *Liberty Hill Victory*."

"Ensign Benjamin Connor, communications officer, *Liberty Hill Victory*."

"Where's the other shavetail?" the commander asked.

"Ensign Vincent Rosetti," Driscoll said. "Engineer, *Liberty—*"

"Answer the question as asked, Lieutenant," the commander snapped. "Where is he?"

Pete said, "He's running with the crew, sir. He should be back…"

"I don't recall asking you, Mr. Maxwell." He shook his head now, openly irritated. "For your information and edification, gentlemen, there are only two things that burn my ass more than smart-ass college boys. Would you happen to know what those are, Mr. Driscoll?"

Driscoll said nothing, glancing at the others for help. None was forthcoming.

The commander's voice turned icy. "Coloreds and commies. Coloreds, commies, college boys—my three 'C's. In my view, groups responsible for all the trouble in this man's Navy."

Connor couldn't help himself. "Well, at least we don't have any communists aboard."

The commander shot Connor a look-to-kill, and the comedy writer seemed to fold in on himself. "Do we *know* that, Mr. Connor? These simple-minded coloreds are easy marks for socialist subversion—over at Port Chicago, we've found union booklets, you know."

Be careful what you wish for, Peter, his mother's voice whispered.

"Enough of this chit chat. I'm Lieutenant Commander John Jacob Egan, commanding officer of the *Liberty Hill Victory.* Does it strike you as appropriate, Mr. Connor, to make weisenheimer remarks to your commanding officer?"

"No, sir. Sorry, sir."

"If you're not sorry now, Mr. Connor, you damn well will be. Give it time." Egan studied the ensign for an agonizingly suspicious moment. "Connor... that's Irish, isn't it?"

"It is, sir," Connor said.

"Somehow you don't look Irish to me, Mr. Connor. *Egan* is Irish, you know."

"Yes, sir. Lot of Egans in my neighborhood, sir."

"What neighborhood is that, Mr. Connor?"

"Brooklyn, sir."

"Brooklyn is not a neighborhood, Mr. Connor. It's a borough. You do know the difference between a neighborhood and a borough, Mr. Connor?"

"Yes, sir."

And the ensign left it at that, having no desire to learn where Jews fell on Lieutenant Commander Egan's hate parade.

The crew rounded the last corner, the runners approaching now. Sarge was still out front, loping along easily, his bald head gleaming in the sunlight. As the group ran back into the grass, many bending over gasping for breath, others dropping to the ground, sweat pearling off dark skin under rolled-up sleeves, Rosetti trotted up to the officers and saluted smartly.

"Skipper, Ensign Vincent Rosetti, engineer."

Egan returned the salute. "Another college boy."

"Don't hold it against me, sir," Rosetti said. "Night school."

Eyeing Rosetti appraisingly, Egan said, "What did you do during the day, then, Mr. Rosetti?"

"Beat cop in L.A., sir."

The lieutenant commander darn near smiled. "Good, good," he said. "Good to hear. That will come in handy in these ... circumstances." He gazed toward the runners recovering over on the grass. "So ... this is our crew."

"Yes, sir," the Fantail Four said as one.

"Well, headquarters warned me about this. We'll just have to make the best of it, right, men?"

Together they said, "Aye aye, sir."

"Leadership is all about making the tough decisions, isn't that right, Mr. Driscoll?"

"Yes, sir."

"These coloreds have just as much right to fight this war as anybody. We'll see they get their chance, won't we, Lieutenant?"

"Aye aye, sir."

He expelled a bushel of air. "Very well. Get them showered and cleaned up. We're leaving for Richmond this afternoon. You have one hour to have them all in front of the HQ building in their dress whites—understood, Lieutenant Driscoll?"

"Aye, sir," Driscoll said. "One hour."

Egan gave them one crisp nod to share among them, then returned to his Jeep.

Driscoll walked over to the crew and introduced himself and gave them their orders, his manner cool but not hostile.

One hour later, the crew had assembled in formation in front of the art moderne HQ building, where a bus and a Jeep waited. Egan exited the building and stepped up to Driscoll.

"You and Mr. Maxwell in the Jeep with me," Egan said. "Ensigns Connor and Rosetti on the bus with ... the crew."

"Yes, sir."

A driver from Treasure Island climbed behind the wheel of the Jeep and another plopped into the driver's seat of the bus. The tiny convoy crossed the Bay Bridge into Oakland, then rumbled north into Richmond, circling around the shoreline of San Francisco Bay till they came to a cyclone fence gate. The fence ran from the bay on one side, passed the gate, then snaked around a corner. A big sign lashed to the fence read:

KAISER SHIPYARDS
STOP
U.S. NAVY SECURITY

A Shore Patrol guard in white helmet and armband came out of the guard shack and approached the Jeep. He had a holstered pistol on his belt; a few paces away, another guard had an M-1 rifle slung lazily across his chest, not quite pointed at them.

Egan reached across the driver and handed the guard several sheets of paper.

"Crew of the *Liberty Hill Victory*," the skipper said.

"Yes, sir," the guard said, reading the top sheet. "Just a moment." The Shore Patrol man returned to the guard shack and, through the glass, Pete could see the guard pick up a phone and speak and then nod.

The guard returned with the papers folded up, handed them to Egan and said, "Pier Eight, sir. Down around the far end to the right. I can have a guard accompany you, if that would be easier."

Egan waved him off. "We'll find it, son. Thanks."

Pete couldn't help but notice that they were "damned college boys," but this guard, an enlisted man, was "son." In his gut, something cold twitched. The skipper's outlook was darn odd, and not just his ranting and raving about "colored and commies." Weren't his officers an extension of him? How could Pete and the Fantailers be Egan's eyes and ears when the old salt seemed so full of contempt for them?

Trying to shake this unsettling feeling, Pete turned his gaze ahead, seeing the masts over the tops of buildings; but it wasn't until they came around the last of the fabricating buildings that he caught sight of the ship named for his hometown.

Long and gray, she sat high in the water, her holds obviously empty. Not as sleek as a destroyer or cruiser, the *Liberty Hill Victory* had a boxy look to her. Pete had studied her specs, and knew her to be just over four-hundred fifty-five feet long with a sixty-two foot beam and a fifteen foot draft, unloaded. Once she had a full cargo of ammo, the draft would be a lot more like twenty-seven feet.

Boxy or not, the ship gave Pete a thrill, seeing the name of his hometown painted on the bow. That was just for the christening, of course. Below the name was the designation AK235, auxiliary cargo hull #235.

Auxiliary meant the *Liberty Hill Victory* would normally have been carrying fruit, canned goods, toilet paper, and what-have-you. These, however, were not normal times and she would definitely be serving as an ammo ship.

The fourteen cargo booms were all upright and lashed down, giving the ship the appearance of standing at attention, awaiting her new crew. Perhaps she was not a great warship, but never had

Pete seen anything quite so magnificent as the USS *Liberty Hill Victory*.

Since the only identification Navy ships showed was the hull number, however, one of their first jobs—ironically enough—would be to paint out the white letters spelling LIBERTY HILL VICTORY.

The Jeep and the bus halted on the pier near the ship.

Egan led as the men piled out of the vehicles and made their way up the gangplank, the line moving slowly as each man stopped at the top to salute the flag before climbing aboard.

From their orders, each man knew his work station, battle station, and billet. Lieutenant Commander Egan, now the captain aboard the ship, had a cabin to himself, as did the first mate, Driscoll, whose quarters doubled as his office. The same was true for Rosetti, the ship's engineer.

Pete shared a cramped cabin with Connor on the port side. The left side of the room was bunk beds with a single bed on the other. Pete, as ranking officer, chose the lower with Connor happy to have the single. By the head of the bunk beds were two wooden lockers; on the same wall as the door, a fold-down desk was below a mirrored medicine chest. A third locker stood at the foot of Connor's bed.

Each bed had a small reading light mounted on the wall just above the pillow, and a small wooden shelf hung on the wall above Pete's bed. One fan was attached to the wall next to the room's only porthole—the only protection they would have against the Pacific heat.

"Not exactly the Waldorf," Connor said, as they both unpacked their sea bags and transferred the contents to their respective lockers.

Pete shrugged.

"Still," Connor said, "must be a treat for you."

"Yeah?"

"Beats sleeping in the barn."

"Are we going to do the 'how many times do I have to tell you I don't live on a farm' routine again? Couldn't you just sell it to Abbott and Costello?"

"My, you Iowa girls are sensitive."

"There *are* towns west of Manhattan, you know."

"Sure. Jersey City. Newark."

"How *ever* did you survive San Diego?"

"Tough, Pete. Tough. If I hadn't found that little deli restaurant, with the great lox and bagels? I'd've lost my mind."

"I've had lox and bagels before."

"Do tell! Where?"

"Hotel Fort Des Moines. They serve all kinds of foreign dishes."

"*Foreign* dishes! Pete … you're pulling my leg, aren't you?"

"A little."

Driscoll poked his nose in. "Can it, George and Gracie. Skipper wants everybody topside, double time. Let's go."

The sun blinded them when they exited the wheelhouse, but the warmth felt good, and they all paused briefly to let their eyes adjust. Egan was waiting for them in front of the bridge.

"Mr. Driscoll," Egan said, "get these people into formation."

Driscoll carried out the order and, in less than a minute, the crew stood in even rows atop wood panels that served as the cover for number three hatch.

Standing with the other Fantailers, Pete wondered if Egan was about to spew the same sort of venom at the crew as he had toward his officers this morning. The captain had his sunglasses on again and Pete wondered if this shielded him from having to look directly at these two C's from his list—college boys and coloreds.

Then—feet firmly planted, chest out—Egan swept the glasses off dramatically, his eyes moving slowly across the assemblage, seeming to take in every single man in the formation, largely a sea of black faces.

"*Stand easy!*" he told them.

Funny, Pete thought. That had been his own first order to these men.

"Most of you don't know me," he said, gruff but not unfriendly. "I am Lieutenant Commander John Jacob Egan, and I'm captain of the *Liberty Hill Victory.* In the time we're together, you'll find me to be a tough captain. You will also find me to be fair, unless you do not deserve fair treatment. That will be your choice."

They all stood silent, water lapping against the hull the only sound.

"Our job in this war is simple. Don't imagine because we are not in battle that we are not fighting this war. Ours is a vital job. Brutally put, the more ammunition we deliver to our troops and our planes and our ships, the more Japs we kill. Kill enough of them, and victory will be ours."

Scattered applause. Egan's face remained a somber mask till the men quieted again.

"We all have the same goal here—to win. Toward that end, I'm going to work you longer and harder than you've ever been worked in your life. The better job we do, the sooner this war will end."

Again, a few of the men clapped and whooped, and Egan waited.

"Now, when we get back to the base," he said, "you'll all be granted twenty-four-hour liberty."

More applause and more whoops.

"But when you come back, be ready to work. Because the war begins then—*understood?*"

"Aye aye, sir!" they said in one voice.

Astounded, Pete could only wonder where the prejudiced horse's ass he'd met this morning had disappeared to. This new

Captain Egan had already worked this crew up to where they'd run through flames for him. Where was the monster who, just a few hours ago, had as much as promised to make all their lives a living hell?

Egan said, "Leadership is about making tough decisions … and sticking to them. And I have faith in the leaders on this ship. Follow my orders, and those of my officers, and you'll be fine."

Pete glanced sideways to see how Driscoll was reacting to the skipper's speech. The exec stood ramrod straight, his face blank as a baby's. Whatever he might be feeling, Driscoll was keeping it to himself.

Egan asked the assemblage, "Do you men understand?"

"*Aye aye, sir!*"

"Back to the base then," Egan said.

The crew applauded, and the captain nodded his thanks, the thin line of his mouth etched in a near smile.

Soon the commander was sitting in the Jeep and waiting while the Fantail Four oversaw the loading of the bus, herding the Negroes in.

Pete was at the front door of the bus, guiding the men up and in. Sarge, with steward's mate Willie Wilson right behind him, paused to speak to Pete.

"Thanks for your help today, Sarge."

"That's what all that money they pay us is for. You goin' out tonight, Mr. Maxwell?"

"Haven't thought about it."

"This ain't San Diego, sir. San Fran's a whole lot different, whole lot better. Places here we can go and wail and nobody will care two shits about what color we is."

"I don't have a horn."

"That's a detail I can handle. What say?"

"… I'll meet you in front of the HQ building."

Sarge flashed a grin. "Yes, sir," he said, then boarded the bus.

Connor stared at Pete as the rest of the coloreds kept climbing up the stairs onto the vehicle. "Don't tell me you got friends on the Globetrotters, Pete?"

"Why not?" Pete asked. "Don't Rochester and Mr. Benny get along?"

"Yeah," Connor admitted. "But that's radio. This here is closer to real life."

FIVE

JULY 17, 1944

The night Pete Maxwell had gone out clubbing with Sarge and Willie in San Francisco had been a revelation. The handful of joints they took in seemed color-blind, Negro and white musicians and even audience members mingling without incident. The two colored musicians knew enough guys on the various bandstands to give the three Navy men plenty of chances to sit in. Pete had borrowed a horn from a colored cat who was so much better than he was, the thought that he was blowing into the same horn as a Negro never occurred to him till later.

What a kick, playing Ellington, Jordan, and Calloway tunes with such a variety of great players till the sun came up. In the four weeks since that golden night, Pete remembered it fondly as the last really great time he'd had, with one exception.

That exception had been a weekend liberty during the brief in-port training period, where Kay rode the train up to see him, and they'd taken a hotel room at the Mark Hopkins no less, and shared room service and made love till he thought his poor pecker would fall off. They'd done a little sightseeing—Fisherman's Wharf, the Presidio—but mostly, when they weren't in bed, they just walked around and kissed and talked like the high school sweethearts they'd not long ago been.

Before he put her back on the train at the Bay Bridge Terminal, they stood kissing on the steam-swept platform like a scene out of half a dozen movies they'd seen, only usually it was the soldier or sailor getting on the train, not the pretty girl.

"Is this the last time we'll have together before you go out to sea?" she asked.

"Probably." Pete really had no idea, and if he had, he wouldn't have been able to tell her; loose lips and ships and all. So he just said reassuringly, "We'll have to come back to San Francisco to reload, eventually, so maybe it won't be so long."

"I ... I have a feeling we did it."

"Did what?"

"It's silly, but ... yesterday afternoon, I just know we made a baby."

"God, I hope so."

She shrugged, her brown hair bouncing off her shoulders, an image that would replay in his mind a thousand times in the days ahead.

"If not," she said, "we'll just have to keep trying."

Then she was leaning out a window waving, and he was doing that stupid routine from the pictures where the lover ran along after the train leaving the station. *Such a silly stupid cliché,* he thought, standing there on the platform, tears on his face, like he was just a kid and not a man.

Other than the two oases of pleasure—music and romance— the last twenty-six days had been Hell, the skipper keeping his promise, officers and crew putting in long round-the-clock shifts, practicing everything from dropping anchor to going to battle stations, to pulling off all the wooden panels that covered the five hatches of the five holds. The colored boys had performed much better than any of the officers could have hoped for. Especially Captain Egan.

The apparent contradiction between the captain's private racist comments (to his young officers) and his public pep talk (to the colored crew) had been cleared up soon after they'd sailed under the Golden Gate Bridge. Once the land was gone and the ocean was everywhere, Egan had called the four officers into his office for a meeting.

The office adjoined the captain's cabin, which was spacious compared to Pete's quarters but still a trick to accommodate five men. An oak desk, a refrigerator, and a safe were among the other accoutrements, but the conference took place with Driscoll and Pete seated on a bench under the porthole and with Rosetti and Connor in bolted-down oak chairs opposite.

Hands on hips, the big crusty Egan stood as if at the head of an invisible table between the bench and the chairs, and they had to crane their necks to give him their full attention.

"You men know how I feel about the make-up of our crew," he said with frigid distaste. "But it doesn't matter a damn that I don't like the way this ship smells—it won't keep me, it won't keep *us*, from doing our goddamn jobs. Do I make myself clear?"

"Yes, sir," they all said.

One shaggy eyebrow rose. "So I did *my* job—I gave the spooks the 'Win One for the Gipper' speech. I got them all fired up, and to their credit, they ate it up like watermelon."

Connor sneaked Pete a look; Pete ignored it.

Egan was saying, "Now, it's your job to keep them that way— nappy and happy. My job is to sail this goddamned ship—you men just keep those colored boys out of my sight and busy, none of this shiftless nonsense. We have a brig for goldbrickers, so don't be afraid to use it. Do I make myself clear, Lieutenant Driscoll?"

"In spades, sir," Driscoll said, a remark the Fantail Four would roar over in the officer's mess but which was delivered straight here.

"Any questions?"

"No, sir," they all said.

Pete had found that treating these men like men, with the respect any man expected, hell, deserved, was all it took to get good work out of them. He extended that attitude to the four white non-coms aboard as well, and so far this crew, black and white alike, seemed hard, dependable workers. Even that big- oted bastard Griffin performed his duties well enough, though he obviously did his best not to interact with the Negroes more than necessary.

As ordered by the President, the Navy had "integrated," but the reality was a sort of segregated integration. Like Pete and the other officers, the four white non-coms had their separate space. None of the Negroes were trained in running the engines, the two steam turbines that drove the ship: that was where Griffin and his buddies came in.

The two men who ran the engines, and that meant the engine room as well, were E-7s, chief petty officers. Tom Whitford was a tall drink of water from Del Rio, Texas, square-shouldered, honest as Abe Lincoln but as prejudiced as his buddy Griffin. The other E-7 was a slightly shorter, stockier guy from Paterson, New Jersey—Albert Blake, who made it known he didn't "give two shits what color you are, as long as you get the fuckin' job done."

Dale Griffin was an E-5, a petty officer second class from Tupelo, Mississippi. Pete had to admit that Griffin was a darn good worker, but it wouldn't have surprised Pete to see the guy show up to shift in a white sheet. The other petty officer second class was from some little town in Missouri—John Smith, with a personality as anonymous as his name.

Griffin and Smith were charged with running the boilers that created the steam turning the turbines. One man manning the boiler and one chief petty officer running the turbines were in the engine room at all times, normally Griffin with Whitford, Smith with Blake. They worked twelve-hour shifts with Blake and Smith usually taking midnight to noon.

When the *Liberty Hill Victory* was at sea, only three of her sixty-plus crew were needed to keep her running: the engine man, the boiler man, and an oiler (a glorified gofer charged with following the orders of the other two, taking care of anything that they were too busy to do).

The oilers worked three eight-hour shifts, and—because this role was carried out by Negroes—the non-coms charged them with the shittiest jobs. This was in addition to the colored oiler's tasks of charting hourly readings and getting sentenced to shaft alley, the darkest, noisiest area in the bowels of the ship.

A fat man's squeeze of a narrow corridor in the absolute bottom of the ship, shaft alley was crowded with steam pipes above and to the side of the massive steel housing that held the spinning drive shaft of the propeller. This dimly lit, dingy hole running half the length of the ship was exactly where nobody wanted to go.

The oilers, lucky them, had to traverse the alley once an hour, making sure that the drive shaft was properly lubricated by taking readings at various stations along the way.

Though most sailors considered this the worst job on the ship, for many it still meant being a seaman and not—as had been typical for Negroes throughout the history of the Navy— lowly steward's mates. Willie Wilson had begged Pete to get him an oiler's job, but you needed a seaman's rating to hold the position, and no steward's mates did.

From 0700 to 1500 hours, the biggest man that Pete had ever seen, white or black, served as oiler. This Negro made the bouncer at the Silver Slipper look like Billy Barty. Hell, "Big" Brown was almost too large to fit into shaft alley. Brown's given name was Simon, according to the crew roster, but the other colored boys and most of the whites never called him Brown, always Big Brown.

An exception was the racist Griffin, who (according to ship scuttlebutt) had once snapped at Big Brown over some screwup real or imagined, "You're the biggest black idiot I ever saw, Brown!"

Big Brown reportedly picked the much smaller Griffin up by both arms and smiled into his face and said, "My friends call me 'Big Brown,' Mr. Griffin."

Whether the story was true or not, Griffin rarely spoke to the intimidating boiler at all, and certainly kept his epithets to himself, apparently understanding that discretion was the better part of valor when Big Brown was around.

The 1500 to 2300 shift belonged to Lenny Wallace, a light-skinned Negro seaman from Seattle. A college student at Seattle Pacific University, Wallace had applied to Officer Candidate School but—after he was repeatedly turned away—settled for being a seaman.

Manning the overnight shift from 2300 until 0700 hours was Orville Monroe, an elfish, articulate, effeminate Negro. When Sarge and Pete had been alone on the fantail one night, smoking Chesterfields, Sarge had asked the officer to watch out for Monroe.

"Poor little guy's queer as a square egg," Sarge had said. "None of the other boys want nothing to do with him. If I hadn't set 'em straight, they beat his ass purple by now."

"You know," Pete had said, "you can be tossed out of the Navy for deviant acts."

"Mr. Maxwell, if every sailor ever sailed up the brown canal got tossed out of the service, there be you and me and maybe Popeye left. And I ain't so sure about Popeye."

"You can't be serious."

"I'm serious about Orville. Poor little punk's caught in between."

"In between what?"

"Let's put it this way—guys like that prick Griffin, meanin' no disrespect, think we're a bunch of shiftless niggers. And about every other Negro on this ship thinks white folk are the enemy, and this war just means a temporary truce."

"Surely it's not that bad."

"It's worse for Orville. Think about it."

And Pete had. On a ship divided along racial lines, Orville Monroe was indeed caught between. Pete recalled that poem from high school: John Donne had said, "No man is an island," but you couldn't prove it by the likes of Orville Monroe, poised to catch crap from both sides.

So Pete had gone out of his way to be friendly and fair with Orville, who'd approached the lieutenant about getting him a transfer.

"Mr. Maxwell," the long-lashed seaman had said, "I'm gettin' ten kinds of holy hell over my intelligence and artistical ways. Is it my fault I'm smarter and more sensible than these gorillas? I learned to type in junior high. Maybe I could transfer to an office somewheres."

"Orville, I'll put in for a transfer for you, but, honestly, we're so shorthanded, the chance that Captain Egan will give up an able-bodied man like you is somewhere between slim and none."

"You consider *me* able-bodied, Mr. Maxwell?"

"Sure. You're small, but you pitch in."

Orville had gone off pleased with himself, and Pete had wondered if his "able-bodied" remark had been taken in some weird sexual way by the sailor. He knew very little about homosexuals, other than that a janitor at the post office where his pop worked back home had been fired for it.

Still, Pete had done what he could for the kid. He got Driscoll to order Wallace and Orville to switch shifts from their original assignments, which had Wallace working overnight. Under the new orders, Orville only spent an hour a day with Whitford and Griffin. Pete hoped Griffin couldn't pile too much grief on the little guy in only an hour.

One might think keeping a born victim like Orville Monroe from being worked to death would be a fairly simple matter; with only five officers—including their recalcitrant skipper, who barely left the bridge or his cabin—they couldn't be everywhere at once.

Plus, the non-coms had a certain amount of power of their own, especially within the confines of the engine room.

The Orville matter concerned Pete enough that he'd asked the rest of the Fantail Four to keep an eye out for Orville's welfare; whatever they might individually feel about (as Rosetti put it) "fairies," they'd all agreed to do their best to keep Griffin and the rest from abusing the sailor.

Now, the shakedown cruise was almost over. Mere hours away from port, Pete entered the officers' mess for a late lunch. On the starboard side of the boat deck, between the officers' pantry and the ship's office, the mess was Pete's favorite room on board.

Not merely the font of food and ever-available hot coffee, the mess was consistently the quietest place on the ship. Even his own cabin was no safe haven—when Connor and Pete weren't on separate watches, the latter had to put up with the former's championship snoring, which sometimes made Pete think he'd sleepwalked down to shaft alley.

The mess offered peace, quiet, and yes, a steaming cup of coffee. The short wall to the left and the long starboard wall opposite the door were home to long, green leather-covered banquettes. Long tables with wooden chairs ran in front of them, bolted to the deck. Two portholes and one fan served to cool the place, but today the portholes were closed and the fan turned off.

July's warmth was offset by their position on the eastern edge of a Pacific storm. For now at least, Captain Egan had successfully outrun the rain, the skies brighter to the east, toward home; but a chill still hung in the air, a stiff breeze stirring choppy swells, making sailing less than ideal.

Pete poured himself a cup of coffee, then dropped into the sheer pleasure of the hard seat. He set his hat on the table.

Willie, in his steward's mate whites, ducked his head in. "Get you anything, Mr. Maxwell?"

"What's for lunch today?"

"Got your favorite, sir. Shit on a shingle."

"Oh Christ. Willie, you know how to ruin a moment."

Willie's mournful mug split into a grin. "I'm just razzin' ya, sir. Cookie made up hot beef sandwiches with mashed potatoes and green beans."

Soon Connor came in and made straight for the coffee urn, then he and his cup of joe slid into the banquette across from Pete.

"Any sign of the Promised Land, Ben?"

Connor gave him a fatigued smile. "Pete, you know my people are only happy when we're suffering."

"And?"

"You're looking at the most ecstatic fucker on this tub."

Pete smiled. "Skipper still making your life holy hell?"

"Aye aye. I think El Capitan has figured out I'm not Irish."

"Really. And to think most people mistake you for Pat O'Brien."

"Sarcasm doesn't really become you farm boys. Stick with slapstick. Slipping in a cowpie, that kinda thing." He sipped the hot liquid. "Seen Driscoll?"

"Sacked out. He's on watch with you tonight."

"Rosetti?"

"Supposed to be running gun practice in…" Pete checked his watch. "…about half an hour."

"Gun practice since when?"

"Since a couple of sea-going tugs are coming out from Frisco to meet us. They'll be towing targets, and Vince and the gun crews are supposed to blow the bejesus out of them."

"Well, I'm glad *somebody*'s getting something worthwhile accomplished."

Willie came in, set their meals on the table and was gone again. The steward's mate's familiarity with Pete was reserved for when no other white officers were around.

"What's eating you, Ben?" Pete asked, filling a fork with potatoes and gravy.

Making sure Willie was really gone, Connor said, "It's these damn Negroes."

"Aw, for Christ's sake—not you, too! You're getting as bad as Dick. These guys are doing the best they—"

Connor stopped him with an upraised palm. "No, no, you're getting me wrong. I don't think every colored boy aboard is dumber than Stepin Fetchit. Not at all. In fact, I've taken your lead."

"What 'lead' is that?"

The comedy writer leaned forward. "I've been talking to these boys, trying to get to know them some. In the process, I've been watching them work, and noticing that they sometimes get even the simplest things wrong."

"I thought you said—"

"Quiet, Andy Hardy. Listen to the judge. I knew they weren't fouling up because they're stupid; they are not stupid. Well, some are, but so are some of us. ... Anyway, I wanted to know why the simple mistakes, oftentimes after they'd done some other thing a hundred times harder ... so I started talking to them. One at a time. One fella to another fella."

"And?"

Connor sighed, leaned back. "These boys are from all over the place—New York, Chicago, St. Louis, the big towns, but also Paducah, Hattiesburg, and towns plenty smaller."

"So what?"

"In the South, the blacks and whites are segregated."

"This is news?"

"Not to me, but the Navy maybe." Connor shook his head, clearly frustrated. "You think their education, their schools, are as good as the white variety? Hell, even Negroes from the North aren't getting anywhere near the same quality as we got."

"I ... I guess I never thought about that."

"Well, they're not gonna teach you about it in school!" Connor, bored with his food, pushed it aside and lit up a Lucky. "One guy, a kid from Georgia, told me how they had a single teacher for all twelve grades—nearly fifty kids and only one teacher! A lot of our boys grew up poor, dirt fucking poor, Pete ... to where they had to quit school in the seventh or eighth grade to work in the fields, sometimes earlier than that. Some of these boys are practically illiterate. Hell—no 'practically' about it."

The terrible possibilities were immediately apparent to Pete. "Oh, hell. You mean, we're going to be dealing with ammunition … high explosives … and the crew can't even *read?*"

Connor shrugged. "Not all of them are illiterate. Maybe only 20 or 30 percent. But we still have got to do something about it."

Pete frowned. "You think the Navy is going to let us disqualify them and get them off the ship?"

"Sure. Right after they send Dorothy Lamour and Dinah Shore to our cabin for a personal USO show."

"Well, if we can't get them off the ship, then … really there's only one alternative."

"That's the way I see it," Connor said.

Pete pointed at the radio writer. "*You're* going to have to teach them to read."

Connor's eyes got bigger than Eddie Cantor doing his Banjo Eyes routine; he thumbed his chest. "*Me?*"

"It was your idea. You're the guy who knows words. You studied literature in college, and—"

"Literature! Literature to these guys is comic books."

Pete shrugged. "Might not be a bad place to start. Beats Dick and Jane."

For once, Pete had topped Connor, who just sat there agape.

"Look," Pete said with a grin, "I won't stick you with the whole job. We'll do it together. I was studying to be a teacher myself. Be good practice."

Connor liked the sound of that and got interested in his chow again. After the two officers had eaten, they began discussing the logistics of what they wanted to do. They were in the midst of this when Willie came in to pick up their plates.

"Willie," Pete said. "Would you mind sitting down with us for a moment?"

"Here?" The steward's mate looked around as if being seen sitting in the officers' mess might get him time in the brig. "With you men?"

"Sure," Connor said. "Nothing against it in the regs, Willie."

"Well.... Let me just take these to the kitchen, first."

Pete said, "Fine. We just want to bend your ear a little."

"Oh kay," Willie said skeptically, taking the dishes out with him.

In a minute or so, Willie was back; he sat on the wooden chair next to Connor while Pete explained the problem and how they hoped to deal with it. But Willie began frowning halfway through and clearly wasn't onboard.

Connor asked, "I can see you have a problem with this, Willie. What is it?"

Willie shook his head. "What you're saying, sirs, and I mean no disrespect, but ... you're saying us colored boys is just a bunch of damn fools."

"No," Pete said, flabbergasted by this response. "God, Willie, not at all!"

Willie's upper lip curled. "Stupid, then."

"Hardly," Pete said. "There's a big difference between stupidity and ignorance."

"Oh, we *ignorant* fools, then ..."

Connor turned and gazed right at Willie. "Ignorance is not stupidity, and it's not foolishness, either, unless you make no effort to correct it. A lot of you fellas can already read. But the ones who can't—who don't recognize the words 'Explosives' or 'No Smoking'—they can wind up hurting everybody, black and white."

By now Willie's frown had turned thoughtful.

Pete said, "We're talking getting a little education to your buddies. To make their jobs easier, and everybody safer."

"Well," Willie said. "That ain't the dumbest idea I ever heard."

Pete had him now. "It'll be helpful to the boys in the long run, too—we're not going to be on this ship forever, Willie. Peace'll come and if these guys can read, they'll have a leg up."

Chin crinkled, Willie nodded. "I can see that."

"Of course," Connor said, "they may react like you did, and think we're just a bunch of smart-ass white boys looking down on them."

"You ain't wrong."

Pete leaned forward. "But, Willie, if leaders among the men—like you and Sarge—step up to the plate, it'll go over swell. It'll go like gangbusters."

"Me and Sarge? How do you figure?"

"You can help sell this to the boys. Explain the safety issue, and what it'll mean for their futures. Anyway, we'll be on a long sea voyage and it beats assholes and elbows, scrubbing down the decks."

Willie was thinking that over.

Connor said, "You and Sarge could even tutor the guys between classes."

"Tutor? You mean, *us* teach, too?"

"You can read, can't you?"

"Of course I can. Sarge can read up a storm—I seen him do it. He's got books and shit."

Connor held out an open palm. "How about it, Willie? You want to fill Sarge in about this for us?"

"Guess I can do that, Mr. Connor."

"I mean, I'd be glad to do it myself."

Willie waved it off. "That's all right. No offense, sir, but Sarge'll take it better from me or maybe Mr. Maxwell. He likes Mr. Maxwell, where he thinks you're kind of a smart aleck. Sir."

They dismissed Willie, and Pete said to Connor, "Can I help it if I'm likable?"

"Shut up and let me suffer," Connor cracked.

"It's what you people do best," Pete said, affably.

Pete spent the afternoon in his cabin trying to catch a nap. Connor was on duty on deck and Rosetti's target practice was over, so getting to sleep should have been a breeze.

It wasn't.

The longer he lay on his bunk, the more he worried over his and Connor's teaching notion. It had come about more or less spontaneously, but now, on reflection, Pete realized they should be running this idea past the skipper. But Egan had made it clear that he wanted as little to do with the colored crew as possible.

Still, this was the Navy, and protocol was protocol, and if the teaching was undertaken and then raised the captain's ire, that risked alienating the crew members, when the classes got rudely shut down.

In his mind he heard Kay's voice: **Why not side step your captain, and take it to your friend Dick?**

Yes! I could present the notion to Dick when we're on watch tonight.

Right. And if Dick tells you to go to the captain with the idea, you do just that.

And if he says he thinks it's a good idea, but doesn't suggest going to Egan?

No problem. Dick liking the idea is tacit approval, and you can go ahead. Any other questions?

Pete and Driscoll took over the watch at 1900, just after dinner. About three hours into their shift, Pete was standing outside the wheelhouse on the port side of the bridge, binoculars around his neck on a lanyard.

Through the open door, he could see Jackson, the Negro helmsman, at the wheel; beyond Jackson in the darkened wheelhouse sat Driscoll in the skipper's chair. The two men were bathed in the soft blue-and-red glow of the instrument lights as they headed toward the Golden Gate Bridge.

Normally, they would have waited for sun-up to sail into the bay. The ship had plenty of headroom beneath the huge structure, but those guiding her still had to be aware of the monstrous pilings buried in the ocean bed. Scraping those, or worse yet hitting them, would be a disaster. Blackout orders kept the bridge darkened at this hour, as well, making the trip a further risk.

Egan had ordered the nighttime approach, however, as new orders had come in for the *Liberty Hill* to report to Port Chicago near San Francisco for loading and refueling, chop chop.

"And that doesn't mean in the morning," Egan had said.

"Aye aye, sir," Driscoll had said.

Now, as the ship approached the bridge in pitch darkness, Pete found himself on edge as he drew up the binoculars in hopes of spotting something. The cities around them—San Francisco, Oakland, Berkeley, and the smaller communities, San Rafael, Richmond—were all under blackout orders as well, and only a few scattered lights dotted the landscape like stubborn fireflies. Pete strained his eyes and finally managed to make out the silhouette of the looming structure.

"Steady as she goes," he called out.

Driscoll echoed the order, as did the helmsman. They were lined up perfectly, and as they eased under the immense structure at quarter speed, Pete gazed up at its underside ominously blocking out the stars above. They crossed under, and as they emerged on the other side, the stars in the sky right where he left them, Pete let out his breath, his entire body relaxing.

He walked into the wheelhouse. "All clear, sir."

"Very well," Driscoll said.

"We've got a few minutes now, sir," Pete said. "Could I talk to you?"

Driscoll nodded and rose in that unfolding manner of so many tall men. "Steady as she goes, Mr. Jackson," he said. "We'll be right outside if you need us."

Jackson said, "Aye, sir."

Pete led the way out the starboard door onto the wing of the bridge where a soft warm whisper of breeze awaited them.

Pulling a pack of Luckies from his shirt pocket, Driscoll shook one out. Pete did the same with his Chesterfields, sharing Driscoll's Zippo, turning their backs to the wind as they lighted the smokes.

"So, Maxie," Driscoll said. "What's up? Cow get loose from the barn again?"

For once Pete skipped any city boy/country boy repartee and went straight to the literacy problem and the solution he and Connor were developing.

After a slow drag, Driscoll held the smoke in his lungs for a long moment, then blew it out through his nose. "You guys seriously think you're going to change the lives of a bunch of poor colored boys by teaching them how to read?"

"That's part of it. Maybe saving our own lives here on the USS *Powderkeg* is another."

Driscoll's chuckle had a patronizing, patrician tinge. "Maxie, these Jim Crows who can't read are, unlike you, *really* right off the farm ... sharecroppers, most of them—what the hell do you think they'll be able to do with this little bit of knowledge?"

"Maybe save lives on this ship. Maybe get a decent job after the war."

"Maxie, haven't you noticed? They're colored. You don't need to read to shine shoes or be a porter."

Pete glanced through the open door to see if Jackson had eavesdropped any of this. But the helmsman's eyes were straight ahead and gave no sign that he'd heard Driscoll's insult.

Pete knew Driscoll's privileged point of view was a wall he couldn't break down. So he stuck to safety.

"Dick, you want somebody to light up a cigarette in the wrong place, because he mistakes 'incendiary' for 'entryway' or 'infirmary' or God knows what?"

"Sounds like a lot of work for minimal gain," Driscoll said. "I mean, here we stand, the two of us running this ship—the captain hardly comes out of his cabin. And what kind of ship is it?"

"A ... a Victory ship."

"An *ammunition* ship. And let me ask you, Maxie—what kind of training in shiploading or handling ammunition or for that matter commanding men have you had? Or me, or Connie or Rosie?"

"None, really. Learn by doing, I guess."

"Has the Navy given us any manuals from which to teach these colored boys about ammunition handling?"

"No."

"We've got the *Red Book* with its codified safety regs designed for peacetime, moving small quantities of ammo. And that's all. Nothing for the men. Do you know why?"

"No."

"Because the United States Navy views these colored boys as expendable. And guess why the complement of white officers and non-coms is so small, Maxie—it's because we, too, have been deemed expendable. How do you like that?"

"Well," Pete said, and swallowed, "I don't. So let's do what we can to help these boys read, so *none* of us get blown to hell."

Driscoll, with that blank baby expression he got, just stared at Pete.

"Or maybe," Pete said, "I should just go to the skipper with it, then?"

The exec rolled his eyes as he tossed his sparking cigarette into the sea. "Jesus, Maxie, Egan will throw a shit fit!"

"If you won't give me the okay, Dick, I at least have to try."

Driscoll raised a palm in surrender. "All right. All right. You and Connie wanna do this on your own time, it's fine by me. I happen to think you're on a fool's errand, but as long as *I* don't have to be one of the fools, go right ahead. It may relieve your boredom on the long days at sea."

"Thank you, Dick," Pete said quietly.

"When have I ever denied you anything, Maxie, my boy?"

Pete tossed his cigarette overboard, and the two officers went back into the wheelhouse.

"Mr. Maxwell," Driscoll said. "Go back out on the wing and see if there's any sign of that tugboat, will you?"

"Aye aye, sir," Pete said and passed through the wheelhouse and out the port side door.

Driscoll was referring to the tug that would bring the harbor pilot out to take over the helm, a local sailor who knew the bay intimately and would steer the *Liberty Hill Victory* through and on up the narrow channel to the appropriate loading pier at the Port Chicago Naval Base.

Raising the binoculars, Pete slowly scanned the horizon, but could see little in the pitch black. They were still short of the area where they'd meet the harbor tug; but, in the darkness, the sooner he could spot that boat, the safer everyone would be.

"No sign of them, sir," he said, glancing back through the door. Steward's Mate Wilson was handing Driscoll a mug of coffee off a tray and had another ready for Pete.

Driscoll said, "Keep a sharp eye."

"Aye, sir."

Pete was still facing the wheelhouse when Wilson came toward him, through the door, the steward mate's hand on the mug of coffee, ready to pass it to Pete.

Over his shoulder, Pete thought he caught a flash of something on the shore, maybe behind the hills in front of the ship.

As he turned, a bigger ball of fire rose three, no, *four* thousand feet, illuminating the sky in bright yellow and red, lighting up the base and the hills, too, so intensely that Pete brought his arm up reflexively to shut out the glare. The ship rocked, and Pete heard the tray and mug crash to the deck just as the sound of the massive blast reached them. Pete lurched to keep his balance and wheeled away from the explosion.

"Lord, my eyes!" Willie was screaming, his hands going to his face as he dropped to his knees as if in desperate prayer.

Pete blinked rapidly trying to dissipate the white lightning bolts that seemed to be going off in front of him. He could barely make out Driscoll diving toward the button that set off the horn as the executive officer screamed, "*Battle stations!*"

"What the hell?" Pete managed as several more smaller explosions went off behind the hills. On the shoreline, tongues of red flame shot out from gray-black plumes of smoke while smaller explosions, shells bursting probably, created an elaborate fireworks display.

Helmsman Jackson yelled, "Jesus Christ, the Japs are bombing the *base!*"

Captain Egan sprinted onto the bridge clad only in his skivvies, yelling, "What the hell's going on?"

The only answer the captain got were smaller explosions that continued for another thirty seconds, though it felt much longer. Every crewman aboard the *Liberty Hill Victory* was in motion now, grabbing helmets and life jackets as they sprinted to their battle stations.

Egan tried again: "What the hell is going *on?*"

But no one responded; everyone, at least everyone who could still see, was staring toward the shore—flames had taken over where, minutes before, the base at Port Chicago had been. Flaming rubble had replaced it and the two ships docked there, the conflagration's reflection onto the water making it seem as if the very ocean had caught fire.

SIX

JULY 17, 1944 – AUGUST 11, 1944

Seaman Marvin Hannah had only just arrived at Port Chicago a week before the explosion. The teenage drummer had kept his word to bandmates Willie and Sarge—and even that nice ofay horn blower, Pete something—and enlisted the day he turned eighteen, two weeks or so after their last gig at the Silver Slipper.

A shortage of men at Port Chicago had seen Marvin rushed through Robert Smalls training camp in a month, and soon—like so many Negro sailors—Marvin found himself not on a ship, but on a dock, loading ammo.

Marvin had spent much of that evening bitching that he'd rather be working nights; in July in California, a clear, cool night like this one, a gentle breeze whispering in from the southwest, would have smoothed out that rough duty on the dock. Right now, the same cargo ship he'd helped load in the day's hot sun was taking on more ammo and explosives, as the boys of Third Division worked under floodlights, chipping away at the 5,000 or so tons of the nasty stuff that needed shifting from boxcars to the *E. A. Bryan*. The *Quinault Victory* had just moored around six, and a hundred guys from the Sixth Division were rigging the ship for loading.

Just before the shit hit the fan, the enlisted men's barracks was still as a photograph, most guys in their bunks and well on their way to dreamland.

Marvin, however, was in the latrine—reading a *Captain Marvel* funny book.

In fact, Billy Batson had just said "Shazam" when an explosion blew the little drummer right off the can, sending him flying one way and the comic book flapping another. He had just enough time to cover his face before slamming into the wall like a bug into a windshield.

He hadn't had time to drop to the latrine floor before a second blast made the first one seem like a warm-up, pinballing Marvin across to the other wall, where he hit at least as hard as before, on his back this time, rattling his teeth and shaking every damn bone in his body.

Guys out there were screaming, and all the lights that weren't already off had gone black, but through the doorway he could see the flash of shards of glass flying like deadly hail, as the many windows of the barracks blew out.

Somehow Marvin got his dungarees up and tottered to the door and looked out to see that that second boom had all but disintegrated the barracks, the whole damn roof caved in, the walls just shaky remnants. Guys were cut and bleeding and staggering around in their skivvies like zombies, except for a few that had managed to get under mattresses after the first blast, and protect themselves from the glass and debris.

Jesus Christ, he thought, hands on either side of the door frame, not sure if it was holding him up or vice versa. *The motherfuckin' Japs have hit! Pounding Port Chicago with guns off warships and bombs from the sky, Pearl Harbor all over again....*

Then a white officer stuck his head in and yelled, "It's the *ships*! It's the *ships*!"

Marvin took quick stock of the situation: the barracks injuries seemed limited to cuts, some pretty bad, but the guys who'd covered themselves with mattresses were out from under and on top of helping the rest; no medics were around, but sheets provided makeshift bandages and even tourniquets.

Getting his belt buckled, glad to be in shoes and not stocking feet, Marvin ran outside into a nighttime turned morning by flames and splotched by dark smoke clouds, and saw a Jeep just sitting there, keys in the ignition.

The barracks, what was left of them, were a mile and a half from the docks. . . .

He jumped in, thinking he had to get down there and see if he could help; it was maybe twenty after ten at night, but the sky ahead was as red as dawn. Sailors, many half-naked, were running around like the end of the world, some bleeding, some burned, some both.

Marvin kept his eyes on the gravel roadway and made sure not to hit any poor fool and he had gone maybe three-quarters of a mile when a Shore Patrolman emerged out of the smoke like an apparition and was standing there, playing crazy-ass traffic cop. Guy even had a goddamn whistle.

Marvin stuck his head out and said, "I want to help! I want to get through and help!"

"*You have to turn around!*" the Shore Patrolman yelled.

"Man, I got to get down to the *docks!*"

The SP came over and leaned in like a car hop and, talking as quiet as he could over the crackle of flames and the screams and the sirens, said: "Go back, son. There ain't no more docks."

"No docks?"

"No ships. No railroad. You keep going straight ahead, son, and you'll finally be a sailor."

"What?"

"You'll drive right into the water."

Marvin could do nothing but turn around and head back into the chaos he'd left. In so doing, he had to pause as two colored sailors were drunk-walking another badly burned black sailor across the road and away from the flames.

But when Marvin took a second look, the black sailor in the middle turned out to be a white officer he recognized as being a real prick down on the loading docks.

Only now he was black, too.

The disaster at Port Chicago was neither an attack by the Japanese, nor was it sabotage, rather a tragic accident, the worst homefront catastrophe of the war so far.

The flash Pete Maxwell had seen over his shoulder had been a small explosion on the pier, the first burst in a horrific display of unintentional pyrotechnics. The second and biggest blast had been the merchant freighter *E. A. Bryan* vaporizing along with the 4,606 tons of explosives and incendiary bombs in her holds. In the bay, beyond the *Bryan*, waiting to take on its "hot" cargo, the SS *Quinault Victory* blew up as well, random pieces of her hull flying so high they were spotted by passing planes, the aft half of her keel landing upside down five-hundred feet from where the ship had been anchored.

Three hundred and twenty sailors and workers on the ships and pier were killed instantly, another 390 were injured. Most of the deceased—202—were untrained Negro sailors loading the *Bryan*. Sixteen railcars of munitions went up in flames, and every single building on the base and in the nearby town was demolished or at least seriously damaged, the seismic shock wave from the detonations felt as far away as Boulder City, Nevada. Of the 7,200-ton *E. A. Bryan*, not a piece remained that you couldn't carry off in a suitcase.

Steward's Mate Willie Wilson, the only injured sailor aboard the *Liberty Hill Victory*, spent two days in sick bay before his vision returned to normal. Twelve others from Port Chicago who had looked directly at the blast had yet to regain their sight.

The Navy had immediately started reconstruction of the base, but until that massive job was completed, Port Chicago's workload shifted to the ammunition depot at nearby Mare Island Naval Shipyard. The *Liberty Hill Victory*, first in line to be loaded, found herself in an unexpected limbo.

Two days earlier, when the Navy had ordered the remaining Port Chicago Negro sailors to resume ammo handling (now at Mare Island), the sailors refused—still untrained in how to handle their deadly cargo, exhausted from the grisly clean-up at Port Chicago, and denied the thirty-day leave granted to white survivors, they said the conditions remained as unsafe as before the explosion. They would do any duty but ammo loading.

Responding quickly and decisively, the Navy immediately arrested all 258 Negro sailors—Seaman Marvin Hannah among them—and threw them in the brig pending courts-martial, with fifty ringleaders earmarked for a mutiny charge and possible death penalty.

Despite Captain Egan's efforts to keep the officers and crew isolated, every man aboard the *Liberty Hill Victory* soon found out what was happening ashore, and the dramatic topic of conversation spread through the ship like the fire at Port Chicago. Opinions on the so-called mutiny were, not unexpectedly, divided largely along racial lines.

During a routine check of the engine room, Pete had overheard Griffin saying to Whitford, "I told you them fuckin' coons would chicken out when push come to shove. Feets don't fail me now!"

Pete also noticed that the only colored man within earshot was the little queer, Orville Monroe. Shaft alley clipboard in hand, Monroe had pretended not to hear, but fear and anger raged in his eyes. With a sigh, Pete wondered how long it would take—minutes, hours?—before the petite sailor put in for his umpteenth transfer....

But Griffin drove the needle deeper, saying, "They're gutless wonders, I tell you—you wait, buddy, they'll refuse to load up the *Liberty Hill,* too!"

Pete came up to him and said, "You're on report, mister."

"Lieutenant, a man has a right to his opinion!"

"In civilian life. In the Navy, I have the right to throw your ass in the brig if you say one more word."

Orville had turned away to hide his smile.

Christ, Pete thought, *am I pandering to these coloreds now?* But he couldn't abide the stupidity and hatred Griffin was spewing, knowing it would sow discontent on all sides.

By assigning the *Liberty Hill* just enough trained men for the engine room, the Navy had inadvertently made it all but impossible for the officers to discipline the only four white non-coms aboard. Still, putting that S.O.B. on report was something at least, and if Griffin earned a stay in the brig, both Egan and the Navy would be forced to do something about an untenable situation.

Wouldn't they?

Hell, even Driscoll had said, "Griffin is as bad or worse than the Negroes. You can't give his white-trash kind that much responsibility—they'll fold under the pressure, every time."

You had to hand it to Dick—his contempt for those beneath his station crossed the color line with ease.

But, man, these last few days had been tense. If the colored crew ever found out how deeply bigoted Captain Egan was, the ship would make the Port Chicago Mutiny look like the *Good Ship Lollipop.* As for Driscoll expressing his casual racism, that was limited to the rest of the Fantail Four, whereas Connor and Rosetti seemed to share Pete's view.

"Guys," Pete had said early on, "if we're going to live with them, we have to treat them fairly."

"It's the Christian thing," the Jewish Connor had said, sarcastic but sincere.

Right now Pete was sprawled on his lower bunk, not wanting to begin another day. Across from him, Connor lay on his left side, looking over at Pete accusingly.

"You're stalling," Connor said.

They could only shave one at a time; this was a regular duel, to see who got five minutes extra in the rack.

"No," Pete said, "it's your turn. I went first yesterday."

"We're not taking turns. It's the first guy up."

"Well, that's not me. Get your dead ass—"

"Maxie, Maxie, Maxie," Driscoll said, sticking his head in, "that sweet little girl you left back on that Iowa farm will be dismayed by your new-found outhouse vocabulary."

"Fuck you, Dick," Pete said. He'd never said "fuck" before the Navy, but lately it came quick.

"I appreciate your sentiment," Driscoll told Pete, invading the little space, "but up and at 'em, you two. Skipper wants to see us all in the officers' mess . . . in ten minutes."

"That's all I need," Connor said, flipping the sheet off and climbing out of the rack. He remained, vaguely at least, on Egan's Shit List—for the sin of looking Jewish with an Irish name—and had gone to some lengths not to piss the skipper off.

"What's up his rear porthole now?" Pete asked, crawling out of his rack as well.

"This may shock you," Driscoll said, "but the captain doesn't share his every intimate thought with his XO." The exec started to leave, then thought otherwise, and shut himself in with them, his manner suddenly confidential.

Connor was a blur in the confined space, trying to shave and get dressed at the same time.

"Look, fellas," Driscoll said, with the disarming grin he could work up if he felt like it, "I owe you something of an apology. You were obviously right about the desirability of teaching this crew to read. Who's to say a 'No Smoking' sign, misunderstood, wasn't the culprit at Port Chicago?"

"Glad you see it that way, Dick," Pete said. He was getting dressed, despite not having access to the shaving mirror yet. "But it was really Ben's idea."

"I'm hearing nasty rumors," Driscoll said. "Seems the white officers were betting on these colored stevedores like horses. Pretty unpleasant, inhumane stuff. You've been right all along, Maxie."

Pete shrugged. "Reading may not be enough. Those guys who got blown to hell, and the ones in the brig waiting for courts-martial, they're just like our guys—no training."

"Why," Connor said, wiping off his face with a towel, "should the crew be any different from us officers?"

"Another thing I heard," Driscoll said, ignoring Connor's all-too-true wisecrack, "is that the Port Chicago boys weren't using work gloves—they were handling ammo barehanded."

Pete frowned. "In that heat, their hands were bound to get sweaty, slippery—and a shell could get dropped, easy."

"There's no detonation pins," Connor said. "Shouldn't matter."

Driscoll raised an eyebrow. "You think dropping a shell of TNT on its ass is a good idea? Anyway, some of what blew at the dock was hot—detonators in."

"Christ," Pete breathed. "Listen, excuse my ignorance, but... do we have work gloves for the boys?"

Driscoll smirked. "Maxie, I *always* make a point of excusing your ignorance... and the answer is no. But I'm going out and get them some from Port Authority if I have to pay for them myself."

"Good man," Connor said.

"Anyway," Driscoll said lightly, "I'm going to rustle up some coffee. When you and Connie come down, Maxie, my boy, would you stop by the skipper's cabin and tell him we're ready?"

"You got it, Dick."

Then Driscoll was gone. Soon the cabin mates were dressed and out the door, Connor going around to the officers' mess while Pete climbed the stairs to the cabin deck and the captain's quarters.

He knocked.

"*Come*," came the familiar gruff voice.

The door opened into a cabin not any larger than Pete's, though single-occupancy. The captain's bed was on the right, above which was a single bookshelf filled with sturdy nautical volumes and a stack of the small oblong paperbound popular novels distributed to servicemen. Opposite as you came in was a small oak closet and a green leather banquette like those in the officers' mess. To the left was a narrow bureau with two sea charts unfolded on top, past which a door led to the adjacent office.

The captain stood shaving at a mirror mounted on the wall directly next to the entry. Egan wore his uniform pants and boots and a white athletic undershirt, a tattoo of an anchor stark against the paleness of his left arm; his uniform shirt hung from a hook, back of the door.

The skipper's brown hair was neatly combed over to hide the thinning top and his chin and cheeks were covered with lather as he drew a straight razor up his neck to his jaw.

"Any particular reason for this interruption, Mr. Maxwell?"

"Sir, Lieutenant Driscoll asked me to inform you that the officers are all present in the officers' mess as requested."

"Good."

Pete stood at attention. Egan had not dismissed him.

Finally, Egan said, "At ease, Mr. Maxwell. So—what do you make of what happened at Port Chicago?"

"A tragedy, sir, for the personnel *and* the war effort."

The captain, face still half-lathered, gave him a sideways, slightly suspicious look. "Did you rehearse that, Lieutenant?"

"No, sir."

"Well, remember it. It may serve you well. How do you think Lieutenant Driscoll held up in the situation that night?"

"Very well, sir. I thought he did the right thing. He did exactly what I would have done, anyway."

"Oh?"

"I think he had to assume it was the Japs, sir. That we were under attack."

Egan took another stroke with the razor. "And you say you would have done the same thing?"

"Yes, sir."

"You would have both been wrong, then."

"Sir?"

"We weren't under attack."

"My first order is to protect the ship, sir," Pete said, trying not to sound defensive. "I'm sure Lieutenant Driscoll feels the same way … and since we didn't know whether we were under attack or not, going to battle stations seems like the right decision."

Egan turned to him now, the brown eyes under the shaggy brows burning. "*Seems* like the right decision?"

"*Was* the right decision," Pete said.

Resting the razor on a ledge below the mirror, Egan toweled the remaining lather from his face. "Good, Mr. Maxwell. You grasp my nuance."

Did he?

"Command is about making the hard decisions, even if you might be second-guessed. Even if you are college boys, you and Mr. Driscoll might turn out to make decent officers yet."

"Thank you, sir. We try."

He held up a forefinger. "No trying, son. Just doing. … Tell the others I'll be down in five minutes."

"Aye aye, sir."

Going back down the stairs to the boat deck, Pete again found himself puzzling over Egan. Were they actually winning the skipper over? Was this the same guy who had ranted about "coloreds, commies, and college boys"? Pete understood that Egan was of another era, and his casual prejudices were perhaps best tolerated, particularly considering Egan was the guy in charge; but the bile their captain spewed really did grate.

Under that crusty exterior, was this career sailor the best friend Pete and the other officers had? Or the opposite? Not knowing which way that coin might flip made something twitch in Pete's gut.

The other Fantailers sat at one table, each with a mug of coffee, but no food. Pete had hoped some breakfast would quell his restless stomach. But, like the others, he knew better than to order a plate when they were waiting for the captain.

Falling into a chair next to Connor, Pete got noncommital nods from the others.

"Captain Blood on his way?" Driscoll whispered.

"Couple of minutes behind me," Pete said.

And almost exactly two minutes later, Egan appeared in the doorway.

Rising, Driscoll snapped, "Ten-*hut!*"

They were all in the process of getting up when Egan waved a benevolent hand. "At ease, gentlemen."

A steward's mate, a young Negro Pete didn't recognize, materialized with coffee for the captain.

Egan asked, "What's for breakfast, boy?"

"Bacon, scrambled eggs, fried potatoes, and toast, sir."

Egan glanced at them, then said, "Bring five plates and don't dawdle."

"Aye aye, sir."

Pete glanced at Connor—the skipper had Connor so buffaloed by now, the young ensign didn't even mention his religion forbade him eating pork.

Soon the steward's mate and a helper brought the servings, after which they filled each officer's coffee cup. Before the steward disappeared, he asked, "Everything all right, sir?"

"Fine, fine. Good job."

The steward turned to leave.

"Wait a minute," Egan said. "What did the crew have this morning?"

"Why, oatmeal, sir."

"Good, good. Dismissed."

The steward left.

Egan said, "We have to keep an eye on the meat. Precious commodity in this war, meat. No point throwing it all away to those boys, and the rest of us do without."

Ah, Pete thought. *There's the Captain Egan we know and love....*

"Dig in, gentlemen," Egan said.

Though the captain's behavior had dulled Pete's appetite, he made himself eat, noticing that every time the skipper looked down to fill his fork, another strip of Connor's bacon appeared on Pete's plate. Glancing at Connor, Pete was rewarded with a pleading look; he managed a half-grin for the mortified comedy writer.

"I hope you all noticed," Egan said, "what a fine job these mess stewards have done for us—getting us this good breakfast, polite and efficient. When that was the colored role in this man's Navy, we were much better served. Much better served."

Connor was agape at this apparently unintended pun; Pete elbowed him.

"Of course," Egan said, "what occurred at Port Chicago was a genuine tragedy."

They all nodded but said nothing.

"A loss of life, yes, and for all the fuss about the Negroes, a good number of white men were lost, too, not that the bleeding-heart newspapers seem to notice. And the *real* tragedy is that it's put us behind schedule. I'm sure you heard, the Port Chicago coons were supposed to be back on the job two *days* ago, but they've mutinied, and they're all going to rot in prison and eventually in Hell. Thoughts?"

No one responded.

"Those black boys getting the rough justice they deserve does not, however, get the *Liberty Hill* loaded. The reason I've called you here this morning is I want to know if you people think our blacks can handle the job, without blowing up Mare Island and us with it."

This speech had left Pete, Rosetti, and Connor so astounded, none of them had a word to say, though all their mouths yawned open.

Fortunately, Driscoll picked up the slack.

"Yes, sir," Driscoll said. "We've got good men. We treat them with courtesy and respect, and they repay us with their hard work. In addition, Mr. Maxwell and Mr. Connor have been working on the literacy level of the less educated members of the crew."

"That so?" Egan asked, the shaggy eyebrows turning toward Pete and Connor.

Pete and Connor exchanged looks; Connor's fear of the captain trumped Pete's belly ache.

"Full credit should go to Ensign Connor," Pete said, and Connor's expression tightened, as if to say, *Thank you so much!*

Pete continued: "The ensign thought it would improve ship safety and I agreed to assist him. It will obviously help if our boys can read the signs in dangerous areas."

Egan wagged a finger at them, but he did not scold the two officers, instead saying, "Well done, Mr. Connor, Mr. Maxwell. Do you think they're up to the task of loading my ship without destroying her, and killing every living thing within a two-mile range?"

"I do, sir."

"Good," Egan said. "It's settled then. We're first in line—and I want us up to the pier by noon, Mr. Driscoll."

"Aye aye, sir."

The steward's mate peered in, came over and refilled the coffees, then again disappeared. They finished their meals in relative silence. With their plates pushed aside, Egan looked at Driscoll; something sly was working around the brown orbs under the shaggy eyebrows.

"Do you think you're ready for command, Mr. Driscoll?"

Driscoll did not hesitate: "Yes, sir."

"Good," Egan said, obviously pleased with Driscoll's decisive tone. "Then this should work out nicely."

A chill washed over Pete as he realized what was coming, and he'd bet a month's pay Driscoll and Connor and Rosetti all had the same nasty goose pimples....

The skipper said, "I've got to go to the base dentist this afternoon—got a tooth's been killing me. And, because I haven't had a leave in over a year, the brass have given me a weekend pass. So, Mr. Driscoll, you'll be in charge of seeing that, while I'm away, the ship is properly loaded."

Again without hesitation, Driscoll replied, "Aye aye, sir."

Rising, Egan gave them the hint of a smile, an expression you see on cats in the process of playing with a captured mouse. The officers rose as well, four puppets on one string.

"Carry on then," he told them, took one last pull at his coffee, and strode out.

With Egan safely out of earshot, Rosetti asked, "Did somebody just fuck us? Usually I get a kiss first and a cigarette after."

"Dick's the one who got screwed," Connor said. "We'd all have been out on that dock, anyway, even if Egan *hadn't* found a loophole to stay away himself—far, far away, leaving any blame to Dick, dead or alive."

Driscoll was brooding.

Connor asked, "No rejoinder, Dick?"

"If we all blow up," Driscoll said, "I hope what's left of us lands on him."

If that was a joke, nobody laughed; but also nobody disagreed.

Egan stayed with the ship until they were moored at the loading dock at Mare Island. Not long after, the captain was striding down the gangplank, and right behind him were the four white non-coms—Griffin, Whitford, Smith, and Blake.

As Officer of the Day, Pete stopped them all before they disembarked to check their papers. By looking over the orders, Pete realized Egan had given weekend passes to the four non-coms, who all smugly saluted before heading to the pier, leaving the Fantail Four to deal with an all-black crew and fifty thousand tons of live ammunition.

With Egan and the non-coms gone, Pete gathered the other three officers and explained this newest development.

"I told you we were expendable, Pete," Driscoll said.

Connor said, "Does he *want* us to fuck up? Does he want this ship blown to scrap metal, and us to Kingdom Come?"

"Why not?" Rosetti said. "The bastard would just get another ship, with an all-white crew, this time."

Connor said, "Those boys at Port Chicago were right to refuse to load ammo under these conditions."

Driscoll turned on him. "Were they? You think mutiny is a viable option, Connie? Allow me to disagree."

Pete said, "Dick's right. We're not going to refuse to load. We're going to do our jobs, and you know it. We've already taught every guy on the ship to recognize 'No Smoking' and 'Explosives' and so on."

"They can also recognize Donald Duck and Robin the Boy Wonder," Driscoll said dryly, referring to the comic-book "primers" Pete and Connor had bought at the Mare Island PX.

"So the skipper and his Klan members get liberty," Connor said, "and we get to load ammo."

"There's a war on," Pete said.

"I'll do the comedy."

"Ladies," Driscoll said, "we're going to do the job we've been assigned. And we are going to goddamn shine."

"Yeah," Rosetti said, "but will the *shines* shine?"

Pete said, "Maybe you shoulda got off with the captain and his bigoted buddies."

"Don't go holier than thou on me, Pete," Rosetti said, frowning. "I know people of every color and get along with 'em just fine. You know every other white boy in Podunk Center, Iowa, so kiss my ass."

"Easy, Vince," Connor said.

But Rosetti was ranting, facing Pete down. "But you know and I know that we have a lot of ignorant boys, and I mean *boys,* teenagers, who are gonna be jumpy as hell after Port Chicago on top of all their other problems. Can they really be trusted to not blow us all to hell and gone?"

"I think they can do the job," Pete said, arms folded, holding his ground. "With our help, they can. And with our captain's help."

"Our captain?" Connor said. "Have the engine fumes gotten to you, Pete?"

"I don't mean Egan, I mean *our* captain—Captain Driscoll here."

Driscoll, head cocked, was eyeing Pete. "What are you saying, Maxie?"

"You're in charge. With Egan, you're defacto captain, right? Like you were of the Harvard football team?"

"I was the captain, yes, my Junior year, before I unwisely went to sea with you lunatics."

Pete shrugged, grinned. "Wouldn't happen to have one of those Harvard pep talks up your sleeve, would you? Halftime in a tight game?"

"You've lost me, Maxie."

"We need these men on our side, Dick."

Rosetti frowned. "They're supposed to be on our side already."

Pete was fired up now. "Well, they would be, if for just one minute they thought we were all on the *same* side—Americans fighting one damn war, and not each other."

"We're listening," Connor said.

"Okay, so I'm from lily-white Podunk, Iowa. Fine. Swell. But I know how I felt when I walked around San Diego and saw signs saying, 'No Sailors.' But there weren't as many of those signs as the 'No Colored' ones—'No Sailors, No Dogs, No Colored.' How did *you* like that, walking down the street in your country's uniform?"

The others said nothing.

"Vince, would they have served your mother? She's Mexican, you said. That's 'colored,' right?"

"Really," Driscoll said. "Your mother was from Mexico, Rosie?"

Frowning, vaguely embarrassed, Rosetti nodded. Then he straightened and said, "No, not from Mexico—she was born here, Mexican American. But after the Zoot Suit Riots, I thought I was going to have to move her to San Diego, to be closer to me, so I could protect her. My dad's still alive, though, and he said he could handle it. He's half-blind but he's strong. He's had to be."

"But if you had brought her down, Vince," Pete said, not confrontationally, "she'd have been just another colored person, right?"

Rosetti swallowed. "You're not wrong."

Pete turned to Ben. "How about you, buddy? You've endured so much prejudice you changed your damn name. Have to sneak the lousy bacon onto my plate, to avoid the captain's evil eye."

"Okay," Connor said. "The world's not fair. That's not a news bulletin, Pete."

"No. It isn't. But think for a second—think about it, and you'll know how our boys must feel. What they've had to put up with, though they've had it a lot rougher than either of you guys. All they want is an even break—to be on equal footing with white folks. And for once, they want to feel like someone gives a damn whether they live or die. Nobody... *nobody*... likes to feel expendable."

"Well," Driscoll said, "*we* certainly care whether they live or die. Because they'll be doing it in our presence."

"Then convince them, Dick," Pete said.

Driscoll gave Pete the blank-as-a-baby expression. "Hell, Pete. You just *gave* the speech ... to us. Give it to *them*."

Pete shrugged. "Fine. But it would mean more coming from you."

"Why do you say that?"

Connor said, "Like the man says, Dick—with Egan gone, you're the captain of the ship."

Driscoll half-smiled. "Maybe I just like hearing you fellas say it. Okay, Maxie—you've sold me. Rosie, round 'em up and I'll give them Maxie's speech. You don't mind if I improve the syntax, Maxie, do you?"

"Not at all, Dick. But give me ten minutes before you start this show. I want to talk to somebody first. Somebody who can make all our lives easier."

"I'm in favor of that," Driscoll said. "Ten minutes."

Before long, standing on the main deck, port side away from the pier, between hatches four and five, Pete glanced at his watch—seven minutes already. He wondered how much leeway Driscoll would give him. Next to him, sucking on a cigarette, Sarge Washington was shaking his head.

Pete had just given Sarge the *Reader's Digest* version of what the Fantail Four had discussed.

Flicking the sparking butt over the rail into the bay, Sarge said, "Know why I like you, Mr. Maxwell?"

Pete said nothing.

"It ain't just you blow a mean horn. I know more than one guy blows a mean horn. It's that you are the craziest white motherfucker I ever saw ... sir."

Pete, weary, laughed just a little. "That's a word I never heard before I got in the Navy."

"Well, it's a rough word. But it has its uses. And you know I mean you no disrespect."

"None taken. Does this mean you'll help us with the crew?"

Sarge nodded. "Oh yeah. Don't wanna get my ass blowed up no more than you white boys do, sir. But I also don't want to face a firin' squad as some damn mutineer. How do you do mutiny on dry land, anyway, Mr. Maxwell?"

Pete ignored that and began ticking off on his fingers. "Five hatches, five men. Five more on the pier side, two shifts. That's twenty men that you choose, Sarge, who you think are the best."

"I understand, sir. When will you want that list?"

Pete said, "Lieutenant Driscoll will be addressing the crew in about two minutes. We'll write the list down later—for now, you just go round 'em up."

"Aye aye."

Driscoll gave the complement of twenty his variation on Pete's speech, and by the time he was done, they were hollering their support.

"You'll work hard," Driscoll said, "and you'll work careful, but fast. You'll load your own ship and do it in thirty-five hours. First thing Monday morning, when Captain Egan gets back, the *Liberty Hill Victory* will have its holds full, ready to sail."

They would work one seven-hour shift before night fell, then two seven-hour shifts each, Saturday and Sunday. Everyone had a job and was expected to do it. They'd have to work together and, more importantly, trust each other.

And everybody knew the consequences of a screw-up—the wreckage was still strewn around the nearby Port Chicago base, where over three hundred men seemed to whisper from the grave to them, every time the wind blew.

SEVEN

Much to the relief of Seaman Ulysses Grant Washington, everything had gone fine on that critical first shift.

Opening the hatches had taken a couple of hours. Removing the wooden covers and the braces down through four decks over five holds was not something that happened quickly, even with sixty men throwing their backs into it.

Once that was done, however, things had picked up. Pallets were stacked with metal cases of .50-caliber bullet belts, others stacked with crates of M-1 clips—literal tons of ammunition loaded one pallet at a time, the first going into hold one, second into hold five, third into hold two, fourth into hold four, and finally the fifth pallet into hold three, before starting the routine again. This way the ship remained balanced as she was loaded.

By the end of the first seven-hour shift, the men were all dragging, dripping sweat and wrung out from breaking their backs with no time off except for two ten-minute smoke breaks on deck, and of course the occasional piss break—otherwise working straight through.

When the shift finally ended, they ate heaping plates of beef stew on deck, enjoying the evening breeze as they passed around rolls and pitchers of lemonade.

Sarge was amazed and even gratified when the officers ate with them, each dripping sweat, too. Lieutenant Driscoll and Mr. Rosetti ate up toward the bow, Mr. Maxwell and Mr. Connor aft with Sarge and his friends. Afterward, Sarge watched as each officer went from man to man telling them what a great job they had done. When Maxwell got to him, they shook hands.

"Hell of a job, Sarge," Maxwell said with a grin.

"Thank you, sir."

"We couldn't have done it without you."

"That is nice to hear, sir."

Maxwell's expression turned oddly shy. "Let me ask you something—do you think the crew would get a charge out of seeing some entertainment from their officers?"

"Well...why not? What kind of entertainment, Mr. Maxwell?"

The twenty ammo loaders sat on deck under the stars while the two ensigns and two lieutenants assembled before them, even the stodgier Driscoll, who'd made himself scarcest of the four during the work day.

Maxwell, a small black circular pitchpipe in hand, stepped forward in front of the smiling if bemused audience and said, "Back in San Diego, we had a quartet. Called the Fantail Four. I know there are some very good musicians among you fellas, and I hope you don't mind us butchering a few of what just might be your favorite tunes, a capella."

Maxwell set the pitch.

They started off with "If I Didn't Care," in a slightly exaggerated but damn accurate impression of the Ink Spots, including the spoken part, and soon the boys were clapping and hollering and whooping and laughing. The quartet, grinning at each other after the tune got huge applause, loosened up and put on a really fine approximation of the Mills Brothers doing "Paper Doll."

What Sarge liked was they didn't coon it up—they obviously had respect for the songs and the singers, and what could have been an embarrassing moment—a bunch of white boys in vocal black face—instead provided a common ground.

The crowd swelled as sailors from below deck, who hadn't been involved in the ammo loading, joined the party. The four white officers crooned and clowned for their receptive colored crew—the biggest laughs coming when the white officers donned mops for wigs as the Andrews Sisters doing "Don't Sit Under the Apple Tree" in exaggerated drag queen moves *("No! No! No!"),* getting howls and cries of "Oh baby!" "Oh mama!"

They went on to perform several other tunes, not imitating anybody, and they had a nice masculine sound, with Driscoll's high tenor surprisingly sweet, and Maxwell providing a rich, almost operatic baritone on several solo parts. "Sentimental Journey" got all the boys swaying and damn if there weren't some teary eyes over "I'll Be Seeing You."

The last tune was another Ink Spots, but minus any imitating, and gradually every sailor on deck joined in, singing, *"I'll get by as long as I have you. ..."* The big male sound rolled over the deck and out onto the water and back again.

Now, in the fo'c'sle, darkness draped the racks of bunks filled with tired sailors, though only a few breathed with the regularity of sound sleep, and fewer yet snored.

In a corner, Sarge sat on his lower bunk across from Big Brown, similarly seated on his own bunk, his big ass making a V for Victory out of the thin mattress.

On the floor, his back resting against the bulkhead, arms encircling knees drawn up to his chest, perched Orville Monroe, the little fairy whose bunk was above Big Brown's. Also on the floor, his back against Sarge's bunk, sat Willie Wilson, in a slumped posture not unlike when he worked his sax. Against the upright between Monroe's and Big Brown's bunks leaned Hazel Ricketts, a tall, skinny kid from a farm outside Water Valley, Mississippi.

Better part of an hour, the quintet had been shooting the shit about, well, nothing at all, really, except the subject on all of their minds: the final day of ammo loading ahead of them, and the Port Chicago explosion behind them.

Orville was gazing up at country boy Ricketts. "How the devil you get a woman's name, Hazel?"

Coming from the effeminate Monroe, the question almost made Sarge laugh.

Ricketts glared at Monroe, eyes gleaming in the darkness like a razor's edge. "It ain't *only* a woman's name, you dumb sissy boy."

Orville ignored the insult; Sarge was well aware the little guy had learned to let a lot roll off his back here on the *Liberty Hill.*

Orville was saying, "I only knew of females havin' that name. I don't mean no insult, man, just askin'."

"Well, mens have that name, too." Ricketts frowned and shrugged. "And it's, you know, also a big nut."

Sarge groaned to himself as he saw the elfin expression blossom on Orville's pretty face.

"How could yo' mama know ahead of time," Orville said, laughing, "that you'd turn out *that* way…?"

Not surprisingly, Ricketts started for the little man, but Big Brown rose halfway off his bunk and glowered up at the country boy, who retreated to his position against the bunks.

"Just joshin', buddy," Orville said, but his smile had curdled some.

"Mama name me Hazel," Ricketts said, folding his arms, "'cause of my eye color. They's hazel brown. Been that way since I was borned."

That put a dead-end sign on this conversational byroad. The five sailors sat thinking their own thoughts for a while, then Monroe gazed at Sarge, bright eyes glittering through the shadows.

"Sarge," Orville said, "why'd you up and join the Navy, anyways?"

Sarge thought about that. He pretty much knew the answer, but he wanted to choose his words carefully.

Before Sarge could respond, though, Ricketts asked Orville, "Why'd *you,* Orv?"

Orville shrugged. "Didn't have no money. Didn't have no future I could see. For a fella with my, uh, artistical nature, N'awlins is a fine place, y'know. People are less likely to judge you. Still and all, I ain't got no real job skills, and all the men was goin' off to war, so people say, 'Orville, why ain't *you* servin'? Ain't *you* a man?' So I had to do something. I went in a line for the Army but they shooed me over to the Navy line. Nobody never said why."

Before Orville could start Chapter Two, Sarge said, "I joined 'cause I believed it when Mr. Roosevelt said he was going to let us fight 'longside the white boys. I thought, here's a fella who believes we're all flesh-and-blood men, who looks at me and sees I'm as good as any man, color be damned..."

They were staring at him in pin-drop silence.

"...Now? Now, I don't know what to think. Maybe I was a damn chump, believing Mr. Roosevelt; or maybe shit just runs downhill, I dunno. Guy like me, seen as much as I have on the South Side streets, shouldn't fool so easy."

"Well," Ricketts said, "it's our war, too. That Hitler makes the worst cracker down south look like *Eleanor* Roosevelt."

Everybody laughed, even Sarge.

But the mirth left Sarge's face as he continued: "Anyway, damn fool that I was, I thought they'd let us be one Navy."

"Ain't we been," Orville asked innocently, "lately?"

Actually, they had.

In these last two and a half days, the crew of the *Liberty Hill Victory* had functioned like your proverbial well-oiled machine. They had been one unit, one entity, one color—Navy blue. And not only had they eaten together, they'd even consumed the same food—bacon and eggs replacing the oatmeal the Negro members of the crew had gotten every single other morning since arriving on this tub, and at lunch they had real turkey sandwiches, just like any other working man anywhere else.

Well, Sarge corrected himself, like any *white* working man anywhere else.

"We *have* been one Navy," Sarge admitted. "But 'fore long, the CO be on board again, and I figure things'll go back the way they was."

"Oatmeal and green meat," Orville said with a shudder.

Nods all around.

Sarge shook his head. "To think I give up a good job in a city I loved, where I got friends and a woman willin' to be my wife, should I be lucky enough to live through this shit. To think I give all that up, all 'cause of Mr. Roosevelt."

"You *believed* that ofay bullshit?" Willie asked, eyes flashing. "You *really* thought they'd let our black asses in the front door?"

"Yeah, I did, you mealy-mouth motherfucker," Sarge said pleasantly. "Just like *you* did."

Willie could only grin, and shrug.

Sarge continued: "Just like we *all* did. We been called shif'less niggers most our lives. And, hell, here was a chance to prove them bastards wrong. Or we thought there was, anyways."

"Nobody ever called *me* shif'less," Ricketts said. "I's a hard worker and has been since I was big enough to pick cotton on my tippytoes."

Orville studied the country boy through half-lidded eyes. "Hazel—ain't you from Mississippi?"

"Born and raised."

"Ever see yourself a white man, 'fore you joined up?"

Ricketts thought about it. "County sheriff, he was white— mean S.O.B. Town mayor, he was white, but I only really seen him once or twice. We 'uns didn't get to town much. Hell, I had to hitchhike all the way to Oxford to join up."

"How far's that?" Sarge asked.

"Near onta twenty miles."

"And you hitchhiked, huh?"

Ricketts shrugged. "Ended up walkin' most of it."

"All so's you could join the Navy?"

"Yup. Ma and Pa, they got too many darn mouths to feed. I figured it was a way to make life easier for 'em. I send 'em my pay every month, naturally."

"*All* of it?" Orville asked.

Ricketts grinned. "What the hell I needs money for on the *Liberty Hill?* I gets meals, and more clothes than I ever got at one time in all my life … and we sure as hell ain't gettin' no liberty, anywheres."

Sarge looked at the skinny kid with new respect. "How much education you got, Hazel?"

"Just what Mr. Connor and Mr. Maxwell been teachin' us in them classes in the mess. By the time I was big enough for school, folks needed me to work the farm."

Finally Sarge turned his gaze on the taciturn Big Brown. "Okay—why'd you join up?"

But Big Brown just shrugged.

"You know," Wilson said, and shook his head, grinning, "those white boys sang pretty good tonight."

"Why, ain't you heard?" Sarge said.

"What?"

"They got natural rhythm."

Everybody laughed and their rowdiness got some grumbles from other bunks.

So Sarge said, "Better get some shut-eye, children. Mornin's comin' real soon, and we got one more big day of not blowin' up ahead of us. …."

Sarge collapsed back onto his bunk, and Big Brown did the same while Monroe and Wilson climbed up to their perches and Ricketts ambled off to his berth.

Trying to lull himself to sleep, Sarge evened his breathing, listening to the men around him settle in for the night.

"Ironic, isn't it?"

The voice surprised Sarge, but so did the choice of words—"ironic" was not the kind of term bandied about among this crew. And here it was coming out of Big Brown, who before tonight hadn't said ten words on the ship, most of those one-syllable.

"What is?" Sarge whispered.

Big Brown kept his voice low, too. "That we're fighting the Axis for persecuting people—for instance, Jews like Mr. Connor."

"Yeah?"

"And we're fighting the Japs, who are slaughtering these island natives like animals, which turns the collective American stomach."

Where had *that* come from?

"Yet in our own home, in our own damn country, which we're defending... how many places are there where we can't go, restaurants we can't eat in, bars we can't drink in... all because of the color of our skin? If that isn't motherfucking ironic, I don't know what is."

Sarge wondered if he was dreaming this. Big Brown's words had been spoken so sotto voce that Sarge was pretty sure neither Monroe nor Wilson had even noticed them talking.

"Yeah," Sarge said, at last. "Motherfucking ironic for sure."

Silence draped the fo'c'sle now. Sarge stared at the mattress above, struck as much by how Big Brown had expressed himself as by the substance of what he said. This beer truck of a man was one quick, smart bastard, and Sarge now realized he needed to be more aware of those around him. Such knowledge might mean the difference between breathing and not breathing.

The more Sarge tried to urge himself to sleep, the more he found himself thinking about home. Here he was, a thousand miles or more from Chicago, and tomorrow they'd be farther away still. And yet even though the ship had turned out to be a mostly Negro crew with a handful of whites in authority, he still believed what Mr. Roosevelt had promised.

They would be one Navy, one congregation of men regardless of color; but (Sarge knew too damn well) even when the President of the United States himself ordered it, some things took time.

After a dawn breakfast, under a hot sun eased by a constant breeze off the water, they were at it again—one pallet at a time, bigger shells today, these for howitzers, getting taken off boxcars in canvas slings, moved to the pier where they were placed in racks on pallets, four to a layer, four layers to a pallet. Then the pallets were lifted by crane up aboard the ship and down into the holds, following the same pattern they had used yesterday.

Sarge stayed on the dock, helping make sure that each shell was seated correctly in its rack, and each layer arranged correctly on the one beneath it. Sweat beaded off black skin like water flung on leather, but no one complained, no one slowed down. For several hours, all went as smooth as the inner thigh of a beautiful woman...

...and then it went to shit.

Orville Monroe was guiding a shell from the boxcar to the pier, the crane arm turning to the right, the little oiler using hand signals to direct the operator, as they moved the two-hundred-pound round. Orville had one hand on the shell and the other slowly waving up high, when the canvas sling suddenly shifted and the shell pitched forward, its pointed nose seeking the target that was the concrete pier.

Sarge's jaw dropped, but before he could otherwise react, someone else did, and decisively: Big Brown—his massive biceps exposed under the torn-off sleeves of a sweat-soaked shirt—materialized like an infielder charging to the outfield to snag a fly ball.

And that was how nimbly the bald, bucket-headed sailor caught the shell, stopping it inches from the concrete.

Then, on a dock gone as silent as the death that impended, Brown lifted the heavy steel bomb gently, as if it were a sleeping baby, and *nobody* wanted to wake this not-so-little fucker ....

With slow steps but no apparent concern, Brown carried the thing over to where Sarge stood gaping and put baby down for its nap in the rack.

All action on the pier had ceased, sailors caught frozen in whatever they were doing, like the citizens of Pompeii when the lava hit, only this was fear out of what just *almost* happened.

Sarge shut his yawning trap, swallowed, sighed hugely, then looked up into the soft dark eyes of the mountain in front of him.

"Not a bad catch, Brown. But I'm gonna have to call it out."

Brown, face running with sweat rivulets, gave up a big grin.

And Brown's grin along with Sarge's words cured the crew's paralysis, though a murmur of relief quickly, nastily, turned into a sea of shouts.

"Fucking *shit!*"

"Jesus Christ, you *see* that?"

"Mother-*fucker!*"

"*Orville!* You dumb-ass queer! You damn near *killed* our asses!"

Connor and Maxwell came running over, frowning.

Mr. Maxwell demanded, "What the hell happened?"

Sarge explained.

But as he did, from the direction of the boxcar, came a shouted, "*Orville, you dumb cocksucker...*"

Spinning toward the sound, Sarge said, "*Shut the fuck up!*"

Clancy Mullins, a lanky Negro from Pittsburgh, jumped out of the boxcar like a wild man and came running toward Sarge with blood in his eyes, hands balled into fists.

Maxwell and Connor tried to get in the middle, between the two sailors, but the crew swarmed forward, sweeping the officers out of the way, driftwood caught in an irresistible tide, indistinguishable yells and shouts erupting.

"Out of my way, Sarge," Clancy said, nostrils flaring. "I got to settle up with that little pansy, and you ain't stoppin' me."

"You turn around and get back to work, Clancy. I ain't givin' you a second chance. Just do it."

Mullins responded by sticking a hand in his pocket and coming back with something shiny. Even over the din of the circle of men, Sarge heard the *snick* as the switchblade flipped open.

"Don't do nothin' stupid now, Clancy...."

"Fuck you!"

And Mullins lunged, blade in his right hand catching sun and glinting.

Sidestepping, Sarge heard the blade go by his ear, then pivoted and latched on to Mullins's wrist while the man was still off-balance, and he twisted that wrist, hard. The wiry sailor screamed as he involuntarily followed his bent wrist and somersaulted onto the pier, the knife flung from popped-open fingers to skitter across the concrete, coming to rest against the pallet of shells.

Wailing in agony and anger, Mullins tried to rise, but never got past his knees as Sarge threw down an arcing overhand right that caught Mullins on the jaw and silenced him, dropping him unconscious to the cement.

Finally Connor pushed through the crowd. "Somebody call the goddamn Shore Patrol!" he shouted as he moved toward the fallen Mullins. "This man's going to the brig!"

Sarge watched as Mr. Maxwell picked up the knife and closed the blade. From Maxwell's face, Sarge could tell both white officers were in agreement on this matter.

"No need for that, sir," Sarge said to Maxwell.

But it was Connor who turned to Sarge, wide-eyed, astonished. "Are you *serious,* man? He just tried to knife you!"

"Please, sir," Sarge said, patting the air. "Clancy was just scared."

"*He* was scared?" Connor blinked. "Weren't you?"

Sarge almost whispered. "Sure I was. But, see—Clancy there, he was the one put the sling around that shell. It was *his* fault that bastard almost fell. He knew it... and he was ashamed, and it made him afraid."

The officers traded a look.

Sarge played on his friendship with Maxwell, saying, "He almost got us all killed, Mr. Maxwell. That would scare the holy hell out of just about anybody."

Maxwell said nothing; but he was clearly listening, considering Sarge's words.

"Clancy ain't no bad-ass," Sarge continued, "he just don't want the rest of us blaming him—so he starts in on Orville, before anybody can start in on him."

"He should go to the brig," Connor said, but without much enthusiasm now.

Down on the concrete, Mullins was coming around, his eyes open but glassy. Groggily, he shook his head and tried to sit up.

Bending down, Sarge put a hand on his shoulder. "You just sit there a minute, Clancy."

Mullins swallowed, nodded sheepishly, but otherwise did not move.

"Orville!" Sarge called. "Get this man some water, will you?"

Sarge might have been foaming at the mouth, the way Orville stared at him. "God *damn*, Sarge, that prick—"

"Don't argue with me, Orville," Sarge said, quiet but intimidating.

After a weight-of-the-world sigh, Orville went over to the water bucket, then brought back a well-filled ladle's worth. He tried to hand it to Sarge, who nodded toward Mullins nearby. Clearly pissed off, but also smart enough not to act on it, Orville handed the water-brimming ladle to Mullins.

"Thanks," Mullins mumbled, hang-dog. He took a sip. He took another sip. Then: "Orv... look... I'm... sorry about that shit. I... I went off my damn head."

"Yeah," Orville said, indifferently. "Sure. Okay."

Mullins rolled his eyes at Sarge and wiggled his jaw with a hand. "Man, Sarge—you got a better right than Joe Louis."

"I dealt with fools before," Sarge said, with humor, helping the man to his feet.

Maxwell stepped forward and held up the knife. "Big trouble, sailor."

The lanky sailor said nothing, chin dropping to his chest.

"Mr. Connor," Maxwell said. "What is called for in this situation?"

Connor said crisply, "Court-martial for attempted murder."

Mullins's eyes widened.

"Hard time and dishonorable discharge," Maxwell said, nodding. "Sarge here says that screw-up with the sling was your fault—not Monroe's. Is that correct?"

"Yes, sir," Mullins said.

"And yet you accused and attacked him."

"… Yes, sir."

Maxwell's chin came up, his eyes came down. "Sarge also says we should let it go. Just look the other way. What do you say to that, Mullins?"

Mullins turned toward Sarge. "He said … what?"

"That we should cut you some slack on this one, Mullins. What do *you* think your punishment should be?"

"I … I don't really know, sir. Something bad?"

Maxwell got nose to nose with him. "Fuck up again, sailor, and it *will* be bad. This knife will fly out of my safekeeping and so will a report on your misconduct. Understood?"

"Aye, sir," Mullins said.

"One tiny fuck-up, Mullins—I mean *anything*."

"Yes, sir," Mullins said, perhaps a bit hastily.

Maxwell took a step back, then held up the knife for Mullins to see; the sailor glanced at it, then looked away.

"Look at it," Maxwell ordered.

Mullins did, and so did the circle of sailors all around.

Then Maxwell said, "Anything, Mullins—dirty underwear, bunk not perfect at inspection, cigarette butt on deck, any goddamn thing that rubs me wrong.... Do you understand?"

"Aye, sir!"

Maxwell pocketed the knife. "Good. Back to work, then—*everybody! Back to work!* We're behind schedule, and we don't want to give the captain any reason to dislike Negroes and college boys any more than he already does."

A score of smiles blossomed.

Mullins said, "Thank you, sir."

Maxwell nodded, his eyes softening slightly. "And for Christ's sake, Clancy, be more careful in future."

"Yes, sir, you don't have to tell me twice, sir, I..."

"Stow it, sailor."

"Aye aye, sir."

Maxwell drew a deep breath, let it out, then said, "Now shake hands with Sarge, and get back to it."

"Aye aye, sir."

The two men shook and Mullins said, "I feel like a goddamn fool, Sarge. And here you always been—"

Sarge squeezed the hand tight until Mullins turned mute. "Next time you pull a knife on me, Clancy, you don't get cut slack, you just get cut."

Mullins nodded and swallowed, and when Sarge finally released his grip, Mullins stumbled off toward the boxcar shaking his hand, probably trying to get some feeling back in it.

From the deck above, Driscoll yelled, "What in the hell is going on down there? Bob Hope stop by on his USO tour?"

Maxwell glanced toward Sarge, then up at Driscoll. "Just taking a smoke break, sir. We're on top of it."

"Try not to smoke around anything that'll smoke you back," Driscoll yelled, then disappeared.

✤ ✤ ✤

Monday morning dawned bright and warm, and Sarge felt more like a sailor than he had since the day he enlisted, when he was still full of hope and naive notions. He was up on deck having a smoke before breakfast when he saw Captain Egan come back aboard. The son of a bitch actually seemed a little disappointed that the *Liberty Hill* and its crew were still there; a rubble pile like what was left of Port Chicago might have suited him just fine.

Instead the salty old skipper was stuck with a ship fully loaded and ready to sail.

But Sarge's smugness didn't last long. By the time they were on their way to Pearl Harbor, with Egan firmly in command once again, Sarge saw these friendly, fair, harmonizing junior officers as the basically powerless people they were. The menu, for example, was back to oatmeal for breakfast, slop for the other two meals, too.

In the fo'c'sle, the steward's mates would come back after their shifts and bitch about the chicken, steak, bacon and eggs the officers got for their meals. This return to second-class citizenship was having an effect on morale: Sarge was hard pressed to find any residual sign of the elation and spirit the crew had felt after loading the *Liberty Hill*.

He would find the right time to bring this subject up to Mr. Maxwell, though right now he wasn't sure the young officer could really do anything about anything. But Sarge had to try....

He lay in his bunk late morning, trying to sleep the four hours remaining before his shift on radar, the fo'c'sle bunks otherwise mostly empty, and was just drifting off when he felt the presence of someone near him. His gift for radar went beyond the gizmos themselves: it came also in the form of a personal warning bell forged by years as a Chicago cop.

With the speed of a striking snake, Sarge snatched the wrist of the hovering figure.

And before his eyes could focus, a simpering whimpering told him Orville Monroe had come calling.

Sarge let go at once, and whispered harshly, "Orville, what the hell, man? You could get killed, sneakin' up on a body like that."

"I'm…I'm sorry." And Orville whimpered some more.

Sitting up and swinging his legs over the edge of his bunk, Sarge said, "Be cool, Orville. You want these boys to hear you?…Why, did I *hurt* you?"

The little man shook his head. Even in the shadowy fo'c'sle, Orville's ironed hair shone, and his eyes were wide with obvious fear.

"You got a problem, son?" Sarge asked.

"I surely do," Monroe said, a tremor in his barely audible voice.

"Tell you what—we'll go up on deck and have a smoke."

"No! No. Best not."

This got Sarge's attention: Orville was a chainsmoker, who normally grabbed any opportunity to catch a smoke, which on an ammunition ship wasn't that often.

"So what's on your mind, Orv?"

Standing there like a school kid in front of the principal's desk, his eyes downcast, Orville wrung his hands one second, tugged his uniform the next, as if trying to adjust the fit. "You know me, Sarge, I mean, you know how I *am*.…"

Jumpy as a shithouse rat is how you are, Sarge thought, but said nothing.

"What I'm tryin' to say is, I don't go out with women so much. I have my…you ever hear the word 'predilections'?"

"Yeah."

"Well, a fella told me once that that's what I got: predilections."

"Okay. Not that I give a shit."

Orville managed a small smile. "I know you don't, Sarge. That's why I like you."

"Whoa, Nelly!"

"No, no, no," Monroe said, alarmed, hands up as if surrendering. "I don't mean it like *that*. I mean, you don't hold it against me, my predilections. You treats me fine, like we's friends. I mean, you is my friend, ain't you, Sarge?"

Sarge thought about it, momentarily, then said, "Sure, Orv. Far as it goes."

Suddenly Orville sat next to him on the bunk. "'Cause, see, I'm bustin' inside, to tell somebody, Sarge."

"Tell somebody what?"

"I ... I been doing sex-type acts."

Oh Christ. "Here on the ship, you mean?"

"Here on the ship."

"Well, if it's between you and some other guy with ... predilections, I don't wanna know about it, 'cause you could get tossed out on your ass, and whoever you're predilectin' with, too ... *and* me, for not tellin'."

"It ain't that way, Sarge ... ain't that way at all."

"What way is it?"

"It's somebody *makin'* me do these sex-type acts ... somebody I don't *wanna* do these sex-type acts with."

"Shit, man, you mean ... raping you?"

"No. Yes. I mean ... it's just, I'm particular. I got to be in love, at least I gotta think I am at the time, even if it's the liquor talking? Otherwise, it's just, you know ... dirty."

Sarge's eyes were wide and he couldn't seem to close them. "Well, now, you wouldn't want to do nothin' *dirty*, Orville."

"No," Orville agreed, Sarge's sarcasm eluding him.

"If some bastard is raping you, Orv, you won't get in trouble—*he* will. A hundred damn kinds of trouble."

"I don't know. He doesn't force me, not ... not *that* way."

"What way *does* he force you?"

"I dunno, it's just…he's a big man. Powerful man. I can't stop him."

"Sounds like force to me, Orv." Sarge shifted on the bunk, put a hand on Orville's shoulder. "Who's doing this, son?"

"I best not tell you. I already said too much."

"I'll help you, son. I got an understanding with Mr. Maxwell. And he'll—"

"No!"

And Orville got off the bunk and was shaking his head, saying, "Forget I said nothing. Forget I said nothing at all."

Then Orville bolted down the aisle and on his way out damn near collided with Captain Egan himself, coming in the hatchway.

"Watch where you're going, sailor!" the captain snarled, and Orville said, "Yes, sir," and squeezed by and hurried out.

Egan, shaking his head in apparent disgust, came over to where Sarge was now on his feet, by his bunk. "What's up that boy's ass? He ran out of here faster than Jesse Damn Owens."

"Nothing, sir," Sarge said. "He's jumpy around any white officer, and seeing the captain must've really goosed him."

"That boy is frightened of his own *captain?*"

"Very likely, sir. Used to happen all the time when I was a cop in Chicago. Perfectly honest man would up and cross the street when he saw me coming. Authority figures make some men jumpy."

Egan frowned, his unruly eyebrows twitching. "It's silly. Not the kind of behavior we expect from a sailor."

"No, sir. But we don't see you down here much, sir."

"You *are* Washington?" Egan asked, Orville forgotten.

"I am."

"Good. You're who I'm looking for."

"I am, sir?"

"I understand you showed great leadership these past few days. You did the job of a petty officer and helped us get loaded under tough conditions. I came down to say you have my thanks."

"Well, thank *you*, sir."

Egan nodded. "As you were."

And the captain strode out.

Obviously Maxwell had put in the good word, and Sarge wondered if a promotion was a real possibility—an officer, a colored officer. That would make Sarge's war, all right.

But in the meantime, he'd grab some sleep, and leave that waking dream behind, Orville's nightmare forgotten.

For now.

EIGHT

AUGUST 26–28, 1944

At full speed, empty, and running for her life, the *Liberty Hill Victory* could manage seventeen knots or just a shade under twenty miles an hour. In the safe waters between San Francisco and Pearl Harbor, they did not run her at top speed. Even so, averaging a steady twelve knots, the fully loaded ship covered the twenty-one hundred nautical miles to Hawaii and docked at Pearl in a week.

Pete Maxwell hadn't seen a box score since they'd left San Francisco and, with the pennant race in full swing, felt left out completely. He had hoped to get a newspaper so he could get caught up with the baseball season while they were in Pearl, but no such luck. They had arrived late in the day, refueled, then joined a small convoy headed to Tarawa, first thing next morning.

The best part about the brief stopover was the waiting bundle of V-mail from Kay. Just as he wrote her daily, she did the same, but their correspondence arrived in clumps, and consisted on both their parts of lots of redundant but no less precious talk of love and missing each other and a rosy if hazy future.

Pete had restrictions on what he could share with her—which is to say, next to nothing—but Kay's letters were filled with both sentiment and incident, the girls at Western Union, her silly boss, her funny aunt, even movies she'd seen (he could tell her about movies he'd seen, too, but there wasn't much you could say about the sixth time you saw the same Hopalong Cassidy picture).

He kept hoping she'd deliver the big news, namely that they had indeed managed to start a family in those last few days together; but nothing, in this batch of letters, even hinted at that. In his bunk, he would stare at photos of her—unlike some of the guys, he did not reduce his wife to a pin-up, these were private to him—and talk to her and she would talk to him.

Some guys prayed, but Pete talked to his wife. It was a kind of prayer at that, he supposed, a prayer that one day soon he would not have to imagine the sound of her voice, or her touch or her kiss, but have her right there with him in the wonderful flesh.

You did the right thing, she told him. **That sailor Mullins was just scared, like your friend Sarge said.**

It could come back to haunt me, he said to her. *What if Mullins lost his head again and hurt somebody?*

He won't.

How can you be sure, baby?

I'm sure because your friend Sarge is sure. You've always had good instincts about people, Pete. Trust them.

Pete knew writing daily letters to a wife or sweetheart wasn't unusual on this (or any other) ship. One of his English students, a kid from Kentucky named Baldwin, begged Pete to teach him enough "so's he could write home to the little woman." Pete did, and Baldwin soon displayed with pride the following letter:

"I loves you baby I loves you baby I loves you baby I loves you baby…" and so on, filling two sides of a sheet.

When you got right down to it, that was a hell of a letter home, and not so different from what Pete wrote Kay.

The *Liberty Hill Victory* and her convoy of two destroyers and another cargo ship averaged fourteen knots, speeding for a little over three and a half days to cover the twelve hundred nautical miles southwest of Hawaii to Tarawa in the Gilbert Islands, nearly to the equator.

The islands of the Pacific served as stepping stones to Japan, the brass knew, and even though it was over four thousand miles east of Tokyo, Tarawa had been the Allies' first step in the march to defeat the Japs. Captured after ferocious fighting in November of last year, the island now served as a fuel and supply station on the trip west.

This close to the equator, the heat pummeled them. White or black, officer or enlisted man, equality found them at last as they all suffered in the sweltering humidity, under an unrelenting sun. Even Orville Monroe—lately a wispy wraith rarely showing himself beyond the engine room and the mess—came out on deck looking for the tiniest hint of a breeze.

Orville, like everyone else aboard, found only disappointment. Had they been part of an earlier exploration, sailing ships moving under wind power, their trip would be stalled for God only knew how long. Pete thanked that same God he'd been born in the present: the idea of sailing around the world depending only on the force of the wind to move your ship seemed a nightmare.

And in the 1640s, as opposed to the 1940s, a wall-mounted electric fan wouldn't have awaited him in his cabin when his shift finally ended on a sweltering evening like this. The tiny contraption lent small solace, but stirring up the hot air seemed preferable to the deathly stillness and insufferable humidity on deck.

Right now, however, his chief concern was the Higgins boat headed their way from the shore. Technically a Landing Craft Vehicle, Personnel (LCVP), the craft was more commonly referred to by the surname of its inventor, Andrew Jackson Higgins. The Higgins boat—used to deliver infantrymen from ships to beaches at not only Tarawa, but Guadalcanal, Normandy, and Saipan—now would hold supplies for the next leg of their journey.

In the Higgins boat were three sailors—a pilot, another enlisted man keeping an eye on the cargo, and a round-faced ensign whose pasty complexion said the guy was a replacement who hadn't been on Tarawa more than a day or two. Of the three, only the pilot didn't wave as they neared, focused on getting next to the *Liberty Hill Victory* without banging into her hull.

The boat eased up alongside, Pete on deck looking down at the crates of meat stenciled MUTTON, BEEF and PORK. He could see the officer and enlisted man gazing up at the colored crew and commenting to each other, but with the engine noise and the activity aboard his own ship, Pete couldn't hear them. Where their approaching visitors had been smiling and waving a minute ago, they now stopped, faces serious, smiles gone.

As the enlisted man tied off the boat, the ensign looked up at Pete. "Welcome to Tarawa," he said without enthusiasm.

"Thanks," Pete said.

"Permission to come aboard?"

"Granted."

The ensign threw a foot into the cargo net hanging over the side and climbed the thick rope onto the deck. He saluted the flag, then turned to Pete and saluted again. "Ensign Jerry Randle."

Returning the salute, Pete gave the man his name and rank.

"I've got some supplies for you, Lieutenant," Randle said. "Meat, as you can see. Watch out for the mutton, though—it's a little ripe."

Pete nodded as he looked at the manifest—in fact, 90 percent of the meat on the manifest was mutton.

"Just a moment, Ensign," Pete said. "This sheet says almost all we *get* is mutton."

Randle nodded back.

"What about the beef and pork you've got there?"

Fidgeting a little, stealing a glance at the enlisted man down in the Higgins boat, standing guard on the cargo, Randle said, "Well, that's ... spoken for."

"Spoken for by whom?"

Randle pointed to a freighter anchored nearby—nearby enough so that Pete could make out the white men moving on deck.

"I see. And how much mutton are *they* getting?"

"They're, uh, getting their share, sir."

"How *much*, Ensign?" Pete asked, his voice sharper now.

"… Ten percent, sir."

"Ten percent. Sounds like that freighter's getting *our* share of everything else."

Randle hesitated for a good ten seconds. Finally, in a near whisper, he said, "Orders, sir. The quartermaster said you officers could feed the mutton to the … to the niggers, sir, and, well, keep the good stuff for yourself."

Pete drew in a breath. He let it out. Then: "He said that to you personally? Are you approximating his words or did he in fact say 'feed it to the niggers'?"

"Yes, sir. He said that, sir."

Pete studied the pale, puffy-faced ensign whose expression was that of a child whose bladder would burst if Daddy didn't stop at the next gas station.

"Understood, Ensign." Turning to his crew, Pete's eyes sought out Seaman Washington. "Sarge!"

Washington hustled over. "Aye, sir?"

"How's your math, sailor?"

"Got me through high school, sir."

"Good." Pete pointed down at the Higgins boat. "Take two men over into that LCVP and load the net with half the meat they're hauling, divided as follows: one third beef, one third pork, one third mutton. Got it?"

"Aye aye, sir."

"Now just wait a minute," Randle protested, moving forward as if about to touch Pete's sleeve.

Pete froze him with a look.

Washington climbed down into the Higgins boat, Willie Wilson and Big Brown right after. The white seaman in the boat almost pitched himself overboard trying to get as far away from the colored boys as he could. As they clambered down, at Pete's direction, Clancy Mullins ran the crane over and lowered a cargo net over the side.

While the three Negroes loaded crates of meat into the net, the boat pilot and his buddy just watched, like victims at a stage-coach robbery, neither uttering a word.

Up on the deck, finally finding a little backbone, Ensign Randle said, "If you carry this action out, Lieutenant, I'll go to the port authority."

Pete leaned in, inches from the other officer's nose. "I invite you to. Please go to the port authority. Come back with the Shore Patrol. Bring the quartermaster. And while you're at it, bring the manifests that show you're clearly discriminating against our ship and our crew."

Randle sputtered a couple of times, then swallowed, and gave up the fight.

Pete and his guest watched in silence as the sailors finished loading the net, then rode it aboard as Mullins raised the crane arm back aboard and lowered it onto the deck. The three sailors jumped free, and soon Washington was standing in front of Pete.

"Is that exactly half the meat in the Higgins boat?" Pete asked.

"Aye, sir," Washington said. "Close as possible without a butcher's scale."

"A third of each?"

"Aye, sir."

Pete said, "Good work, Seaman Washington."

"Thank you, sir."

Turning to Randle, Pete said, "Thank you, Ensign, for the delivery. Much appreciated."

"Do you really believe you can get away with this?"

"If anyone questions it, ask them if they think denying proper supplies to Negro sailors is a good idea, in the wake of the Port Chicago incident. Quote me, if you like."

A much disconcerted Randle climbed over the side, down the cargo roping, without further comment.

Washington, Wilson, and Big Brown stood there grinning at Pete.

"Why are you men standing around when there's work to do?" Pete barked. "Get this meat down to the locker before it spoils in this sun."

"Aye aye, sir," they all said at once, then each picked up a crate of meat as other crewmen appeared to pitch in.

Within the hour, comedy writer Ben Connor had dubbed the incident "Much Ado About Mutton," and shortly after that the *Liberty Hill Victory* was at sea again, this time part of a much larger convoy traveling through more dangerous waters toward Eniwetok atoll on the far western edge of the Marshall Islands.

The crossing was to last five days, after which they would begin the final leg of the journey to Guam, where they would finally disgorge their load of ammunition as close to the front as they dared get.

Though the Marshall Islands were now under control of the Allied forces, the Japs had a nasty habit of turning up where they shouldn't. Pearl Harbor had taught all Americans that much, so everyone on the ship was getting edgier as they drew closer to the action, traveling under radio silence now, signalmen using flags to communicate between ships during the day, and signal lamps at night.

Halfway through the thus-far quiet voyage, Pete drew the night watch—a black moonless sky, heat of the day having dissipated into a chilly evening as a storm front bore down from the west. Still they plowed along, the rest of the convoy barely outlined in the darkness.

Even a hick from Liberty Hill, Iowa, knew the difference between city dark and country dark, the desolate blackness of the ocean on the edge of a storm making it seem as if Pete and the other two men on the bridge were alone at the edge of the world.

Egan slept, as did Connor and Rosetti, while Driscoll was now checking on something (in the engine room, he said), leaving Pete on the bridge with the helmsman and the radar operator. With binoculars, Pete peered through the porthole, but saw little beyond the wakes of the other ships and the occasional flash of lightning behind distant clouds.

"Mr. Maxwell, sir?"

Turning, Pete saw Washington in the wheelhouse door. "What is it, Sarge?"

"Could we talk a minute, sir?"

"Lieutenant Driscoll isn't here and I can't leave the bridge. What is it?"

Washington pondered momentarily, then said, "That's all right, sir—guess it'll keep."

The Negro sailor left through the starboard door, his unasked question hanging in Pete's mind; then seconds later, Driscoll came in, port side.

"All clear," Driscoll announced.

"Except for the weather," Pete said. "Another hour, we'll be in the middle of one hell of a storm."

"You sound sure."

Pete gestured with the binoculars. "Been through enough storm fronts to know a bad one when I see it coming. Barometer's dropping, and this bastard's headed right for us."

Driscoll frowned, lengthening his already long face. "Should we wake up the skipper, you think?"

"No ... not yet anyway. We can handle it."

Driscoll shrugged fatalistically. "All right," he said, as if Pete and not Driscoll himself were the boss.

"Look," Pete said, "I've got to take care of something before the storm hits."

"What?"

"I'm not sure what, frankly. One of the crew wanted a word."

"And that can't *wait*?"

"We've got time. I'll be back in ten."

"All right," Driscoll said. He held out his palm and Pete filled it with the binoculars.

"Keep an eye on the wind," Pete added. "Waves'll start getting choppier."

"Ten minutes," Driscoll said, and turned the binoculars toward the front porthole.

Pete left the bridge through the starboard hatch, following the route Washington had taken onto the bridge deck. On a hunch, Pete took the stairs down to the boat deck and found Washington, just outside the galley, having a smoke, his hand shielding the orange tip.

"What's up?" Pete asked.

In the subdued light leaking through the galley door, the seaman's eyes were jewel bright. Taking a long drag, Washington seemed to ponder Pete's seemingly innocent question for a long moment. Finally, he exhaled smoke through his nostrils. "Mr. Maxwell, we might have ourselves a problem."

"Look, I know it's a new ship with a new crew, but this storm—"

"Ain't talkin' about the weather, Mr. Maxwell."

Lightning divided the sky, and in the split second of bright light, the scars on Washington's cheeks seemed to glow. Then kettle-drums rolled overhead.

"It's about Monroe, sir."

"Little Orville?"

"Yes. He's in a real mess."

Pete frowned; storm of the century heading their way, and Sarge wanted to talk about that little fairy's problems. Still, he said, "What kind?"

Washington moved to the rail, wind ruffling his clothes (and Pete's), silence following him there for several long moments before he said, "Orv's cornered me three times now and hardly said a damn thing."

"Sarge, can we talk about this another time?"

Washington's scarred mask of a face swiveled toward Pete. "I believe somebody's taking advantage of the little guy. Bad advantage."

"How so?"

Pinching off his cigarette and letting the butt drop over the side, Washington said, "Somebody's using him like a goddamn sex slave."

The phrase was so unexpected to the small-town officer that he shook his head, not sure he'd heard right. Then Pete studied the seaman's somber face and dread washed over him as he realized his hearing was just fine. "My God. Who?"

"He won't tell me. He just says somebody big and powerful is making him do sex things."

"Another…homo?"

"A jailhouse homo, maybe."

Pete squinted. "I don't follow."

"In the jailhouse, in prison? Guys put away for years got the same needs as you and me on the outside. They don't have no women, so a small, weak girlish man like Orville can get handed around like a motherfuckin' bottle of beer."

Horrible, Pete thought, but what he said was, "He didn't tell you who?"

Washington glanced around, then said, "Every time it seems like he's going to, somebody shows up and spooks his ass. First time, when Captain Egan come around; next time it was Mr. Connor; last time Mr. Driscoll."

"And Orville clammed in each instance?"

"He didn't just clam, sir, he skedaddled. Like he seen a ghost."

"Why do you think?"

The wind was whipping now. "Hell, Orville's afraid of his damn shadow and a thousand other fuckin' things, but he's *most* afraid of white officers."

"We've been decent enough to you men, haven't we?"

"That's not the point, Mr. Maxwell. White men, especially white officers, make the boy...jumpy."

"*I'm* an officer. Orville and I get along fine."

"I noticed that. Well, he trusts you, sir. Of course, he trusts Mr. Connor, too, and even Mr. Rosetti. But around Captain Egan or Lieutenant Driscoll, Orv turns into Willie Best."

"Who's Willie Best?"

"Feet-do-your-stuff darkie in the moving pictures."

"Oh." Pete got a Chesterfield going, despite the wind. "Any idea who might be forcing Orville to do this shit?"

Washington shook his head. "Could be damned near anybody. Sounds like Big Brown, from the description, but I find that hard to buy."

"This sex stuff...is that why Monroe's always trying to get a transfer?"

"Makes sense, don't it?"

Rain began to pelt them now—big heavy drops driven by an increasing wind like an obnoxious God flicking them in the face every few seconds.

"Where the hell," Pete asked, trying to protect his smoke from the raindrops, "is there enough privacy on this cramped ship to commit sex acts?"

Washington shrugged elaborately. "I've got no damn idea. Seems like, no matter where you are, somebody's movin' around somewhere on this tub. If somebody was getting blowed or cornholed, they have to worry about gettin' walked in on, just about anywhere."

This was a conversation Pete had never imagined having, not even in this man's Navy. And the very fact that he understood exactly what Sarge was talking about showed how far Peter Maxwell had come...or fallen.

The waves no longer lapped at the ship but crashed into her, the chop steadily rising, the rain driving now. Washington and Pete stepped into the wheelhouse.

"You better get below, Sarge—this storm's getting out of hand."

"Aye, sir. What do we do about Orville?"

"When this damn squall's behind us, Sarge, I promise you, we will figure this shit out."

And Pete held his hand out and Sarge took it, shook it, and the men grinned humorlessly at each other before Sarge headed off down the stairs.

Pete went up to the bridge deck, cutting through the communications room, and onto the bridge from the rear. The pilothouse hatches were shut and locked now, rain pounding against the portholes. The two Negro crewmen on the bridge stayed steady, the helmsman's forearm muscles knotted as he fought the wheel, sweat beading the radar operator's face, his fear apparent but controlled. Driscoll in the captain's chair appeared calm, but his eyes betrayed him when he looked to Pete.

"Good to have you back," Driscoll said.

"Where's the rest of the damn convoy?" Pete asked the radar man.

"Still holding formation, sir," the crewman said. "But they's wrestling the storm, too."

The waves were higher now, the ship rolling on the choppy water, the storm's intensity building. Pete could barely hold his balance as the ship lolled left, then right, then left again, lurching like a drunken sailor, then finally, blessedly, got sober and just plowed straight ahead. For the moment.

Pete asked his XO, "Did you wake the skipper?"

Driscoll shook his head.

"We better do it now."

"Agreed. Go rouse him, Maxie."

At the intercom, Pete pushed the button. "Captain Egan?"

A moment later, a groggy voice answered, "What the hell time is it?"

Pete ignored the question. "There's a storm, sir, a pretty bad one. Mr. Driscoll is asking for you on the bridge."

"...Be right there."

Five minutes later, his eyebrows wild but his eyes steady, Egan marched onto the bridge, uniform cleaned and pressed, hair combed, though he hadn't stopped to shave. Still, Pete wondered how the crusty old S.O.B. did it. If Pete had been the one rushing onto the bridge from a sound sleep, he'd be lucky to remember his pants, especially the way the storm was tossing the ship around like a goddamn toy boat.

"Situation report," Egan barked, fighting to keep his own balance.

Driscoll rose from the captain's chair, explained what had been happening and what they had done to prepare for the storm.

"Convoy still intact?" Egan asked the radar man.

One of two men who shared the job with Sarge Washington, Louis Frye was a light-skinned Negro about twenty, with short hair, muscular arms, and a perpetually curious baby face that made him seem about fifteen years old (when he was in fact nineteen). Sweat stained his shirt and he was clearly scared shitless.

"I'm losin' the front of the convoy, sir. Can't tell if they're pullin' away from us, or if the formation's breakin' up under the weather. Waves are too high to get an accurate reading."

Egan nodded. He went to the intercom and pushed a button. "Engine room, this is the captain—ahead two-thirds."

"Aye, sir," came the crackly reply.

Wind and rain kept lashing at the ship, and the more the ship rolled, the more trouble these men had keeping their balance. Several times Pete slammed into the wall until finally he held one arm up against it, to steady himself.

"Wind's coming from port?" Egan asked.

"Aye, sir," Driscoll said. "Thirty knots with gusts to forty."

"Ship's pushing to starboard—we need to correct that. Helmsman, bring her left ten degrees."

"Aye, sir," the helmsman said. "Bearing left to course 280."

Pete watched the helmsman battle the wheel as the ship continued to pitch over the choppy sea, but he finally steered the ship onto the proper course. They all turned as the wheel in the center of the port-side hatch began to spin.

Connor and Rosetti both burst into the pilothouse from the port bridge wing, jerking the hatch shut behind them. They were soaked head-to-toe and Rosetti shook himself like a wet spaniel, water going everywhere. Then the ship dipped and he almost dropped to his knees.

Egan turned on them. "Mr. Rosetti, get down to the engine room."

"Aye, sir," Rosetti said, going out the way he came in, spinning the hatch wheel from the outside.

The course change, Pete could feel, had little effect on the waves crashing into the ship.

Egan waved Pete over. The journey of a few feet was compromised by the pitching and bucking, and Pete grabbed whatever it took to get across the bridge. Then Egan spoke just loud enough to be heard over the howling.

"Are you confident our cargo is secure, Mr. Maxwell?"

"Should be, sir."

"Better make sure—send some men down into the holds. Any of these coloreds you can trust?"

"Yes, sir. That group who handled the loading should do very well—and I can supervise it myself!"

"Can't spare you on the bridge—with Mr. Rosetti in the engine room, I need my other officers with me. Any non-coms up to the job?"

"I know a man who can handle it, sir," Pete said, though he didn't mean one of the non-coms.

"Good, good," Egan said.

Pete maneuvered awkwardly over to the squawk box and called Washington to the chart room. Two minutes that were a jostling eternity crawled by and then Sarge was trotting up the stairs from the cabin deck. Pete sent the radioman—who had little to do, anyway, under radio silence—onto the bridge; the lieutenant needed to speak to Washington alone—wouldn't want talk of jeopardy over their explosive cargo panicking the crew.

"Sarge," Pete said, "we both know you're the leader among the colored boys."

"Wouldn't say that, sir."

"False modesty isn't an allowable luxury, right now—this storm is a goddamn roller-coaster ride, and it's not going to get any smoother, soon."

"Had that feeling, sir."

"I mean no offense when I say those boys down below are probably nervous as hell right now—and I don't think color has anything to do with it. A white crew, stuck down there off-duty, would be pissing and moaning, too."

"No argument, sir."

"I need you to go down there and tell those men that everything'll be A-number-one."

"Yes, sir. Will it, sir?"

"Should be. Captain Egan may have his faults, but he's a hell of a sailor, and he'll get us through this. Biggest danger may be our cargo."

"You mean, this ship blows up and shoots enough fire in the sky to put out the storm?"

Pete nodded glumly. "We should already be secure down there, but hell, you can feel the pitching and rolling."

"Yes, sir."

"Take some men you trust, including anybody left down there that helped us load, and check that cargo. Understood?"

"Aye, sir. You want us to babysit them bombs?"

"No. Determine they're secure, then get on the horn and let me know."

"Aye, sir."

"If the ship turns upside down, we're dead anyway—burn or drown, take your pick. But short of capsizing, we will make it."

"Aye, sir," Sarge said, and went out into the storm.

NINE

Heading down the stairs, fighting the sway of the ship, Seaman Ulysses Grant Washington mentally assembled his team as he made his way forward to the fo'c'sle, fast as the rocking ship would allow. He had about fifty feet of main deck to cross out in that nasty-ass weather, rain lashing him, deck slippery as Chicago sidewalk in an ice storm; he hung on to any secure piece of equipment he could as he traveled: the winch behind the number three hatch, then (rain stinging his eyes and blurring his vision) the winch in front of hatch three; next a ventilator, then the winch behind hatch two.

Finally, the fo'c'sle blocked the wind enough for him to throw open the hatch, hurl himself inside and slam the hatch shut.

Big Brown was already heading toward him and Sarge met him halfway.

"Getting a South Seas tan out there, Sarge?" the big man said, working his bass up over the monster banging at their door.

Sarge said, "Thought I spotted a mermaid—*everybody*! Gather 'round!"

Around Sarge now were any not-on-duty crew members, displaying faces that ran the gamut from nervous to terrified. Somebody threw him a towel and he wiped his face—they didn't need to know the moisture was as much cold sweat as rain.

"Just come from the bridge," he told them, loud and casual yet confident. "Skipper's got everything squared away. Storm is a motherfucker, but they good sailors up there."

This elicited some nods, but also a good deal of uncertain frowns.

"And they's good sailors down here, too. I talked to Mr. Maxwell and he say no need to worry."

"You believe him?" somebody yelped, maybe Orville Monroe.

"I do," Sarge said, willing confidence into his voice.

Relief washed most faces now, though skepticism and fear painted the remainder.

"Yeah," that same voice said, definitely Orville, "but does you *trust* him?"

"For a white boy."

That drew general laughter, easing the tension.

"But got to do our share," Sarge said. He explained to them the need to check the cargo in these conditions. "They's twenty of us. They's five holds. Mean four men a team. Willie, Clancy, Big Brown, Hazel, and me will head 'em up."

Immediate nods came from Wilson, Clancy Mullins, Hazel Ricketts, and Big Brown.

Gesturing with the appropriate fingers, Sarge said, "Hazel, hold one; Clancy, number two; Willie, number three; Big Brown, number four." He jerked a thumb to his chest. "Last one's mine."

The Mississippi farm kid, Ricketts, was the least experienced, so Sarge wanted him in the nearest hold. Most dangerous would be the final hold, farthest from the safety of the fo'c'sle. Before they dispersed, he sent six sailors to the forward stores to get each man a flashlight—no lights on in the holds. When the men returned, the teams made their way to their particular areas.

Sarge assembled his team: John Kelley, a handsome, slender Negro from western Illinois who'd been a steam-fitter before the war; Mason Gray, a coal-black Negro from South Carolina who'd taught at an all-Negro school; and Leon Boudreaux, Omaha truck driver.

Sarge and his men took different staircases, weaving down the decks until they were at the bottom and just outside the forward end of the hold. Even here, five decks below the bridge, the storm battering the ship kept up a constant reminder of the danger they faced.

Sarge opened the hatch, switched on his flashlight, and entered the hold, dark but for a slant of light coming in the open hatch from the passageway.

Sarge sent a beam of light to his right: wooden boxes, twenty inches high by thirty inches long by twenty inches wide, chock full of small arms ammo, were stacked five high and ten wide, covered with cargo netting secured to the bulkheads, each net around eight feet high and sixteen feet wide, with six netted bundles on the port and starboard sides. The cargo netting allowed for loads to shift slightly with the motion of the ship, yet stay secured.

"Mason," Sarge said, "you and Leon take the port side, John and me'll take the starboard. Make sure everything's secure, sing out if it ain't. When you get to the other end, wait for us, then we move up to the next deck."

"You bet, Sarge," Mason Gray said.

Sarge and Kelley moved slowly down their side, casting their lights over the netted cargo, tugging on the nets to test they were secure, then moving on to the next bundle. They finished before Gray and Boudreaux and waited while the others checked their last bundle.

"Everything okay?" Sarge asked.

"Tight as a tick," Gray said.

They climbed to the next deck, where at the far end were pallets like the one that had damn near been dropped during loading, stacked two high, four shells in a rack, four racks to a pallet, with heavy chains running over them, front and back, attached to the deck on either side.

Sarge hoped the other teams were running as smooth as his men were. He and Kelley kept moving, Gray and Boudreaux ahead on the other side. Then the ship lurched to port with sudden force and Sarge almost went ass-over-teakettle. He heard scraping to

his right and, as he steadied himself, swung his light around—
one big shell, top row of a pallet, was sliding toward him....

"Mother-*fucker*!"

The other three swung their flashlights toward the startled
Sarge, then followed the beam of his flash to where the shell was
still sliding, until it tipped precariously toward the deck.

As it did, however, the ass end of the shell rose to catch
against the chain with enough pressure to keep the shell from
dropping out of its cradle as Sarge, dumping his flashlight to the
deck, leapt toward the teetering shell and got his hands under it.

"John!" he yelled.

But Kelley had already moved to the side of the pallet and
was training his beam on the back chain-puller through which
the shell had slipped, and was loosening it. A few seconds later,
Kelley aimed the flash at the front chain-puller, which kept the
links taut, and was the only thing keeping this shell from dropping in Sarge's lap.

Kelley called, "You got it, Sarge?"

The shell felt heavy as a Buick, but Sarge had the thing cradled in both hands, knees bent, and knew he could hold it, since
the alternative was to let it blow itself to bits.

"Yeah, John," he said, voice betraying no fear, "loosen that
son-of-a-bitch come-along, and slide the shell back, and then we
tighten her down, right."

Kelley loosened the chain-puller, and the extra weight over-
whelmed Sarge, the strain more than anticipated, as the shell
tried to tip off; but he lifted with his legs, and—with a manful
grunt that echoed in the hold—managed to get the shell back up
in the rack. As he slid the shell home, Sarge could only marvel
at Big Brown's strength—on the dock, the sailor had lifted one of
these things like a damn toy.

They got the chains in order, and Kelley cranked the front
come-along down nice and tight. Then, they tightened the back
one again, just to be sure.

"Let's see that bastard move now," Kelley said.

"Let's not," Sarge said.

Gray and Boudreaux came rushing over.

"Jesus," Gray said. "You okay, Sarge?"

Sarge shrugged aching shoulders. "No big deal."

Boudreaux began, "If that damned thing hit the deck—"

"Well it didn't," Sarge said. "And probably won't go off, anyhow. Ain't armed till the detonators go in."

"Tell the boys at Port Chicago," Kelley said.

The rest of Sarge's check went without incident, and all five teams gathered in the mess to compare notes. Each team leader agreed the cargo was secure, which Sarge reported to Mr. Maxwell via the squawk box.

"Thanks," Maxwell said. "Skipper wants you guys to patrol the holds until the storm passes, just to be sure."

Babysitters, after all, Sarge thought. But he said, "Aye, sir," and turned to the others, who had already heard their orders.

Truth be told, Sarge was a little uneasy after playing catch with that shell in hold five; just the same, he felt better knowing somebody had their eye on their volatile cargo while they rode out the storm, even if the eye had to be his.

On the bridge, Lieutenant Driscoll was saying, "Maybe we should radio the others, sir."

Egan's eyes burned into his exec. "Our orders are radio silence, mister, and we *will* obey our orders."

"Aye, sir," Driscoll said meekly.

"Radar," Egan said. "Where's the convoy?"

"All ahead of us now, sir," Frye said. "Moving southwest—heading into the storm."

Pete knew at once that every captain in the convoy was likely doing the same thing as Egan—the storm was coming out of the southwest, the convoy's original course had been northwest, and by turning, even slightly, they presented a thinner target to the oncoming waves.

The last thing they wanted was to get hit broadside by a pounding sea.

The other captains had turned even further than Egan, trying to take the storm head on, presenting the narrowest profile possible to swells now up to twenty-five feet. Out the porthole, Pete could see waves crashing over the port side and the bow.

Egan saw the same problem. "Helmsman, course 225."

"Aye, sir, bearing left to course 225."

Pete watched helplessly as the helmsman fought the wheel, but nothing seemed to be happening.

"She's not answering," the helmsman said, a note of panic in his voice.

Egan stepped to the intercom and pushed the button again. "Engine room."

"Aye, sir?"

"Full speed ahead."

"Aye, sir."

Pete knew that speeding up the ship would actually increase her maneuverability, but the waves were growing steadily higher and—if Egan didn't find a way to turn the *Liberty Hill*—sooner or later, they would flounder.

"She's turning, sir," the helmsman said.

The ship suddenly lurched to port so sharply Pete wondered if something important in her workings had busted. But she settled onto her new course, and though they still struggled against the high seas, they were aimed into the storm, the bow cutting the waves rather than those waves crashing broadside into the ship.

Egan moved to the intercom. "Engine room, slow to two-thirds." Then, he turned to Driscoll and Pete. "We'll ride the storm out. We should be fine now."

They waited for a reply from the engine room, got nothing.

"Engine room!" Egan bellowed into the intercom.

Finally, Rosetti came on the intercom. "We've got a problem, sir."

"What is it?" Egan demanded.

"We're not sure, sir."

"That's no answer, sailor."

"When we went to full power," Rosetti said, "the bearings started over-heating. It's a hitch we noticed on the trip to Pearl, but it hasn't reared up again, until now. Thing is, we can't go over half-power … and probably shouldn't be pushing it *that* hard, till we isolate the trouble."

"All ahead half," Egan said, then—without any note of exaggeration in his voice—added, "And work fast, Mr. Rosetti, we're fighting for our lives up here."

Egan had succeeded in steering directly into the storm and they were safer, yes, most definitely; but with the engine problem, whatever it might be, they were falling farther and farther behind the convoy … and Egan refused to break radio silence.

Driscoll looked sick, Connor scared, and the two Negroes in the pilothouse shared an uneasy aspect; but Egan stoically faced the storm, occasionally giving an order to keep the ship heading into the wind. It wasn't "Damn the torpedoes" exactly, but (Pete had to admit to himself) their captain looked pretty impressive, moving the injured ship forward.

The next morning, when the storm finally broke, the sea gave up the fight and went calm, though the *Liberty Hill* still steamed under a threatening gunmetal sky of low-hanging clouds.

No question about it: by steering into the storm, Egan had saved the ship. Despite a crippled engine, they had fought the storm all night and had, per Egan's orders, maintained radio silence. The only problem now was that the engine was still limping along and the convoy was nowhere on the horizon.

Whether the other ships had all steamed off, leaving the *Liberty Hill Victory* behind, or whether every other vessel had floundered and sunk in the storm, no one knew. Either way, they were well beyond radar distance, and—under radio silence—had no way to contact the others to see where they were and if they were okay.

Meanwhile, the lube oil temperature of the forward HP (high pressure) journal bearing had climbed to a dangerous level. This should have been repaired when they were at Pearl Harbor, but time had not allowed and, anyway, the problem had seemed minor … until the storm.

Rosetti had recognized what was happening and—by forcing the captain to slow the rpms of the engine—gave them some power to maneuver, rather than blowing the engine completely. The calm-for-now weather gave them time to investigate the situation.

Finally, Rosetti reported that the oil flow to the bearing wasn't the problem, as the sight glass showed plenty of flow. Still, the temperature rose when the engine was pushed above one-third.

"I tried to shift the lube oil strainer," he told the captain. "But it wouldn't budge."

"How long to repair?" Egan wanted to know.

"A day."

"A day?"

"Maybe longer. I'll get back at it …"

Good news was they knew where the convoy was heading and, most likely, were just a few hours behind, though the *Liberty Hill* was losing more distance with each passing moment. Bad news was they had been blown an indeterminate distance off course, and couldn't absolutely pinpoint their new position. The Pacific was, after all, a big ocean and—with no sun, stars, or islands in sight—they would have to count on Egan's dead reckoning, at least for now.

The day passed quietly, with Rosetti and Connor staying down in the engine room, until—just before supper—the pair discovered that the engines were supplying only partial power.

Maybe they could get the monster fixed at Eniwetok atoll, assuming they could ever find the Marshall Islands; but for now, half-speed was full speed—and then only for a short time.

They had all been up all night. Egan stayed on the bridge while Driscoll and Pete slept during the day. When they got up to take over the evening watch, Rosetti and Connor finally hit the rack after spending over twelve hours straight in the engine room.

The ship steamed northwest again, back on its original heading of 290. The shift went by as quietly as the day had, Pete on the bridge now, Driscoll taking another round of the ship.

Just after midnight, Ben Connor came in to relieve Pete.

"You look surprisingly good to me," Pete said.

"You do nothing at all for me," Connor said, handing him a steaming cup of coffee.

Pete grinned. "Thanks." He took a long drink. "It's good."

"Have you always had this way with words?" Connor asked, rhetorically. Then a real question: "Where the hell is everybody?"

"Skipper's asleep. Driscoll's ..." Pete looked at his watch. "I guess I don't know where Driscoll is. Haven't seen him for over an hour."

Connor smirked. "Maybe he's off writing the captain a note of apology for all the terrible things he's said about him."

Pete looked meaningfully at the helmsman and radar man, and Connor got the hint: his sarcasm might be lost on the colored boys, so stow it.

"I'll be in the officers' mess," Pete said. "Doing shift reports. You see Dick, send him down."

"Will do," Connor said.

An hour later, the call came over the intercom. Hunched at the table where he'd fallen asleep, Pete woke slowly, lifting his head from folded arms that had served as his pillow, report forms plastered underneath. He pushed the button on the intercom. "Say again?"

"Captain wants you in the engine room, Pete," Connor said.

"Right away!" Connor's voice had gone from bass to a higher pitch, indicating excitement and, maybe, alarm.

"What now?" Pete moaned.

"Something's happened to Dick."

Wondering if he was being set up for a practical joke, Pete said, "What, did one of the colored boys ask him out for a date, after that Andrews Sisters routine?"

There was a long silence.

"Ben, what the hell is going on?"

Connor said, "Pete...Dick is dead."

The words hit Pete like a punch.

"You *there*, Pete?"

It took a moment, but Pete pushed the button on the intercom. "What in God's name happened?"

"You just get down to the engine room on the double...and not a word to anybody on the way."

"Aye," he said numbly.

He went through a boat-deck door down a short flight of stairs and came out in the engine room. With the ship reduced to half-power, the engine room ran slightly quieter than usual—in other words like being inside an explosion. When the phone down here rang, that "ring" was more a foghorn going off—the only way it could be heard by the engine man.

Albert Blake, chief petty officer in charge of the overnight shift, stood near the intercom cubicle, his skin a ghostly white. Over by the boiler, John Smith kept his eyes on the temperature and refused to look up.

"At the bottom," Blake yelled, pointing toward the floor.

Pete nodded and descended four more flights of stairs to get to the bowels of the ship, just outside shaft alley. The overnight oiler, Orville Monroe, sat on the deck, a towel covering his face—was he weeping?

Yes.

"Where is Mr. Driscoll?" Pete asked.

Orville pointed toward the open door to shaft alley.

Despite the engine-room heat, a chill traveled through Pete Maxwell as he peered down the dimly lit corridor. If ever he might feel claustrophobic, this was the place—illuminated only slightly better than a tomb, the corridor was nearly two hundred feet long with a forty-watt bulb every thirty or forty feet. Most of the alley was taken up by the drive shaft and the steel casing that surrounded it.

Pete could only marvel that anybody the size of Big Brown could maneuver in such a tight space as this. At the far end, Pete could make out two men in uniform standing over something on the deck. His stomach somersaulted and he had to work to keep everything in it from making a return trip.

He stepped over the coaming into shaft alley and, oh so consciously, put one foot in front of the other, not at all anxious to see what awaited him at the other end.

TEN

AUGUST 31, 1944

Pete Maxwell could never get used to the cramped hell that was shaft alley, its overhead nest of pipes (some wrapped, some not), its recessed walls providing space for fire extinguishers, more pipes and various tools, and a passageway along the massive shaft of the ship that could accommodate one man, but just barely.

As he drew closer, Pete saw Captain Egan and Vince Rosetti standing over something down on what was the ship's lowest deck, regarding it with a sort of solemn disgust—Egan closer to the brown-uniformed sprawl, his back to the massive shaft, while Rosetti stood back-to-the-wall just down from the captain, closer to the approaching Pete.

Even though he'd been warned, Pete couldn't make the shape be a human body until he was about ten feet away.

Egan turned toward Pete and acknowledged him with a nod and a crisp, "Mr. Maxwell."

"What the hell is this?" Pete asked, stopping a few feet from Rosetti, filling the gap between the other two officers in their staggered positions in the cramped passageway. "Some kind of horrible accident?"

"If so," Egan said, "call Ripley."

"What?"

Egan gave Pete a ghastly smile. "For this to be an accident, Mr. Maxwell, your friend Driscoll would've had to walk through here with a knife in hand, trip and fall, accidentally slit his own throat, then manage to hide his knife before he died."

The awful gallows humor echoed off the metalworks of shaft alley. Metallic, too, was the iron-tinged scent of blood in the otherwise oily air.

"It's murder, Pete," Rosetti said, numbly. "Some lousy bastard cut Dick's throat."

In the abstract at least, Pete Maxwell had expected to see killing when he went to war—but he had not expected to see murder. He had known he almost certainly would, serving his country, witness carnage, that he would see death and blood and terrible wounds; he had even accepted (again, in the abstract) that he himself might be wounded or killed or kill someone else. But a fellow sailor, a fellow officer, slain by someone on his own side—another American? Never.

Never arrived as Pete forced himself to look down at the lifeless body of his friend. Driscoll had folded up on himself in the confined space, apparently kneeling, then falling forward and tipping onto his side, a thin scarlet gash across his throat, dripping into a modest pool of scarlet.

Softly, in a dazed sort of mumble, Pete said, "Not as much blood as you'd think."

Rosetti said, "Killer probably missed the jugular and carotid, but did sever the windpipe."

"And that'll kill you?"

"Yeah. In half a minute or so."

Pete was working to keep his breakfast down. The blocky Egan revealed nothing behind a typically stoic mask. Obviously, Rosetti had seen his share of violent death, patrolling the streets of Los Angeles. Still, was Vince looking a little pale around the gills, or was that just the spotty incandescent lighting?

"Well, Mr. Maxwell," Egan said with dry sarcasm, "you're our new executive officer now. Congratulations."

"Aye, sir," Pete answered, his tongue thick.

"And your first duty is to find the black bastard responsible."

The *Liberty Hill Victory's* new XO gaped at the captain. "Sir...?"

Egan raised one unruly eyebrow and gave Pete something that might have been a smile but was more likely a sneer. "Do I stutter, Mr. Maxwell?"

"No, sir."

"You are in charge of the inquiry into Mr. Driscoll's death." The captain's chin came up. "You are to take whatever measures necessary in order to find the kill-happy jigaboo who has turned my ship into a goddamned slaughterhouse. Do I make myself clear?"

"Yes, sir. Uh, sir?"

"What?"

"You seem convinced it was one of our colored crew. I don't believe I should exclude the white officers and non-coms in my inquiry. Sir."

The pouches under Egan's eyes tightened. "You're right. You need to be thorough. But may I suggest that if in fact one of these black sons of bitches has killed one white officer, he may not hesitate to kill another, and another? Has it escaped your attention, Mr. Maxwell, that we are seriously outnumbered here? That the white teeth floating in the darkness of the *Liberty Hill* do not belong to the goddamned Cheshire Cat?"

"Yes, sir. Understood, sir."

"You may certainly include the whites in your inquiry. But it is well-known that a knife or razor is the preferred weapon of niggers north and south, and I would suggest you start there."

Rosetti said, "We haven't had a bag inspection since San Diego."

One hundred knives had been confiscated before the *Liberty Hill* left port.

"That might be wise," Egan said, eyes slitting beneath the out-of-control brows. "Now, Mr. Maxwell, I'm going to my cabin, where I have paperwork to do. If you need me, you'll know where to find me."

"Aye, sir," Pete said.

Egan waggled a thick finger at Pete. "Remember, Mr. Maxwell, I don't care how you do this thing, just get it done. We're in the business of shedding Jap blood, not our own."

"And my other duties, sir…?"

"Temporarily suspended. In the meantime, Mr. Connor and Mr. Rosetti… and myself, of course… will take care of the ship."

"Aye aye, Captain."

Shoving past, Egan strode out of shaft alley, wide enough to damn near fill it, leaving Pete and Rosetti staring at each other with the corpse of their friend slumped nearby.

"He's passed the fucking buck again," Pete said, upper lip peeled back over his teeth.

Rosetti shrugged. "Captain's prerogative."

Instinctively the two officers moved away, a few yards, from their dead comrade, almost as if they were afraid Driscoll might eavesdrop.

Pete frowned at Rosetti. "You really believe this had to be the work of one of the colored boys?"

"They do outnumber us palefaces something like eight to one. But why would one of 'em single Dick out, in particular?"

"Why would anybody? Dick could be a sarcastic snob, but that's no murder motive." Pete let out a long sigh. "Vince, I'm going to need your help on this. You're a pro at this stuff—I'm a rank amateur."

"Pete, buddy—I was a *beat* cop! You know what I did at murder scenes? I waited till Homicide got there, the plainclothes boys—I don't know shit from shinola about *solving* crimes."

"And I *do?*"

Rosetti patted the air with two palms. "My job was just to make sure nobody did anything stupid till the dicks arrived.

What you need is a *real* detective—an honest-to-God Sam Spade, and where exactly are you going to find one on *this* bucket?"

"Well…hell." Pete found himself grinning, even with dead Dick Driscoll so nearby: Vince didn't know how right he was. "We do have one."

Rosetti frowned. "Who? *Connor?* Pete, he wrote for *Jack Benny,* not *The Shadow.*"

A certain irony was not lost on Pete—Driscoll had been killed with a sharp blade; yet it was the knife-scarred face of Sarge Washington that had come immediately to mind.

"The skipper said I should take whatever measures were necessary to catch this killer, right?"

Rosetti's eyes narrowed. "Yeah…that's what he said. Why am I suddenly nervous?"

Pete answered this rhetorical question by telling his friend who the detective on the *Liberty Hill* was.

Rosetti's mouth dropped open; when he got it working again, he managed, "You got to be fucking kidding me, right? A colored shamus? What is he, black Irish?"

Pete said nothing.

"*Is* there such a thing as a black detective? Where the hell do they have 'em?"

"South Side of Chicago, for one. How do you think he got the nickname 'Sarge'? Not in the white man's Navy!"

But Rosetti was past his initial astonishment now. "He was a sergeant with the Chicago PD, you say?"

"He was," Pete said. "Detective bureau, too."

Rosetti sighed, shook his head. "I don't know, Pete. None of that cancels out the fact he's colored. Here we are, sitting on that powderkeg Dick Driscoll always talked about, and you think it's a good idea to have one of the enemy goin' around lighting matches on the subject!"

"*Who's* the enemy?"

"Well...in this situation, these coloreds. You know damn well Egan's right—one of them did it. Got a white officer alone and took out a razor and got even for hundreds of years of—"

"Of us assuming the worst about them? Calling them 'coloreds' and sticking razors in all their hands?"

Rosetti scowled. "Don't you go making *me* out a bigot! I got friends in L.A. every damn color in the rainbow—how many pals you got back in Iowa who aren't as pasty-faced as you, Pete?"

This was rich, coming from somebody as pasty-faced as Rosetti about now; but Pete let it pass.

Instead he said, "Let me grant you that the Negroes are our major suspect pool. But if we want to get cooperation out of them, how better than having one of their own handling the inquiry? They'll see their interests fairly represented, and know we're not just assuming the worst."

Rosetti said nothing for fifteen or twenty seconds, really thinking over what Pete was saying. Finally, he said, "All right, I'll admit you got a point, Mrs. Roosevelt...but do you really think our local Klan reps, Griffin and Whitford, will stand for questioning by a colored seaman?"

Pete gestured with open hands. "Well, what if Egan promoted Washington? If Sarge was a petty officer, then Griffin and—"

"Listen to yourself, Pete. You *really* think Egan's going to promote a black? And about the time the captain gets wind of you turning his precious investigation over to a colored boy, you'll be knocked back to seaman yourself!"

Knowing his friend was right, Pete said, "Okay, then. One of us'll have to stay at Sarge's side, and work with him, and make sure everybody—black *and* white—cooperates. And since you have police experience—"

Rosetti grinned nastily. "You may be the XO now, Pete, but the captain himself is the only one gets to pass the buck on this bucket. You heard Egan—him and me and Connor run the ship, and you run the investigation."

"Come on, Vince, be reasonable…"

"Reasonable don't enter into it. The captain was specific about your duty—you will have to officially lead the inquiry, with Washington helping or advising or what-have-you."

Pete just looked at his friend; then finally he grinned, shook his head, and said, "Thanks for everything, you miserable prick."

Rosetti grinned back at him, but something bittersweet was in it. "Dick was right—your language is going to hell. You are officially salty, my friend."

Pete smiled, shook his head again, then turned, leaving Rosetti with the body of Richard Driscoll.

Rosetti frowned at his back. "Where the hell are you going?"

"To find a real detective. Not some damn beat cop."

"And what am *I* supposed to do?"

"Make sure nobody does anything stupid," Pete called over his shoulder, "until the dicks get here."

Pete started up to the bridge to summon Washington on the intercom, but saw the sailor on the main deck, near one of the winches, deep in conversation with a couple other Negro crewmen. They all snapped to attention as he approached, then saluted.

He returned the salute. "Sarge, a word?"

Washington glanced at the other two sailors, who did a quick disappearing act. The officer and the seaman moved to the rail where Pete offered Sarge a Chesterfield.

Washington took it, and Pete lighted him up with his Zippo, then lit his own smoke.

"Mr. Maxwell, afraid I don't have nothin' for you yet, where Orville's concerned. I buttonholed him this morning, and the boy still won't spill who's been messing with him. Fact, he told me to just forget about it."

"This is something else," Pete said, waving that off. "Another problem. Bigger problem."

Washington's eyes narrowed. "What's happened, Mr. Maxwell?"

"It'll get around the ship soon enough—for now I need you to stay mum about this."

"About what?"

Pete exhaled smoke. "Sarge, we've had a killing below deck. A murder."

"Jesus Christ. Who?"

Pete told him.

Washington shook his head. "Damn. Somebody murder the exec? Who in hell would do a damn fool thing like that?"

"That's what I need your help to find out."

"My help? Hell, Mr. Maxwell—I'm just another colored seaman."

"No you aren't, and you sure as hell know it. Right now you're one valuable seaman, colored or white, because of what you did in civilian life."

Shrugging, Washington said, "Wasn't Mr. Rosetti a cop, before the war? Better an officer, a white officer, do this thing."

"Vince walked a beat. We need a detective."

"You mean you need a colored detective, to help keep the peace on your slave ship."

"I didn't say that. And I think I deserve better than that."

"You probably do," Washington said, sighing smoke. "Who found Mr. Driscoll?"

"Orville did."

Washington gave Pete a hard look. "You said this wasn't *about* Orville."

"Far as I know, it isn't. A body turns up in shaft alley, one of the oilers finds it, happens to be Orville. Now you know as much about it as I do."

Washington smirked mirthlessly. "Does seem like that little fairy turns up wherever and whenever there's trouble on this ship."

"Well, he's the first man you'll talk to, then."

Washington's eyes and nostrils flared. "That's it, isn't it? You already decided a Negro did this, and I'm appointed Uncle Tom, to put a black face on this necktie party."

Pete sent his cigarette sailing over the rail. "Listen to me, Washington. That's not who I am, and you damn well know it. I make no assumption that this was the work of a Negro."

"Then you're a fuckin' fool—it's mostly Negroes on the ship, and the weapon's a knife. We both know—even if Captain Egan don't—that the last mix-up on this ship was a knife fight … 'tween me and another colored sailor."

But Pete was already shaking his head. "I'm not trying to put a black or a white face on this inquiry. I need *a* detective and it's my damn luck that you're the only one around. All I want, Mr. Washington, is to find the truth of this, and to find the son of a bitch who killed my friend."

A humorless laugh rumbled up out of Washington's chest. "You after truth or revenge, Mr. Maxwell? Best make up your mind."

"Call it what you want, Sarge. But I promise if you can help me find the killer, black or white, we will lock him up until we get to port, where he'll face court-martial. You have my word. Nobody gets lynch-mobbed on my watch."

Washington's gaze was cool and hard now. His voice had a surprising lightness of tone as he asked, "You really think I'd help you put a black man away, Mr. Maxwell."

Pete met the sailor's gaze. "Yes. I believe you would put away your mother, if she did a crime."

Shaking his head, Washington said, "Now you're flat-out wrong, Mr. Maxwell. I'd let my mama walk." He grinned suddenly. "Now everybody else? They is fair game."

"Good. You'll help me, then."

"I will. Got a condition or two, Mr. Maxwell."

"Let's hear them."

"First, you're with me every step of the way. I'll be your colored Sherlock, but I need me a white Watson."

"Wouldn't have it any other way."

"Second, we finish this no matter where it leads."

"Sarge, I already told you ..."

Washington held up a hand. "No matter who did this, looking into this murder, we gonna have to tear this ship apart ... and this ship, this crew, will tear itself apart at the same time. You get my meaning?"

Pete frowned. "I don't think it has to. We'll be fair and straightforward and—"

"Mr. Maxwell, right now this crew be eating oatmeal and spoiled mutton, you hadn't stepped in. So now is not the time to pass the piss and say it's rose water. We both know this is an ammo ship full of Negroes run by white men that could go off any time; we start pokin' around, we just might light the fuse."

"You're saying, we put a Negro sailor in the brig on a murder charge and we could have a race riot on our hands."

"Yeah. I am."

Pete exhaled smoke. He thought for a moment or two. Then: "We're in the middle of the Pacific in the middle of a war, Sarge. We can't ignore the murder of an officer by a person unknown on this ship. Who'd be murdered *next*?"

Sarge raised an eyebrow. "More likely you than me, Mr. Maxwell."

"Maybe. Maybe not."

"What do you suggest?"

"That we do our job. I have my orders, Sarge, and now you have yours. We go ahead and light this goddamn fuse, and do our best to find a way to snuff it out, before she blows."

Dark eyes fixed on Pete for what seemed forever, and was probably ten seconds.

Finally, Washington grunted something that wasn't quite a laugh. "You know, sir, I guess I was wrong about you."

"How so?"

"For a time there I was thinkin' you was maybe the craziest white motherfucker I ever met. Turns out? You way crazier than that."

And Washington held out his hand for Pete to shake, which he did.

"Partners in crime?" Washington asked.

"Partners in crime," Pete said.

The two men spoke fifteen minutes more, going through another cigarette each as Lieutenant Maxwell shared everything he knew (which wasn't much) with the Chicago detective. Then Sarge followed the lieutenant down into the engine room.

Blake and Smith, the two white non-coms at work there, eyeballed the colored intruder as he came through the door.

When Maxwell came looking for him, Sarge had already known about the murder; he'd acted suitably surprised, which wasn't difficult, because Sarge had been as scared as every other Negro on the ship, every one of whom now felt a suspect in the murder of a white officer.

Though the crime had not been announced—and how exactly the news had spread no one seemed to know—every colored crewman aboard was well aware that Lieutenant Driscoll had gotten his throat cut down in shaft alley. And each and every Negro onboard had figured the white officers would pick one of them out to take the rap.

Now, judging from the furtive looks Sarge was getting from Blake and Smith, the handful of white crewmen on the ship must have felt just as scared as the Negroes—*whose white throat would be slashed next?*

Still following the lieutenant, Sarge passed Orville Monroe, slumped outside the hatch to shaft alley. The small-framed oiler had a seasick look. Sarge figured this was natural, considering

Orville had found the body, but said nothing as he followed Maxwell through the hatch into the dank confines.

As they moved down the tunnel toward where Mr. Rosetti stood guard near the body, Sarge asked, "Has anybody interrogated Orville yet?"

"No," Maxwell said, his voice echoing in the tight quarters. "Nobody's been ... interrogated yet."

That explained Orville's sick expression—the little fairy had found the body, so the white officers would assume he did the killing. Orv would hardly be the first colored boy to get strung up for being a black face in the wrong place at the right white time.

"Finding the body doesn't make Orville the only suspect," Sarge reminded the lieutenant, who glanced back and gave a perfunctory nod.

The body lay in a heap at the far end of this endless corridor— throat neatly slit by someone who knew what he was doing.

"We don't got much blood," Sarge said, "'cause our killer slit Mr. Driscoll's windpipe without cutting the carotid artery."

Maxwell and Rosetti exchanged quick smiles.

What was that about? Sarge wondered.

"Sickening damn crime," Sarge continued, "but still ... you got to respect the skill of this bastard. Knew enough to do this without getting much red stuff spraying, so's he could make a getaway without wearing half of Mr. Driscoll's blood on him."

"Go on," Maxwell said.

Sarge gestured behind him. "If this is the only way in here, Mr. Maxwell, why not just ask the men in the engine room who come in here after Driscoll?"

"That's the problem," Rosetti said. "Way you came in is not the *only* way in."

"I don't see no other door."

Rosetti motioned for Sarge to step over the body with him. They did this, then moved to the absolute back end of the tube next to the wooden ring surrounding the drive shaft as it exited the ship out to the propeller.

Once there, Rosetti withdrew a flashlight from his pocket and directed the beam toward the low ceiling. Sarge could see the beam disappearing up a long, dark shaft.

"What the hell is that?" Sarge asked.

"Escape tunnel for the oiler," Rosetti said. "If there's a fire, he can climb out."

"To where?"

"Main deck, boat deck—take your pick."

"Hell. If our killer gone up there, he could come out damn near anywhere without anybody seeing him."

Rosetti nodded. "About the size of it."

Sarge turned back to Pete. "Like I said before, we got ourselves one smart killer—clean way he cut Mr. Driscoll, now this escape tunnel? Says he's smart. How many men on ship knew about that tunnel?"

Shrugging, Pete said, "Anybody could have."

"I didn't."

"Well, it's plainly visible on the cutaway view in the officer's mess. And the oilers and engine room guys, they definitely all know—it's their lifeline."

Sarge frowned. "Who's seen the cutaway?"

"All the officers, certainly ... and anyone else who happened by, or asked to see it."

"So, who asked?"

Pete shrugged again. "Nobody that I know of ... but any sailor could've talked to any officer and found out. In fact, the killer could've learned about the tunnel from Dick himself."

Sarge grunted, then returned his attention to the body, saying to Rosetti, "Sir, lend me that flashlight, please."

Rosetti handed the light over and Sarge knelt, in the tight quarters near the body, as best he could. He got a closer look at the fatal wound: short, neat, accomplishing its objective with both finality and a macabre grace.

"Thin blade," Sarge said. He looked up at Pete, then raised the beam of the flashlight to shine on the lieutenant's face. "You still got Mullins's switchblade, Mr. Maxwell?"

"Why," Maxwell said with grim humor, wincing at the light, "am *I* a suspect now?"

"Who ain't? Me included. And if you done it, Mr. Maxwell, you picked the wrong man to head up this dog-and-pony show."

"That's not funny," Maxwell said, blocking the beam with a hand.

"Maybe not, Mr. Maxwell, but the question still stands. Do you have that knife?"

"It's hardly the only knife on this ship. We were just saying we hadn't had a bag inspection since—"

"You have the knife, sir?"

"Yes. That is, I locked it up in the ship's safe."

"And if it's still there, it'll go a long way towards clearing you." Sarge's hand was on Driscoll's wrist. "Body's still warm. Dead maybe two hours."

Rosetti's eyebrows were up. "What's that, your expert opinion? You're a coroner, now?"

Sarge shifted the flashlight beam over to Rosetti. "I didn't ask for this job, sir. You going to fuck with me, or help out?"

Rosetti didn't blink at the harsh white light filling his face. "That remains to be seen—I don't know you from the next colored boy. Pete says you're a Chicago dick, but he's from Podunk Center, Iowa, and is easily fooled. I'm from L.A."

Sarge rose and locked eyes with the ensign. "I was a cop in Bronzeville over ten years. Investigated near sixty homicides and got forty-nine convictions. Four resisted arrest and never made it to trial, one killed himself while I was knockin' on his door to arrest his ass, another is as far as I know still running, but I figure the war won't last forever and then that son of a bitch will be mine, too."

Rosetti's eyes were wide now.

Maxwell, amused, asked, "What, you don't believe him, Vince?"

But Rosetti had held up a traffic-cop palm. "Seaman Washington, if there's any way I can aid you in your investigation, say the word."

"Appreciate it, sir. First thing you can do is tell me where you was two hours ago."

Rosetti offered no protestations about any status he might have as a suspect. "In the galley drinking coffee," he said, "making out reports on the engine incident. That's where I was when the captain came through, on his way to the engine room, and told me to fall in."

"How long were you in the galley, sir, before the captain come through?"

"I went into the galley before midnight and never left. The steward's mate, Wilson, can vouch for me. He brought me a late dinner and coffee."

"Why the galley, not the officers' mess?"

"Privacy. I wanted quiet, and the cooks were gone and I figured I'd be done with my reports before they got back."

Sarge nodded, glancing from Maxwell to Rosetti. "Okay. Now, what are we going to do about the body?"

"What *should* we do?" Pete asked.

"Know anybody with a camera on board?"

"I have one," Rosetti said. "Nothing fancy—little Brownie."

"That'll do fine. Know anything about taking photos at the scene of a crime?"

"Well, I've seen it done enough times."

"Swell. Then you know to snap from every angle you can—get good and close on that wound. When you're done, get a couple men to sew Mr. Driscoll into a sheet and stow him in the meat locker."

Rosetti merely nodded at that, but Maxwell blurted, "Meat locker? Are you kidding?"

"Can't leave him here," Sarge said, "or he'll get riper than that mutton. ... Now, Mr. Maxwell, let's us go talk to Orville and those two white non-coms."

Back in the engine room, where Blake and Smith were doing their best to keep the ship running at one-third power, Maxwell went first and Sarge took the rear as the pair escorted Orville Monroe up the stairs and into the passageway outside the engine room.

The little guy was oozing sweat and his eyes looked everywhere but landed nowhere. The heat was oppressive, especially in the engine room, and Sarge and Maxwell were fairly sweat-soaked, too; but Monroe might have gone overboard and just been hauled on deck, wet as he was.

"Seem kind of jumpy, Orville," Sarge commented. "Even for you, son."

The engine noise was slightly muffled in the passageway with the hatch closed; but even then—and with the engine in bad shape—the roar might have been an airplane landing. "Hell yes, I'm jumpy," Monroe said. He was trembling. "When did I ever see a dead body before?"

Sarge studied him for a while. Then he asked, "Is that what's give you the jitters, Orv? Seeing a dead white man?"

Orville turned and fixed his nervous gaze on Maxwell. "What is this uppity nigger asking the questions for? Why ain't *you* asking, Mr. Maxwell?"

"Never mind why," Maxwell said. "Just answer Sarge."

With no help forthcoming from Maxwell, Orville gave Sarge his full attention. "Don't bullshit me, Sarge, you know and I know that there's a dead white officer down in shaft alley, and some poor black bastard on this ship is going to pay for it."

"And since you're the poor black bastard who found the body," Sarge said, "you figure you're first in line."

"Hell yes!"

"Well, you're wrong, Orv. Mr. Maxwell and me, we're investigating what happened, and we ain't making any assumptions about nothing."

"No?"

"No. Now you just calm down, and take it easy, and tell us what happened."

"From when?"

"Start of your shift."

Orville took a deep breath, then let it out slow. The way he was shaking, he might've been outside an igloo in Alaska, not an engine room in the blistering South Pacific.

Maxwell shook out a cigarette from a deck of Chesterfields and used his lighter to get it going for Orville, who thanked him. The gesture, Sarge thought, was a smart one: all three knew it was against regs to smoke here, but the investigators needed to calm their subject, and this was a good start.

Orville sighed smoke, then said, "Well, I got down to the engine room just 'fore shift started at twenty-three hundred. Wallace give me a report about his shift."

"You're doing fine," Sarge said.

"First thing I did, when my shift really got goin', was check the main bearing journal. Strainer's been causin' the problem with the engine. So, that was my first job."

"Then what?"

"Well, I checked the bearings on the drive shaft in shaft alley, of course."

"And that's when you found Mr. Driscoll?"

Orville frowned, shook his head vigorously, and puffed away at the cigarette, not really inhaling—kid smoked like goddamn Bette Davis, Sarge thought.

Orv was saying, "Everything looked swell at first. I just checked the bearings, then got right back to the engine room— got to keep an eye on the lube oil strainer, y'know. So, anyway,

I didn't find Mr. Driscoll until my *second* round through shaft alley."

Sarge nodded. "Did you see Mr. Driscoll come into the engine room, then go into shaft alley?"

"No, but he might have. See, I was busy. Coulda missed him. Maybe Mr. Blake or Mr. Smith saw him."

"And you didn't see anybody else go in there?"

"Not a soul."

"Didn't hear anything?"

"You out of your mind, Sarge? *You* been in that engine room. It's louder than Basin Street at Mardi Gras."

"Yeah, it is loud. By the way, Orv, you own a knife?"

"No! Check my bag, check my bunk, I don't carry such things. I am a gentle artistical type, Sarge, as you damn well knows."

Sarge patted Orville on the shoulder. "Okay, son. You done fine. That's all for now."

Orville blinked and then blinked some more. "You done with me?"

"Might be some more questions later. Unless there's anything you think might be helpful to us, Orv, that you mighta left out by accident?"

"No! Nothing."

"Maybe you want us to take a couple minutes, then, so's you can tell Mr. Maxwell here about that *other* trouble. About the fella that has been—"

"No! You was told in confidence, Sarge, and anyways that don't have nothing to do with this here."

"Okay. One other thing…"

"What?"

"Put the cigarette out, Orville. And police the butt."

Orville did as he was told, then turned toward the engine room hatch.

"Send Blake out, would you?" Sarge asked.

"Okay," Monroe said and disappeared through the hatchway.

Perhaps a minute later, Albert Blake came through the hatchway and closed it behind him.

Blake was almost as short as Orville, but stockier, more muscular. His ready smile softening a shovel-shaped face with heavy dark eyebrows and regular five o'clock shadow, Blake had a reputation for getting along with the colored boys. Seemed he'd seen enough hard times during the Depression that duty on the *Liberty Hill,* largely Negro crew or not, felt like a step up.

Maxwell led off. "This is Seaman Washington."

"Radarman, right?" Surprisingly, Blake extended a hand and they shook.

"Sarge has a police background," Maxwell said, matter of fact. "So he's helping me look into Mr. Driscoll's murder."

"Makes sense," Blake said, and leaned back against the passageway hall. "What do you fellas need from me?"

Sarge asked, "Did you see Mr. Driscoll come into the engine room tonight?"

"You know, I didn't. Sorry."

"Could he have come in without you noticing?"

"He could've. But, honestly, I doubt he did. I don't miss a lot."

"Is it possible?"

"Yeah ... doubtful, though."

"What about Monroe?"

"What about him?"

"You see him go into shaft alley?"

"I saw him—twice." Blake frowned in thought. "Well, to be more accurate ... once. Little queer was in there already when our shift started, then came out. Then he went back later, and that's when he run out hollering about finding Mr. Driscoll's body. He was pretty worked up, but who can blame him?"

Sarge nodded. Then: "Notice anything unusual about how Orville did his job tonight?"

"You mean did he act more nervous than normal? He's kind of a jumpy little feller to begin with."

"Yeah, but was he more worked up than usual?"

"Not till he came running out screaming like a schoolgirl that somebody killed Mr. Driscoll."

"Other than that, anything unusual you notice tonight?"

"No."

"And you didn't see Mr. Driscoll come through the engine room?"

"I did not." Blake got a rag out of his back pocket and worried it between his fingers. "Closest thing to unusual, I guess, was Orville being on shift."

"Why's that unusual?"

"It's not. It's just that Orville, he always works slow in shaft alley, but then he's slow when he *ain't* in shaft alley, too."

"Lazy, you mean?"

"No, I'm not saying that. Washington, I don't think all coloreds are lazy or stupid, but some *are*—like some white men are. And Orville is small and slow. That's just the way it is. Now, Wallace and Big Brown both get done in there way faster than Orville does. Truth is, they're faster than him in every part of the job. As for Mr. Driscoll, he must have come down the escape tunnel, because he never came through the engine room."

John Smith, the boiler attendant from Missouri, had green eyes, wavy red hair starting to recede and a wide, flat nose. Maxwell told Smith that Sarge would be asking the questions and he accepted that.

The boiler attendant echoed pretty much everything Blake had said. "Mr. Driscoll did not come through the engine room. Neither did anyone else, for that matter. Monroe's slow, but I think it's on account of his nerves. You may not have noticed, but he has got a permanent bad case of the heebie jeebies."

"Thanks," Sarge said.

As Smith went back into the engine room, Rosetti came out with a Brownie camera in hand.

Rosetti announced he'd finished the photos, then said, "I've got three men putting Dick in a sheet and sewing it closed. They should be bringing him out any time now."

"Maybe we should clear a path," Maxwell said.

But it was too late.

The hatch swung open and three Negro sailors passed through, carrying the white sheet that shrouded Driscoll's body. Sarge and the two white officers plastered themselves to the wall so the impromptu funeral procession could squeeze by.

A *white man in a sheet,* Sarge thought, *never bodes well for Negroes.*

Even though this one was dead.

No, *especially* because this one was dead. ...

ELEVEN

AUGUST 31, 1944

Pete Maxwell couldn't remember the last time he'd eaten or slept, but he was committed to this inquiry and would be Sarge Washington's Siamese Twin until Dick Driscoll's killer was locked in the brig. But some aspects of the inquiry were harder than others....

Like right now, Pete standing poised outside Captain Egan's cabin, ready to knock at his door. Fist frozen in midair, he turned toward the patiently waiting Sarge Washington and asked, "You're *really* going to insist I do this?"

Even to Pete it sounded pitiful.

The scarred sailor nodded solemnly. "No free rides in a murder case, Mr. Maxwell. You asked for a professional job, well, this is how it goes."

Pete had already submitted to interrogation by the Chicago cop, right after the questioning of second-shift oiler, Lenny Wallace. Next up would be the day-shift oiler, Big Brown, then the other two engine-room sailors, Griffin and Whitford; but first, as Sarge said, "We got to get you ruled out, Mr. Maxwell."

This apparently involved going over the business about the knife again and again....

"After you and Mullins mixed it on the pier," Pete had told Washington, "I confiscated that knife—that is, picked it up, put it in my pocket until we were back onboard that night. After supper, I got Mr. Driscoll to open the ship's safe in the captain's office; and I placed the knife inside, on the right-hand side of the second shelf."

"You don't know the combination?" Sarge had asked.

"No. Of course, I can't prove I don't."

"Yeah, and I can't prove you do. That one's a wash."

That was when Sarge had said they'd settle it by going to see the captain and find out if that knife was still where Pete said he'd left it.

And so, finally, Pete knocked on the captain's cabin door.

"*What?*" came the familiar gruff voice.

"Maxwell, sir. I need—"

But the door sprang open before Pete could finish.

"You've found the killer!" Egan said, grinning—the grin combined with those wild-and-wooly eyebrows to make the captain's happy face as bad as any of his darker ones.

Egan's uniform had a slept-in look—chances were he'd caught a nap in the hours since they'd spoken over Dick's body in shaft alley, when the captain had pledged to retreat to his cabin till further notice.

"No, sir. Working on that right now. May we come in?"

Scowling now, Egan stepped aside and gestured for Pete to enter, which he did, Washington trailing behind him.

Once inside the cabin, Washington came to attention and saluted.

Egan returned the salute. "At ease, sailor. Mr. Maxwell, what's this?"

"Seaman Washington," Pete said.

"I know who he is—I commended him not long ago for his leadership on the pier. But what's he *doing* here?"

Pete felt suddenly awkward that Sarge was being spoken of as if the man were a potted plant, unable to explain himself.

"Sir, I've recruited the seaman to help out in our inquiry."

"Really," Egan said, and the wild eyebrows rose. "And why would that be?"

Pete told Sarge to fill the captain in, and Washington did so, crisply: "Before I joined the Navy, sir, I was a detective with the Chicago Police Department. Handled a good number of homicides."

"That so," Egan said, studying the sailor with no apparent skepticism.

"It is, sir," Washington said.

Nobody said anything for a while, and Pete wondered how much trouble he was in. He'd known it was a risk to bring Sarge into the investigation, and had hoped to fly under the bigoted captain's radar. But Washington himself had insisted they come, because of that goddamn knife in that goddamn safe....

Egan grunted something that was damned near a laugh. "You know, Mr. Maxwell, I've underestimated you. I gave you carte blanche on this inquiry, and you have outdone yourself."

Not convinced this wasn't sarcasm, Pete nonetheless said, "Thank you, sir."

"Bringing on board a man with a professional background, that's an excellent decision. The kind of hard decision a leader needs to make, as we've discussed, so often."

"Yes, sir. Thank you, sir."

"And using a Negro to question Negroes is politic in the best sense of the word. Congratulations."

"Thank you, sir."

"But woe betide both your asses if you don't produce." Now he looked sharply at Washington. "If you're here for my permission to proceed, you have it. Carry on, men."

"We're here for more than your blessing, sir," Pete said, "though I'm gratified to get it."

Egan frowned. "Oh?"

Washington said, "Sir, we're here to check on Mr. Maxwell's story. He's a suspect like the rest of us."

Egan laughed again, a more obvious one this time. "Well, I'll be damned...." Then his smile turned cold as he turned his shaggy gaze on Pete. "Mr. Maxwell, if you're expecting an alibi out of me, well … Mr. Washington, the XO was not here with me during the time that murder must have occurred."

"I know that, sir," Washington said patiently. "May we have a look in the ship's safe?"

"The safe?" Egan frowned in confusion. "Mr. Maxwell's alibi is in the ship safe?"

Washington risked a small smile. "In a way it is, sir."

"Well, then," Egan said, gesturing grandly, "by all means, let's have a look. …"

The captain led the way through the door that joined the captain's cabin with his L-shaped office. Egan ushered them in and opened a door on the right, revealing the ship's boxy safe, about the size of a table-top radio, resting on top of a three-drawer oak file.

Egan leaned down and spun the dial and turned the crank and swung open the squeaky door. "You tweaked my interest," Egan admitted. "What could be in here that would alibi Mr. Maxwell?"

Washington came forward, Pete right behind: they spotted it at the same time, resting on the right-hand side of the second shelf—Mullins's switchblade.

Egan frowned. "Where the hell did *that* come from?"

Pete withdrew the knife and handed it to Washington, who began to examine the weapon. In the meantime, Pete informed the captain of the truncated scuffle on the dock, the final day of ammo loading, omitting the names of the participants.

"There was a fight involving a knife," Egan said coldly, "and no one went to the brig over it?"

"Sir, the morale of the men was my chief concern—we had another half-day of ammunition loading ahead of us."

"And you did not tell me about it?"

"No, sir. I felt if at some point the incident became known, I should be the one to take the brunt of the blame."

Egan thought about that. Pete hoped this line of bull would pass muster with the captain, because protecting Egan had been the last thing on Pete's mind, really. But it sounded good.

"You take risks, Lieutenant Maxwell."

"Yes, sir."

"But you stand behind them. I respect that."

A *snick* signaled Washington opening the knife. He examined the blade. "No dried blood," he said. "But we'll hold on to it…"

Washington folded the knife shut, and placed it back on its shelf.

"… 'cause the Navy lab boys may find something, when the time comes."

Egan, vaguely amused, asked, "Does this mean Mr. Maxwell is innocent?"

"Might not be enough for a court," Washington said. "But I'm comfortable ruling him out."

"Good. Now, how do we know *you* didn't do the crime, Seaman Washington?" Egan's tone was genial, almost friendly. "As a leader among the crew, you might have had the occasional run-in with a hard-ass exec like Richard Driscoll. Not difficult to imagine."

"Fair point, sir," Washington said, not rising to the bait. "My best guess is, Mr. Driscoll got killed around midnight, between 23:45 and 0:15. Right then, I was busy and in the presence of witnesses."

"Be more specific," Egan said.

"Sir, I was playing craps in the fo'c'sle with half a dozen other crewmen."

Amusement played on the captain's thin lips. "Of course you know gambling is illegal on a line ship of the United States Navy."

"I do, sir, it surely is illegal. But I'd rather face court-martial for gambling, sir, than a murder I had no part of."

The captain and the sailor stared at each other, eyes locked in a silent, motionless dance—like a snake and a mongoose, only Pete had no idea which was which.

"I could," Egan said mildly, "instruct Mr. Maxwell to lock you in the brig for running a game of chance aboard my ship."

"That's a fact," Washington said, his tone as easygoing as the captain's. "But, first, you might consider a couple things."

"Which are?"

"One, I never said I ran the craps game. I just said I was playing. To stay out the brig, I just got to say I was only watching, which ain't illegal...but I didn't. I give you the straight dope, Captain."

"And the second thing?"

"That's the main one," Washington said, and risked a white smile. "Lock me in the brig and you'll never catch Mr. Driscoll's killer."

Egan smiled back. "Pretty sure of yourself, sailor."

With a little shrug, Washington said, "Mr. Maxwell knows my background and he's satisfied. Can I ask you something, sir? Meaning no offense?"

"Go ahead."

"Do you trust your officers? Do you back their judgment?"

Egan drew in breath through his nostrils; the eyebrows were quivering so much, Pete thought they might take flight. Finally, Egan said, "I do. And you are correct in assuming that I stand behind Lieutenant Maxwell's decision to involve you in this inquiry."

Washington smiled again, no teeth this time. "Thank you, sir. Now, if you don't mind, we'll get back to work."

"Please do, men. Dismissed."

Neither seaman nor lieutenant moved as Egan closed and locked the safe. When the captain turned to go back into his cabin, Washington was on his heels, Pete trailing.

Turning to them, Egan said, "I said, dismissed."

Pete said, "Sir, you dismissed us to return to our job. The inquiry into Lieutenant Driscoll's murder."

"Yes. Of course."

Washington said, "We need to interrogate the next crew member on our list, sir."

"And who would that be?"

Pete grinned feebly and said, "We thought, while we were here, sir …"

Washington said, "*You,* sir. Need to rule you out as a suspect, sir."

"Are you out of your mind?" Egan demanded.

"There are times, sir," Washington said, "when I would welcome a Section 8. But right now, I need to ask you some questions. You see, you worked close with Lieutenant Driscoll—he was your XO. You two mighta had problems that was never heard about."

Egan's mouth was open and so were his eyes; he seemed to be trying to decide whether to be outraged or bust out laughing.

"Sir," Washington said, "where were you between 23:30 and 00:30 last night?"

Egan swallowed thickly. Then he said, "You're well within your rights to ask. I was here in this cabin, in bed, asleep."

Pete asked, "No one saw you, sir?"

"Mr. Maxwell, I'm not in the habit of inviting the crew of this ship in to tuck me in, read me a bedtime story, and stop in periodically to see how well I'm goddamn sleeping."

"Yes, sir. Not a good question, sir."

Egan's expression turned shrewd. "A guilty man would have a better alibi—isn't that right, Mr. Washington? In your experience?"

Washington said, "A guilty party would have a better alibi ready than that, sir, if he thought he was going to need one."

"Exactly."

"'Course, that assumes the murder was planned. Spur of the moment is something else."

Egan scowled at the Negro detective. Pete cringed, wondering if Egan would throw his two investigators into the brig and start over.

Washington asked, "When did you get the call about Mr. Driscoll?"

"Right around 00:30," Egan said, settling down, perhaps sensing that Washington was helping him build an alibi.

"Before that, who saw you or talked to you last?"

"One of the Negro corpsmen," Egan said. "He brought me a bicarbonate around 21:00. I had an upset stomach. I took the bicarbonate and worked on the ship's log until 22:00, then I went to sleep."

"Which corpsman?"

Egan shrugged, his voice matter-of-fact as he said, "You boys all look alike to me." Then, as an afterthought, he added, "No offense meant, sailor."

"None taken," Washington said, but Pete detected a faint cold edge in his voice. "Does it for now, sir."

"Good," Egan said with a nod. "You fellows find the killer and find him fast. Ship like this has tensions enough without a goddamn maniac aboard. Sooner he's locked up, sooner we'll all be safe."

In tandem, Pete and Washington said, "Yes, sir."

Out in the passageway, Pete said, "Sorry about the 'all look alike' remark. Guys his age, well, they grew up in another time. Still...I really don't know how you can put up with that kind of horseshit."

They were going down the stairwell from the bridge deck to the boat deck. At the bottom, Washington turned, his eyes cool in the hard scarred mask of his face.

"Pete, certain kind of white man ain't happy just hating us—has to all the time try and prove he's better than us. Hell, I been dealing with the captain's kind since I could crawl."

"But how do you take it?"

Washington shrugged. "Had my whole life to get used to it, and I know the Captain Egans of this world are flat-out wrong about us being some damn inferior race. And when I catch Lieutenant Driscoll's killer? Egan'll know he's wrong, too."

Pete nodded.

"And so will you," Washington said quietly.

"Hell, I already *know* he's wrong."

Nodding, Washington said, "Is that why you didn't say anything in there? You waited till we was outside the captain's office, 'fore you called him on that bigoted jibe of his."

"Well, he is the captain. There are a lot of things I don't correct captains on."

"True enough. But next time you hear shit like that, and it's not coming from the captain or your boss or somebody high up like that... but just some buddy of yours, spouting off about stupid niggers? Do us both a favor—*call* him on it."

"Okay," Pete said, feeling vaguely hurt. "What next? We have more interviews..."

Washington yawned. "Know what? We ain't neither of us slept in God knows how long—we get bone tired, we'll screw up, and we can't afford screwing up. So let's take a few hours and get some sleep."

"Good idea," Pete said.

"Meet you at the officers' mess in four," Washington said, then disappeared around the corner to head down a flight of stairs to the main deck.

Pete went to his cabin with a lot more to think about than he'd had for some time. On his bunk, he got Kay's picture out—the one of her in a white bathing suit that he wouldn't show anyone—and focused not on her curves but her lovely face.

So *is Sarge right? Am I a bigot like Egan?*

Darling, no—you're not perfect, but you do your best. You've always treated everyone with respect you came in contact with.

Maybe so, but the things I've done for the crew—the reading lessons, the food I fought to get for them, just treating them fair and square—was it out of fear?

Maybe a little—you're a smalltown boy, Pete, don't run from that—it may be your best quality. Men with black faces are new to you, you're bound to be a little afraid.

Or have I been decent to them just so I could feel better about myself? Am I just some patronizing jerk?

If so, you're my patronizing jerk, and I'm proud of you. …

He tucked her photo away in his wallet, and lay on his back, elbows winged out, body exhausted but his mind buzzing. A sudden, awful wave of guilt washed over him.

Dick was dead.

In all the talk of alibis and bigotry, of evidence and race riots, Richard Driscoll was gone forever, his remains sewn in a white-sheet sack, his handsome looks no good to him or anybody, his breeding, his droll wit, useless. The Fantail Four were no more, and the trio remaining—Pete and Vince and Ben—hadn't even had time to discuss it, to mourn, to raise a glass of anything to his memory.

"Sorry, Dick," he said, and he was weeping when he finally fell asleep.

The officers' mess became their de facto interrogation room. Pete sat in a leather booth with the witness in a bolted-down chair opposite. Washington preferred to stand. To hover.

"I like the high ground," he'd told Pete.

Four hours of shuteye didn't sound like much, but Pete had slept deep and now felt refreshed and alive—refocused, ready to go. Washington seemed equally fresh and on top of his game.

The first man they interviewed was Big Brown, who had to duck to make it through the door. The day-shift oiler ran a hand over his bald head, as if checking for new growth, and took in the room with sweeping eyes—except for the green leather banquettes along two walls, the officers' mess mirrored the crew's one deck down.

"Take a seat," Washington said.

Big Brown managed to wedge himself in across from Pete, a great big grown-up sitting in a little child's chair.

Washington stood alongside the table, putting himself between both men. "Know what this is about?"

Big Brown nodded. "Mr. Driscoll."

"How'd you feel about him?"

Big Brown shrugged.

"What kind of answer is that?" Washington mimicked the big oiler's shrugging gesture. "Don't play your tough boy games with me, Brown. What did you *think* of the man? Like him? Hate him? What?"

"Never gave it much thought."

"How much thought *did* you give it?"

"Mr. Driscoll was an officer," the oiler said, "I wasn't." This, for Big Brown, seemed to sum it up.

"Ever see him down in shaft alley?"

"Can't say I did."

"How about the engine room?"

"Once or twice, maybe."

Pete said, "You don't mince words, do you?"

The big man said nothing.

Washington leaned in and glowered at Big Brown. "Maybe he's just shy, Lieutenant Maxwell. Or maybe he's a big lummox with nothing to say."

Ignoring the goading, Big Brown sat placidly, his eyes meeting Washington's but showing no apparent anger, no resentment.

Washington surprised Pete by flinching first. "Back in Chicago, we feed boys like you the goldfish."

Pete had no idea what Washington was talking about.

Big Brown said, "Rubber's in short supply."

"Maybe so, but I bet I can find something around here to slap some sense in your black skull."

"You can try. Many have." Now Big Brown gazed directly at Washington, brown eyes burning. "However, I believe that would be a mistake on your part."

"So," Washington said, pleased. "At last. The real Brown comes out to play."

Stunned, Pete sat forward and said to their subject, "I'll be damned—an educated man."

"I never said I wasn't," Big Brown said. His expression was peaceful, even angelic.

"Then why," Pete blurted, "do you persist in this monosyllabic bullshit!"

Big Brown sat forward as best he could in the cramped seating conditions. "Mr. Maxwell, I do appreciate, even admire what you're doing, helping these poor fellows learn to read. But I'm not one of their ignorant breed. I have a degree from the University of Cincinnati—football scholarship, but also an A-minus average."

"I'll be damned," Pete said. He glanced over at Washington, standing there quietly amused. "I heard you were a bouncer at the Bucket of Blood in Cleveland."

"I was," Big Brown said.

"But … with your brains, you could do anything."

"I will, but being a bouncer at the Bucket of Blood was lucrative, and filled in nicely where my scholarship came up short."

"I'll buy that," Pete said. "But why stay so quiet on ship? And why keep your education a secret?"

"Lieutenant, what does that have to do with your murder inquiry?"

"Maybe nothing. But please answer."

Big Brown heaved a sigh, more bored than irritated. "When my education got me no greater status in the white man's Navy than lowly seaman, I assumed the role I'd been assigned. Simple as that."

"Is it?"

"Ask Seaman Washington here—it's a role Negroes often play, built on the assumptions of white people. A black man is stupid, slow. A *big* man is stupid, slow. And a big black man? That's the idiot jackpot—and people say and do things around the likes of us that they would normally hide."

Eyes narrowing, Washington said, "So what have you seen or heard lately?"

"Might be I heard those two white boys, Griffin and Whitford, calling Mr. Driscoll a nigger lover."

"Dick *Driscoll?*" Pete shook his head. "No, that can't be right."

Washington said to Pete, "He was no bigot like our captain. Was he?"

"No, he wasn't," Pete insisted. "But he *was* a terrible snob. I mean, I liked him, he was a good guy, could be fun to be around. But deep down, I believe he thought all of us on this ship—hell, in this *country*—were beneath him."

"Not a matter of color, then," Big Brown said. "More of class distinction."

"Bingo," Pete said.

Washington, looking thoughtful, said, "Maybe it's time we talk to Griffin and Whitford."

Pete nodded.

"Then I can assume," Big Brown said, starting to get up, or trying to, "you're finished with me?"

"No," Pete said. "Stay seated, please. Where were you between 23:00 and 00:30 last night?"

The big man shrugged. "Sleeping. I go to work at 0700. I got up at six, went to the mess for breakfast, and that's where I was when I heard about Mr. Driscoll. It's likely others saw me asleep in my bunk. I was there all night."

Washington said, "We'll check it out."

Big Brown frowned—an unsettling sight. The oiler said, "Are you calling me a liar, Sarge?"

"I ain't even callin' you a suspect, son," Washington said. "But we're still going to check out your story—no insult, just fact. Anyway, I got one more question."

"Do you?"

Washington leaned in. "If you hear so much, Mr. Brown, maybe you've heard something about Orville Monroe."

"Such as what?"

"Such as something bad enough we might want to know about it."

"Pertaining to this inquiry?"

"Orville found the body. He's in this."

Big Brown sucked in a bushel of air, let it out through his nostrils. Pete would have sworn he felt his hair ruffle. Finally, Big Brown said, "Not directly."

"Indirectly, then?" Pete asked.

"I don't know. Perhaps."

"Perhaps?" Washington asked. "What the hell is 'perhaps' supposed to mean in the goddamn scheme of things?"

Big Brown did his best to shift in the cramped chair. "Some of the boys were talking about finding Orv in the head... crying. They asked him what was wrong, but he wouldn't talk about it. Scuttlebutt is, the boy's losin' his grip. Griffin and Whitford weren't the only ones giving Orville a bad time. He was getting plenty of grief from our guys, too. World's not easy for homosexuals, you know. Negro homosexual in the service? Recipe for tragedy."

"Any talk of Orv getting forced to do things?"

"Such as?"

"Sex acts."

"No. No, nothing like that."

"What, then?"

"Like I said, he gets picked on. I stick up for him sometimes, but I can't be everywhere. I'm not Superman."

Even if he did have a secret identity.

Washington sighed. "Well, thanks, Big Brown—we'll let you know if there's anything else."

"If I think of something I'll tell you," he said. "Can't be having our officers butchered onboard—even white ones."

The big man extricated himself from the little chair, and trundled out.

The two white sailors were brought in separately. Washington figured Whitford was weaker than Griffin, and if either non-com had something to hide, the two investigators would have a better chance of prying it out of the former than the latter.

On the other hand, if Whitford hadn't talked, Griffin wouldn't know it, and might be buffaloed into thinking his pal had "ratted him out." Washington's thinking seemed convoluted to Pete, but he went along, having no better suggestion.

Whitford entered the mess.

Lanky, with a dirt-brown butch haircut and blue-gray eyes, he was bow-legged and rolled a toothpick around his mouth. Taking the same seat Big Brown had, Whitford faced Pete and tried his best to pretend that Washington wasn't even there.

He had a West Texas drawl, which gave a lilting countrified music to his speech. "And what can I do you for, Mr. Maxwell?"

Pete gave him a slow, easy smile. "You can answer a few questions."

The toothpick traveled. "Glad to."

"Seaman Washington will be asking them."

Whitford stared blankly for several seconds, then blinked a few times, the toothpick hanging limply from his lower lip. Finally he said, "Now that's going to be a problem."

Pete raised an eyebrow. "If you don't answer him, it will be. Because I'm giving you a direct order to do so. Understood?"

Whitford shrugged and sneered, just a little, as if to himself.

Pete leaned across. "Want to keep those stripes, or would you rather go from petty officer back to seaman? Word from me, your gear gets moved in with the rest of the crew members. How does that sound?"

The implication was clear: answer Washington's questions or go in with the Negroes.

Captain Egan had given the petty officers two cabins whose doors had locks. In the fo'c'sle, Whitford would be at the mercy of men who'd heard the white petty officer's openly racist remarks.

"Like I said," Whitford said, with the sickest smile Pete had ever witnessed, "glad to help, any way I can."

His scarred face an unreadable mask, Washington gazed down at their subject. "You worked till midnight last night?"

Whitford did not look at Washington, staring straight ahead, just past Pete's ear. But the man spoke: "Yeah. Midnight."

Washington continued: "Did you see Mr. Driscoll go into shaft alley?"

He worked the toothpick. "Nope."

"Anybody else?"

"Just that little nigger cocksucker, Monroe …"

Washington backhanded him.

Whitford got halfway out of his chair, his eyes going to Pete, who sat with arms folded, immobile. The Texan's toothpick was missing in action.

"You *saw* that, sir!" Whitford said, voice harsh as broken glass. "This fucking nigger—"

Pete's slap cut off whatever the rest of that was going to be. He'd gotten to his feet in a fraction of an instant and caught Whitford on the other cheek with an open hand, an enforced version of the Christian turn-the-other-cheek rule.

"You keep your language within bounds, Whitford," Pete said crisply, seated again. "Understood?"

Wide-eyed, still half out of his chair, Whitford said, "Yes, sir."

Whitford might be a white man but his face was largely scarlet.

"You may think you're in the Navy," Pete said, "but you're not. You're behind closed doors in a murder investigation, dealing with the two sorry bastards given the job. Washington used to be a Chicago cop, by the way, and they have distinctive methods of interrogation. Now, sit your ass down and try again."

Clearly frightened, Whitford did as he was told; he touched the cheek Washington had slapped. "What did you ask me? I ... I forget."

Washington said, "You saw Orville Monroe ..."

"Yeah, Monroe went into shaft alley. Just before midnight."

"When did he come out?"

"Honest, fellas, I don't know—my shift was over."

Washington paced a little patch near the table. "We hear you and your friend Griffin called Mr. Driscoll a 'nigger lover.' Is that right?"

Nervous, not wanting to get slapped again, Whitford said, "That's a load of horseshit. We *never*—"

"We heard this from Big Brown, by the way." Washington shrugged, smiled. "I'd feel obligated to let him know you called him a liar."

"I never said it! I swear to you, I never said it."

"How about your friend Griffin?"

"He ... he mighta used that particular turn of phrase a time or two."

"What did he mean by that? Nigger lover?"

Whitford shrugged. "Nothin'. Just that Driscoll seemed to take a shine to some of them shines."

Realizing what he'd said, Whitford winced; but nothing happened.

"Any *particular* shine?" Washington asked.

"I saw him talking to the little fag...to Orville."

"Guy talking to a fag," Washington said, "guy talking to a *nigger* fag...ain't that a lynchin' offense back home where you come from? And when no rope's handy, there's always a knife or a razor...."

Whitford's eyes went wild. "Whoa, whoa, hold on a minute, just hold on—we didn't kill *nobody*!"

The petty officer looked petrified now. Taking a couple slaps for slips of the lip was one thing, getting court-martialed for murder another.

"You fellas ask Griffin. Him and me were on deck, smoking after our shift; then we went and talked to Mr. Rosetti about the engine problem. Griff thinks he might know a way to fix it. Anyway, you can ask Mr. Rosetti. He'll vouch for us."

Washington hammered the shaken Whitford for another fifteen minutes, but the non-com's story stayed the same.

When they were alone, Pete said, "Did you have to slap that jackass?"

"Did you?"

"Had to back you up, didn't I? Jesus, man, he outranks you."

Washington shrugged. "He ain't an officer. Petty officer's just another enlisted man, with a better pay grade. Anyway, behind closed doors? Nobody outranks me."

Pete shook his head, but had to grin.

When Griffin was brought in, his story paralleled Whitford's. In an interview devoid of the melodramatics of the previous one, the other engine-room sailor took questioning from Washington without complaint and was smart enough, in the face of a murder inquiry, not to indulge in race-baiting.

When Griffin was gone, Washington got Pete and himself coffee, then flopped into the chair opposite. "Damnit! Sons of bitches're telling the truth."

"Easy enough to check with Rosetti." Pete sipped the hot black liquid. "So if Vince backs 'em up, have we lost our best suspects?"

"You mean our best *white* suspects, don't you?"

"No."

"Sorry." Washington was stirring sugar into his coffee, already loaded with cream. "You and Mr. Rosetti and Mr. Connor were in that quartet with the victim, right? Mr. Driscoll was your friend?"

"Yes he was. Meaning there's no reason to think Vince would lie for Griffin and Whitford—he's as anxious to nab Dick's killer as anybody."

Washington hit a fist on the tabletop; the coffee cups jumped. "We're chasing our damn tails. We interviewed everybody around the engine room, time of the murder ... and nobody says they saw Driscoll *or* his killer go into shaft alley."

"If all our witnesses are telling the truth," Pete said, "then the only way Dick and his killer could've got in shaft alley was by going down that escape tunnel. *Both* of them."

"Yeah," Washington said, and gestured with empty hands. "Only why in hell *would* they?"

Pete was trying to find a reasonable answer to that one when the battle-stations horn brayed and he plunked his coffee cup down, half-spilling what was left of it. He came out of the booth on the run, heading for his cabin to get his gear.

Right behind him, Washington dogged Pete's heels till they got to the staircase, which the seaman flew down while Pete rounded the bend.

Inside his cabin, Pete grabbed his helmet and life jacket—Connor's were already gone. Soon he was sprinting up to the bridge where Connor met him in the chart room.

"Lookout spotted a Jap Zero," Connor said tightly, eyes bright. "Circled once, seems headed back for us."

Pete stepped from the chart room and onto the bridge just in time to hear Egan say, "Battle stations ready?"

The radioman next to him said, "Aye, sir. All guns reporting manned and ready."

Everyone on the bridge had on their life jackets and light-blue helmets, the radioman's brain bucket oversized to allow for his headset. Frye was on radar with another Negro, Andrews, behind the wheel.

The radioman announced, "Lookout reports Zero off starboard bow, coming in low and fast."

Egan, voice surprisingly calm, said, "Fire when ready."

Moving through the bridge, Pete slipped out onto the starboard bridge wing. The .20mm guns coughed their bullets and the .50 cal on the bar ripped away as well, its report deeper than the twenties.

Then Pete saw the Zero right where it was supposed to be, high in the sky with sun glinting off a glass-covered cockpit. Machine guns erupted on each wing and spat yellow fire just as Pete realized he made one hell of a target out here in the open, and scrambled to try to correct that.

TWELVE

AUGUST 31, 1944

Bullets clanged into the ship's bulkheads and *whinged* off the hull as Pete Maxwell went diving through the hatch into the pilothouse, hot slugs hissing past him like pissed-off snakes.

He landed on his side, his uncinched helmet flying off, clattering across the bridge, his left calf stinging like hell; he jerked his knee to his chest as the phone talker bounced forward and slammed the hatch shut.

The metallic cacophony continued all around him as he checked out the small tear in his pants leg; then he ripped it wide to reveal a small laceration where a ricocheting bullet had skimmed across his leg, going in one side of his pants leg and out the other.

He glanced up to see Egan glowering down at him with an odd mingling of concern and irritation. "You all right, Mr. Maxwell?"

"Just a scratch, sir," he said, getting to his feet and testing the leg. Yes, the wound stung, but nothing more; wasn't even bleeding much.

Pete scuttled over to pick up his helmet, and slammed it back on, but the insistent chatter of machine-gun fire was coming strictly from his own ship now, doing its damnedest to bring down that fucking Zero.

Then the world went quiet, like the unsettling silence that follows a thunderstorm, and Pete peered through the front-bridge porthole, seeing nothing beyond the *Liberty Hill's* gun crews in their pods and the ship.

"He's circling around again," the phone talker announced.

Connor came into the pilothouse. "Where the hell'd he *come* from? Middle of damn nowhere."

Upper lip curled back, Egan said, "We'll discuss that *after* we get him off our ass."

"Be easier if we had more power," Connor muttered.

"Thank you for the pointless observation," Egan snapped. "Helmsman, commence a zig-zag course. Won't do much good, but it's something."

"Aye, sir," the helmsman said, and spun the wheel to starboard.

That this was an ammo ship would be unknown to the pilot, and anyway their explosive cargo was unlikely to be ignited even if a bullet beat long odds and penetrated their hull, its speed slowed into impotence. Still, it never felt good, sailing Dick Driscoll's USS *Powderkeg,* getting blasted at.

The phone talker, in a terrible matter-of-fact monotone, said, "He's coming for another pass, sir."

Without waiting for further orders, the ship's machine guns again fired away. Their rat-a-tat report might have reassured Pete if he hadn't also been able to hear the approaching plane's propeller. Through that porthole he could see the plane bearing down on them, directly along the line of the bow. The .50 caliber on the bow was firing as were the twenties on either side.

Seeing the flashes of the Zero's machine guns, Pete knew the pilot was targeting the bridge, and yelled, *"Duck!"* as he hurled himself to the deck.

Everybody except Connor, who dove into the chart room, responded wrong, glancing at Pete and not immediately taking his advice before four portholes across the front of the bridge had time to shatter under the Zero's firepower, bullets tearing through the safety glass and *whanging* off the gray metal around them.

From the deck, Pete watched aghast as the helmsman slapped at his chest, like swatting a fly, but this was no insect bite—a telltale red mist emerged around fingers as the helms-man crashed into the back wall of the pilothouse and sagged to the deck.

Near the helm, the radarman plunged from the path of bul-lets chewing up the wall behind where he'd stood. Off to one side enough to avoid the bullets, the phone talker had nonetheless taken a shard of glass in his cheek, embedded there like a jagged chunk of ice, and he dropped to the deck, screaming.

Throughout the fracas, Captain Egan stood fast, a statue, as an awful storm of glass and blood flew all around him, and yet he never so much as flinched. Pete was amazed—was this man incredibly brave, or a complete idiot?

The roar of the plane flying over signaled the stoppage, for now, of enemy bullets; what had seemed like ten minutes to Pete had been perhaps ten seconds. He got himself to his feet as Egan knelt next to the phone talker, taking the man's headset. Around them, the ship's machine guns continued to grunt their angry response into the sky.

Into the headset, Egan, his voice firm but calm, said, "Corpsman to the bridge, corpsman to the bridge." Then, turn-ing, he said, "Mr. Maxwell, take the helm."

Looking down at the dead helmsman, Pete fought against being sick and, for now, won. He dragged the body out and climbed into the narrow space between the wheel and the rear bulkhead of the pilothouse. He took the wooden wheel in both hands and felt the stickiness of the dead man's blood, still hang-ing in scarlet droplets on the spokes.

Every ship in the Navy had to have a corpsman, if not a ship's doctor. The *Liberty Hill Victory* had been put on line so fast, dur-ing such a shortage of doctors, that the closest thing they had were two Negroes who'd taken Navy advanced first aid.

They also had Rosetti, who was first to make it to the bridge; his police background had included some medical training. Anyway, he didn't need a degree from Johns Hopkins medical school to pronounce the helmsman dead. The radarman was frightened but otherwise fine, and the only other injury was the phone talker with the piece of glass in his cheek.

"It's deep," Rosetti said, not to his patient but to the captain. "I'll get him down to the sick bay and get a corpsman to get it out."

As Rosetti helped the injured man to his feet, Egan got on the headset again. "Phone talker to the bridge, any available phone talker to the bridge. Helmsman to the bridge, any available helmsman to the bridge."

Putting the injured man's arm around his shoulders, Rosetti led the in-shock sailor out through the chart room and down the stairs. Shortly after, Connor came in, from the chart room.

"Radio's shot to shit, sir. Took two hits."

"Thank you, Mr. Connor," Egan said. "Mr. Maxwell! The lookout is reporting Zero coming around again. Zig-zag course."

Again firepower erupted from the shipboard guns. Hot wind blew through the broken portholes, and Pete could see the plane bearing down on its inexorable death-and-taxes path. He waited for the next burst from the plane's machine guns before he spun the wheel to the left, taking them out of the line of fire, he hoped ... but at one-third power, it was more prayer than hope.

He braced himself for the next wave of bullets, but it didn't come—instead, the sputtering of the plane's engine told a new story, as did the whoop that went from the crew. Through the porthole in the starboard hatch, Pete caught a glimpse of the Zero as it staggered down that side of the ship, a trail of black smoke behind it.

Egan spoke into the headset again. "He's turning away? Good, good. Pass the word—remain at battle stations, but stand easy."

"We got him?" Connor asked.

"We did," Egan said, as if reporting that *Fibber McGee and Molly* would be on at eight tonight. "Bastard's not dead, but he's hurt and won't be back—trying to save his Jap ass." Then, into the headset, he said, "Do we know who scored the hit?" He listened. "Send him up here—I want to shake his hand."

Helmsman Jackson came onto the bridge and relieved Pete, who stepped over beside Connor.

Through the doorway into the chart room, Pete could see the radio, two bullet holes like black eyes staring back at him. Already the *Liberty Hill* was sailing on Egan's dead reckoning alone, thanks to the low clouds that'd dogged the ship since before the storm. They were off course, that much was certain; but how far was anybody's guess and, now, without the radio, calling for help was out.

Their best hope lay with the clouds clearing, giving them the chance to get a bearing by stars or sun.

From outside the pilothouse, cheers announced that the man who'd made the vital shot was getting an ovation on his way to the bridge. The starboard side hatch opened and the entire crew of the three-inch .50-caliber gun from the bow rolled in. Four were seamen with whom Pete had dealt only minimally; but one was Big Brown, another, country-kid Hazel Ricketts, and trailing in came delicate little Orville Monroe.

Dutifully, Egan shook each black hand as the gun crew crowded onto the bridge, lined up and snapped to attention.

"At ease," Egan said.

They relaxed, slightly.

"Which sailor made the shot?" Egan asked.

The perpetually nervous Monroe stepped forward, his eyes lowered as if the captain were the pope.

"I guess it was me, sir," he said, his voice barely a whisper.

Big Brown said, "It was Orville, sir. He gets the kewpie doll."

Egan stepped forward, and shook the little man's hand, vigorously, all the while Monroe's gaze remaining shyly on the floor.

What's it take to make this little guy happy, anyway? Pete wondered. The crew that'd made Orville's life miserable since

June was now cheering for him—the "little fairy" was a big hero! *Too little too late, maybe?*

"That was a hell of a shot, young man," Egan said.

"Thank you, sir."

"Damned near ripped the end of the wing right off," Ricketts put in, grinning. "That Jap wasn't flyin' nowhere near straight, when he lit out!"

The gun crew and the captain shared some nervous laughter.

"Well done," the captain said. "Well done all around."

An awkward few moments followed—if the gun crew was thinking Egan would promise them commendations or medals, Pete figured they were mistaken. They'd done a good job, but in this captain's eyes, these were still "coloreds." Orville Monroe alone seemed to know that, stealing an occasional glance at the dreaded captain—reflecting, as Sarge had explained to Pete, the usual trepidation this young Negro felt around the white officers.

"Anyway," Egan sighed, "good job, all of you. Let's stay alert in case our wayward Jap comes back with friends. Dismissed."

The gun crew filed out the starboard hatch with Monroe as eager to lead the way out as he'd been to bring up the rear coming in.

The cheering started again as soon as Orville and his crewmates stepped through the hatchway. Pete hoped the crew would remember that this little guy had saved the ship, and grant him belated acceptance, never falling back into their own prejudices. But he had his doubts.

Although the Zero was a memory, its trail of black smoke long since dissipated, the ship stayed at battle stations for another two hours, after which the captain settled for double lookouts and let the remainder of the crew get some rest.

Except for Pete.

Egan instructed his XO to resume the murder inquiry, at once, which Pete would have done, anyway. He was soon scouring the ship for his fellow investigator, but found no sign of

Washington—not in the fo'c'sle or on the boat deck, not even back on the bridge. Pete tried down on the main deck, moved aft on the port side, then forward up the starboard side.

Nobody seemed to have seen Sarge.

Finally, out of desperation, he checked the different rooms in the wheelhouse, winding up at sick bay.

A handsome Negro named Jasper Jensen sat at his corpsman's desk in a corner near the hatchway, working on a report under a small lamp. The sick bay lights were otherwise out, making it easier for the wounded to rest.

The deceased helmsman—whose corpse had been temporarily moved into the meat locker with Driscoll's—had been the only fatality; but there'd been other casualties.

The phone talker Rosetti brought down here for stitching up was doing fine, asleep on his cot. Next cot over lay a gunner's mate who'd caught a bullet in the leg, and on the cot beyond, much to Pete's dismay, rested Seaman Ulysses Grant Washington.

Sarge had a bandage across his forehead, Spirit of '76 style, stained scarlet at left, along his temple; his eyes were closed and, in the sick bay's dim light, Pete could barely make out the rise and fall of his friend's chest. At least it *was* rising and falling. ...

Jensen materialized at Pete's side.

"How bad?" Pete whispered.

"Not so bad," the corpsman said, also sotto voce. "Bullet skimmed off his head. Got himself another scar, and maybe a concussion, but I can't see as he'll have no permanent damage."

"Thank God."

"'Course," Jensen said good-naturedly, "I ain't no doctor. Leastwise my pay don't reflect it."

"We're all grateful for what you *do* know, Corpsman. Okay I talk to him?"

"You can sit there. If he wakes up, just keep it short, will ya?"

"Sure," Pete said.

The corpsman moved away and Pete pulled up a folding chair. Almost immediately the bandaged seaman's eyes flickered open, and he got a feeble smile going.

"Thought I hear your deathless baritone," Washington said, voice a little raspy.

"You sound lively enough. How do you feel?"

Washington winced. "No worse than if Big Brown tore off my head and took a shit down my throat."

"Makes sense. About how you look."

Washington grinned. "Here I was hoping Lena Horne might drop by and instead I get one of the Three Stooges."

"Fantail Four, you mean."

"No. Only three of you now. And don't look at me to fill in— I'm no tenor. Didn't happen to run into our killer during that little air raid?"

"No. But I think maybe that Jap drilled some sense in me. Because I came up with a few new questions."

"Every investigation needs questions. You think maybe *I* got the answers?"

"Maybe." Pete leaned in. "Everybody we talked to so far has an alibi, right?"

"More or less."

"And we've checked them all out?"

"Best we could."

"And they all seem to hold up?"

"Far as it goes. 'Course, we ain't talked to everybody yet."

"How many men have we not interviewed?"

"A bunch…but we *have* talked to them we know was anywhere near the engine room last night."

Pete lifted his eyebrows. "Still, could be somebody on the ship who's got nothing to do with the engine room—right?"

Washington's expression was either thoughtful or a sign of discomfort. "Yeah, sure, right.…Help me with this fuckin' pillow."

Pete did.

Sitting up better, Washington said, "I had prettier nurses."

"You're welcome," Pete said. He sat forward. "How many men knew about the escape tunnel, you suppose?"

Washington grunted a laugh. "I asked you the same damn thing down in shaft alley, and you didn't have no answer."

"Not sure I've got one now. But I do know *I* had no idea that damn passage existed. And *you* didn't know about it, either—right?"

Washington risked a shrug. "Didn't need to. If you didn't work down there, why would you?"

"Wouldn't you say that's true for 99 percent of the crew, too?"

"I'll give you that."

"Which means we should concentrate on those aboard who *did* know about that passage—the oilers, boiler men, engine room chiefs. What's that, seven guys?"

Washington's eyes were steady and a little cold. "Don't forget the officers, Lieutenant. The white officers?"

"The officers didn't necessarily know about the passage, but they had access to the information, if they had any reason to...." Pete stopped himself, considered for a long moment. "Maybe...maybe we've been looking at this wrong."

"What way?"

"Let's go back to Orville."

Washington gave up half a smile. "Kid was a hero today, I hear."

"Yeah. But he took his praise up on the bridge like a whipped puppy. He's still scared, and not just little-colored-fairy scared—I mean scared for his life."

"Scared that this big guy who's been using him like a plaything is gonna keep on doin' the same?"

"Not that. I'm wondering if there's a connection between Orville's 'problem' and Dick's death."

Washington frowned, tried to sit up even more. "What the hell could it be?"

"Well, we wondered where there could ever be enough privacy on a crowded ship like this for what Orville said was going on. Engaging in perverted acts like that, aboard a Navy ship, can—"

"Get a man killed?"

"Right. Or thrown out of the service, and the best you could hope for is every other guy on the crew knows about it and rags you every day and night."

"But the crew *has* been raggin' Orville."

Pete nodded. "They have, but if somebody actually *saw* him performing these acts, ragging would just be the start—there'd be beatings, for sure. God knows what they'd do to the likes of Orville, such a case."

Washington's expression was somber. "So these sex acts got to take place somewhere *really* fuckin' private."

Pete nodded. "Like shaft alley."

"Like shaft alley. And it was Orville's shift. ..."

"Right. Maybe Dick caught the guy, with Orville, and tried to bust it up, and got killed for his trouble."

Slowly Washington began to nod. "So we need to talk to Orville again."

"*I* need to. You need to feel better." Pete got to his feet. "You rest—I'll report back."

Washington was sitting up without the pillow's aid now. "Mr. Maxwell—that's a good theory you come up with, but keep in mind—it's just a theory. Seaman Monroe was in that tunnel and unaccounted for, too. Just because he didn't have any blood on his clothes or hands when he come out don't mean *he* couldn't have been the killer. So you keep that in mind when you come up against him, or maybe that Jap won't be Orville's only kill today."

Pete's eyes narrowed. "You think *Orville* could be the killer?"

"Little guys who get picked on make real good killers. And you need to ask yourself what Mr. Driscoll mighta been doin' in shaft alley with Orville."

"... What are you saying?"

Washington shrugged. "There is other kinds of big, powerful men than the likes of Big Brown and yours truly. Officers are big, powerful men, too."

"Dick Driscoll! Don't talk crazy—"

"Don't get yourself all riled, Lieutenant. A little colored feller like Orville would do most anything a big white officer like your Mr. Driscoll tell him to."

"Dick was no queer!"

"Hey. Easy now. No offense meant. But you ever see him with a woman?"

"Well, sure ..." But actually Pete wasn't at all sure.

"And, remember, men at sea with no women is like men in prison with no women. Orville's got a pretty mouth and he's got his predilections. Your late friend might have been jailhouse queer."

Pete wanted to be angry. Wanted to be indignant. But he knew Washington had a point.

"Might have been some other way," Washington allowed. "Mr. Driscoll might come along and seen Orville with some other white officer—Mr. Rosetti, maybe. Mr. Connor."

"Are you trying to piss me off?"

"I'm trying to make you think like a detective, because the real detective here is on a goddamn cot with his head half shot to shit. Can you carry the weight, Mr. Maxwell?"

Pete swallowed. "I can carry the weight, Sarge."

"Good. Do it, then."

And, for the second time today, Pete scoured the ship. The job was harder now, in the fading light, though day turning to night under the low ceiling of dense, dark clouds made only a shade of difference.

Again, Pete started in the fo'c'sle, wandering up and down the rows of bunks until he got to Big Brown and Orville Monroe's. Brown was on the bottom, but Monroe's upper was empty.

"Any idea where Orville is?"

Big Brown was stretched out, obliterating his bunk, hands behind his head, arms winged out with massive muscles like the work of a master sculptor. Eyes closed, face serene, he just shook his head, not even changing expression.

"It's important. Any idea where he might be?"

Finally, Big Brown's eyes came open. "He's a hero now. Nobody's bothering him."

"Where is he?"

"I don't know. You can order me to tell you, and I still won't know."

He closed his eyes again.

Over the next few hours, Pete did a complete lap of the main deck from the fo'c'sle back along the port side and all the way to the stern, then came back starboard. Along the way he encountered three clusters of crew, but nobody knew where Monroe was, or at least wouldn't say.

He checked the galley, the mess, the various cabins on that deck, then made his way up to the boat deck and cut through the officers' mess, past the cabin he shared with Connor, and around the corner and then, as he neared the door to Rosetti's cabin, he noticed something glimmering darkly on the deck of the dimly lit passageway.

Something that was almost certainly blood.

Apprehension spiked through him as he backtracked to his own cabin, which he found empty—Connor not around, probably on the bridge pulling another watch. Pete opened his locker and got out his .45-caliber automatic pistol.

All the officers had service-issue .45s, and they had practiced with the heavy weapons every two weeks back in San Diego—every one of the Fantail Four a crack shot. He pulled the clip out of a spare boot and slapped it into the pistol, then racked a round into the chamber.

He kept the pistol's safety on and tucked the gun behind his back in his waistband. He checked himself in the mirror, toweled the sweat from his face, then left the cabin and returned to the passageway just outside Rosetti's cabin.

He looked down at the drops, convinced that they were indeed blood.

He knocked on the door and got no answer. He waited, knocked again, and again heard nothing. He opened the door and stepped in, finding the light on, but the cover down over the porthole.

Behind the door, a familiar voice said, "What the hell?"

Pete moved into the room and whirled, his hand going behind his back and settling on the butt on the .45, ready to whip it around if necessary. Rosetti stood at the fold-down desk behind the door, a scarlet-stained towel around his left hand.

"Jesus, Pete!" The ex-cop seemed half-amused, half-irritated. "Don't they teach you to knock in Iowa?"

"I saw blood on the deck—thought there might be a problem."

"Sarge's turned you into a regular Junior G-man," Rosetti said, pulling the towel away from his hand, revealing a long laceration along his palm—not unlike the fatal wound across Dick Driscoll's neck.

"What happened, Vince?"

"Working on that goddamned engine. We were taking the lube oil strainer out to replace it with the one from the low-pressure side, when it slipped and ... I don't know ... somehow it got me, and I ended up with this fucking thing." He held the hand out as evidence.

"Why aren't you in sick bay?"

Rosetti gave him a chagrined grin. "Suppose I figured the corpsmen were too busy, and frankly I know as much about it as those boys. So I came up here to stitch it up myself. You seem on edge, pal. What's going on?"

"I'm looking for Orville Monroe. Seen him?"

"No. What do you need that little fairy for?"

"Answer some questions about Dick's murder. And by the way, that 'little fairy' saved all our asses today."

Rosetti made a face. "Yeah, I heard. You're right. Kid deserves better than a crack like that. You think Orville can help you find Dick's killer?"

"Maybe."

Rosetti shook his head. "Doesn't seem possible, does it? Dick gone. Butchered like that. Funny thing, I keep hearing us singing 'I'll Get By'... on deck, for the colored boys?"

"Last time we ever sang together."

"Damn. Not the way to go, not even in war." Rosetti daubed at the wound again.

"You okay? Maybe sick bay isn't a bad idea."

"I'll be fine. After pulling half a porthole out of that phone talker's face and stitching him up, this is small potatoes."

"You did the stitching yourself?"

"Yeah. Corpsman's hands were shaking. Poor phone talker'll curse me every day of his life, when he looks in the mirror to shave."

Pete frowned. "Maybe so, but you can't stitch that hand yourself. Let me get you a corpsman."

Rosetti, looking a little pale, considered that advice. "Maybe you better at that. I'll... I'll wait here."

Pete nodded and left the cabin. When he walked to the stairs, he was following the path of the blood drops; down would take him to sick bay and a corpsman.

But the blood trail stopped on the landing, nothing on the steps Rosetti would have used coming up from the engine room. Yet the stairs leading from the bridge deck *did* have blood droplets....

A sick feeling flooded through him as Pete followed the trail of droplets up the stairs, and then across the hall to the door of the cabin that had been Executive Officer Richard Driscoll's.

As if in a dream, with a sense he had done this a thousand times before and would do it a thousand times more, he turned the knob, swung open the door, and stared into the cabin....

...at utter blackness. The porthole in here had its cover down, as well.

He flipped the light switch, somehow already knowing what he would see—and gazed into the open, unseeing eyes of Orville Monroe, sprawled on the floor, on his back, the little man's mouth a slit not unlike the one in his throat, and again Pete was reminded of Driscoll's fatal wound.

Pete knelt to take a pulse but there was none; the body, though, remained warm. The blood pooling near the wound was again surprisingly minimal.

In his mind's eye, he saw it: *Orville came to Rosetti's cabin, the two men struggled and Orville met the same fate as Driscoll, the would-be savior who had come upon Rosetti forcing himself on Orville in shaft alley, Dick interceding on Orville's behalf and getting killed for the effort.*

Then Rosetti carries the body up the stairs and stows it in Driscoll's currently out-of-use cabin.

The captain had been right: they had a maniac on board, and insane as it seemed, that maniac was Vince Rosetti.

Who Pete had just left, one deck below!

Pistol in hand, Pete sprinted down the stairs. He swung around the corner, bolted down the short passageway, and burst into Rosetti's cabin without knocking.

The burly ex-cop was gone.

THIRTEEN

AUGUST 31, 1944

Pete Maxwell flew out of Vince's cabin and took the stairs to the main deck, then hurried down the port side passageway to sick bay. He had to tell Washington, *right now,* that he finally knew who the killer was. As he neared the door, he became aware of the pistol still in his hand—had he encountered anyone along the way, he'd have looked like a homicidal maniac himself, on the run.

Weapon at his side now, he entered sick bay and looked toward Sarge's cot, past a khaki-clad figure, then realized Ensign Vincent Rosetti was blocking his view.

Reflexively, the .45 came up and its snout seemed to level itself of its own free will at the chest of his once-trusted friend, the second tenor of the Fantail Four Minus One.

"Pete!" Rosetti blurted, shocked, alarmed. "What the hell?"

Rosetti stood at a stainless-steel table where the seated Negro corpsman, Jasper Jensen, was about half-finished stitching up the ensign's left palm. Both men froze under the aimed automatic, whose blocky, bulky no-nonsense design seemed at odds with the trembling hand wielding it.

"Vince…" Pete shook his head; he boiled with rage and yet sadness was intermingled, and he had to struggle not to fucking cry. "How the hell could you do it?"

"Pete," Rosetti said softly, patting the air with his good hand, "just lower that, buddy. You're confused. I didn't do *anything.* What do you *think* I did?"

"You know."

"I don't."

He worked hard to keep the .45 steady. "First Driscoll, now Monroe. You must be some kind of damn psychopath. I should shoot you where you stand, you sick son of a bitch. ..."

From the corner of an eye, Pete discerned only one other patient in sick bay—Sarge Washington, in t-shirt and rumpled dungarees, climbing with some difficulty off his cot. He staggered toward them like the Mummy, one eye shut under his skull bandage, possibly against the throbbing pain of a concussion. "Easy now, Mr. Maxwell! What's this you say, 'bout Orville?"

"Sarge," Pete said, "just stay where you are, okay?"

Rosetti was shaking his head, his voice tight as he insisted, "I didn't kill Dick. He was my friend, Pete, *our* friend. I didn't kill *anybody.*"

Pete thumbed back the safety with a tiny click that was somehow deafening. "I think you did. I *know* you did. ..."

"Mr. Maxwell," Washington said, moving in beside the seated corpsman. "Don't do nothing stupid. No reason not to talk about this. Now tell me about Monroe. ..."

Pete ignored Washington, his eyes locking with Rosetti's, which were wide and wild and indignant and terrified. "Vince, you and the other guys used to love to kid me about being a farm boy."

"You're no farm boy," Rosetti said softly.

"Maybe not, but I know what the farm boys do with a rabid dog." And he raised the weapon and trained it between Rosetti's eyes.

"Stop it," Washington said.

Pete stared expressionlessly at Rosetti, who was shaking his head and muttering, "No, no, no. ..." To Washington, Pete said, "He killed Dick and he killed Orville. No witnesses left, right, Vince? Except for the blood trail from your cabin to Dick's— that's where I found Monroe's corpse stowed. ..."

Washington held up his hands as if surrendering and took a step toward Pete. "You listen to me, Mr. Maxwell. We're partners in this. Fact, you made me the lead investigator. You need to take a breath and listen."

"You're a casualty, Sarge. I had to step up to the plate myself... and as goddamn much as I *hate* it, my friend Vince here killed—"

"*Nobody,*" Washington said, his voice deep, his tone authoritative. "Listen! I checked out Mr. Rosetti's alibi myself—my pal Willie Wilson vouched for him. *You* know Willie, Mr. Maxwell—he don't lie. And when Mr. Driscoll was murdered, Mr. Rosetti was sittin' in the officers' mess, all the while. Willie *saw* him."

Rosetti said, "It's the truth, Pete. You're mixed up about this. I'm no goddamn killer."

Pete took it all in, but he did not lower his aim, the nose of the .45 trained at the white space between Rosetti's eyes. "I know what I saw," Pete said. "And what I saw was a blood trail from Rosetti's cabin to Driscoll's cabin, where I found Monroe with *his* throat cut."

This news froze everything for a moment.

Then, some desperation in his voice now, Rosetti said, "I *told* you, Pete—I cut my damn hand in the *engine* room. There were three witnesses!"

"That right?"

Rosetti ticked them off: "Blake, Smith, and Big Brown."

"Doesn't explain the blood. I know what I saw."

Rosetti, half-crazed with fear, held up his partly stitched hand, lurching forward half a step. "Then look at this, you dumb son of a bitch!"

"Get back!" Pete demanded, waving the .45.

Rosetti did.

But Washington stepped forward, moving in between the two men, blocking Pete's aim.

"Goddamnit, Sarge, get out of the way!"

"No. You settle down. You ain't had enough sleep last couple days to know your own name. You been shot at and tripping over dead bodies and generally thinking about as straight as a two-year-old with a temperature."

"Out of my way, Sarge ..."

"What, you gonna shoot *me*? That'll go over big with the other colored boys. Listen, 'fore you go off half-cocked, ask yourself this—what if that blood trail was *from* Mr. Driscoll's cabin down *to* Mr. Rosetti's, not the other way around?"

"That doesn't make sense ..."

"Doesn't it? Killer couldn't have got himself cut in Driscoll's cabin, then bled as he went back to his own cabin?"

"What, you mean—got cut scuffling with Orville? How much fight could *Orville* have put up?"

"*Any* man facing a blade can put up a fight. But chew on this—what if the real killer wanted you to *think* Mr. Rosetti murdered Orv?"

Pete's mind reeled—he'd been so positive that he'd figured out what happened, yet here were two possibilities that he was wrong, or had overlooked something. ...

He was no detective. But Sarge was.

Maybe he should listen to the real detective. ...

Washington was saying, "Mr. Rosetti here has got a tight alibi for the first murder, and plenty of witnesses to say how he cut his hand, for the second."

In a daze, almost a dream state, Pete sensed the gun in his hand easing itself down as Washington lowered the weapon's snout toward the deck; and Pete didn't fight when Washington gently lifted the gun from his hand and snapped the safety on again.

Rosetti fell into a chair near the stainless-steel table and sat there, looking exhausted, the half-stitched hand cradled in his lap by his good one. Pete's eyes met Rosetti's, but Pete was too close to what he'd thought and felt moments before to realize just what he'd put his friend through.

But Rosetti knew, and just as his fear had turned to relief, now that relief turned to rage. "You fucking moron, Maxwell. I ought to wring your scrawny fucking neck, stick a gun in *my* face!"

Yet Rosetti stayed seated, while Pete just stood there, with no idea what to say, not even entirely sure that Washington was right, though what the detective had said seemed to make sense. . . .

So Pete and Rosetti faced each other, one with a blank hang-dog expression and the other turning a seething red, their friendship disintegrating in the space between them.

Then the sound of the pistol clattering to the deck drew their mutual attention.

Washington had toppled.

Both Pete and Rosetti started for the fallen man, but the corpsman, Jensen, beat them to him. He took Washington's pulse and looked up at the two. "Just passed out. Mr. Maxwell, could you help me get him back to his cot?"

"Sure," Pete managed, and without thinking about it retrieved his .45 from the floor and tucked it in his front waistband. Then he and the corpsman got under Washington's arms and hoisted him to his feet and drunk-walked him back to his berth.

"Sir," the corpsman called to Rosetti, "can you get me a damp towel?"

"Where from, son?"

"Over there, far corner—see that little sink? Clean towels on the table next to it."

Rosetti did as instructed.

Pete asked the corpsman if Sarge would be all right.

"He's a strong one," Jensen said. "But meanin' no disrespect, you're done in here, sir. My job is to watch out for these men, and you got to go. You can't come in my sick bay, waving a goddamn gun, sir. And you better know I'll report this incident to the captain, soon as I finish with Mr. Rosetti's hand."

"I'd expect you to, corpsman."

Rosetti came over and handed a towel to the corpsman. He didn't meet Pete's eyes, still seething, if in control.

Jensen said, "Mr. Rosetti, you go back to the table, I be there in just a minute to finish up your hand."

"All right," Rosetti said. "Thanks."

Like a whipped puppy behind its master, Pete fell in behind Rosetti, following him to the stainless-steel table.

"I don't suppose," Pete said, " 'sorry' will cut it."

"Not hardly," Rosetti said.

"You understand, I was just trying to … that I got caught up with … Vince, sorry is all I've got."

"Noted."

The corpsman approached the table. "Mr. Maxwell, you need to leave—*now.*"

Pete stepped into the passageway, but he did not leave, instead waiting outside sick bay for a good fifteen minutes before Rosetti finally exited. The burly engineer did not look thrilled to see him. "What the hell do you want?"

"Vince, I need to talk to you about your accident."

"Go fuck yourself."

Rosetti started off and Pete put a hand on his shoulder, and the ex-cop whirled and brought his fist back to swing and Pete just stood there.

The fist froze in midair, and Pete shrugged and said, "Do what you have to. Because I have things *I* have to do, too."

Rosetti's fist dissolved into fingers and his limp hands hung at his sides and he seemed genuinely hurt, almost near tears as he said, "Jesus, you pointed a gun at me! You saw two men with their throats cut and you thought I was *capable* of that! I'm your friend, or I was, anyway. You're supposed to fucking trust me!"

"Dick probably trusted somebody. Little Orville probably trusted somebody, too. And they're dead. And whoever did that is still on this ship. And the captain said it was my job to figure it out. You're the cop, and I get the goddamn job! You could've stepped up, Vince, but you didn't. I'm sorry. That's all I have. That's all you get."

Rosetti just stood there, his expression blank; finally he let out a sigh that started at his toes.

"Hell with it," he said. "I been there. Sometimes you can't even trust your fellow cops. You don't know who to believe, anymore. Well, neither do I. But you ask me your questions. I'll do my best to answer 'em."

"First, are you okay? How is your hand?"

"I'll be fine. Just the meat of my palm. Like I said, I did it trying to replace the goddamned lube oil strainer. Thing lurched and fell. Edge caught my hand. Looks worse than it is."

"You said there were four of you in the engine room, right?"

Rosetti nodded. "Blake and Smith, Big Brown, and me."

"What happened when you got hurt? How did the others react?"

"Blake and Smith were useless as screen doors on a submarine. Hell, I thought Smith was gonna faint or maybe puke at the sight of blood."

"And Big Brown?"

"He waded right in. Grabbed a clean engine rag and put pressure on the cut, right away. That lummox take first aid or something?"

"That lummox has a degree from the University of Cincinnati."

"No shit! Big ape hasn't said word one since we left port."

"I know. Keeps to himself, but he's smarter than just about anybody else on ship, us two included."

"There's a ringing endorsement. Anyway, he put pressure on the gash, got the bleeding stopped, for the most part. If those two worthless white peckerheads had been my only chance, I could've bled to death before anybody figured out what to do."

"Who else knew you were hurt?"

Rosetti frowned in thought. "I got no idea. Why? What's that got to do with anything?"

"Just a hell of a coincidence that blood turns up outside your cabin, right after you've cut yourself."

"But I don't think that was my blood, Pete."

"If you're right, somebody tried to frame you."

"There were three *witnesses* to me getting cut!"

Pete shrugged. "What if you'd already cut your hand, struggling with Orville, and faked injuring it in the engine room? Or really got hurt and used that as an excuse to leave your post and go deal with the little guy?"

"You can't believe—"

"No, Vince. I've come to my senses. But you've got to admit, somebody in the middle of a couple of murders might see you as the perfect patsy."

"No more Bogart movies for you, Pete," Rosetti said with a sick smile. But he wasn't disagreeing.

"I think you were a frame of convenience. That's why it's important we figure out how many men knew you cut yourself."

Rosetti held up the Boy Scout salute. "Just those three guys in the engine room."

"Didn't see anybody on your way back to your cabin?"

Rosetti frowned in thought. "Don't think so."

"Did the corpsman call anyone on the squawk box after you got there?"

"No," Rosetti said. "But that'd've been too late, anyway, wouldn't it? Hadn't you already found the blood?"

"Right, right." Now Pete was frowning. "And when I came into your cabin, you were there.... Did you go straight to your cabin from the engine room?"

"Yeah."

Pete shrugged. "Then one of your three witnesses has to be the killer."

Rosetti smirked. "Like *I* had to be?"

Pete could only wince. "You know, you're right. I need to go run this thing past Washington."

"Suuuure," Rosetti said, "That corpsman's gonna be thrilled, letting you back in sick bay."

Rosetti had a point.

Pete said, "Kid said he was going to report me—maybe when he goes up to the bridge to do that, I could sneak back in ...?"

"He's probably already reported you over the squawk box."

"Christ, I hadn't thought of that. I bet he has."

"Maybe not." Rosetti grinned, put his good hand on Pete's shoulder. "Look, you head back to your cabin, and I'll run this past Washington, and report back."

Pete wasn't wild about that, but had little choice—corpsmen Jensen wasn't likely to welcome him back and Washington wouldn't be leaving there any time soon.

"Okay," Pete said. "Good of you."

"What are friends for?" Rosetti asked, and headed back to sick bay.

In his cabin, Pete found the wait interminable and had about made up his mind to storm the corpsman's bastion when a knock came at the door. His hand went automatically to the gun in his waistband, but he decided to leave it there as he answered.

"Me," Rosetti said.

Pete let him in and Rosetti rushed in, adrenaline clearly pumping.

"I was getting worried," Pete said.

"Got back as soon as I could. You might want to avoid that corpsman for the immediate future—he's scared shitless that you're Driscoll's killer, and invaded his sanctuary to kill one and sundry."

"You straighten him out?"

Grinning, Rosetti sat on Connor's bunk. "No! I told him that was the best theory I'd heard all day, and would look into it."

With friends like you—"

"Look who's talking. Anyway, I told him it'd be best he didn't report your conduct to the captain till I finished my own investigation."

"Thank you, I guess." Pete sat on Connor's bunk across from Rosetti. "So, what did Washington think?"

"Oh, he thought it was pretty funny. Told me the routine I did with Jensen was better than 'Who's on First.' Ben would be proud."

"I meant," Pete said tightly, "about the murders."

Rosetti, apparently finished taking his revenge (at least for the moment), said, "Sarge agreed that my three witnesses were our best suspects... but not the only ones."

"And?"

"And he said you need to talk to those three, find out what they did after I went off to my cabin—that'll tell you how, and how fast, word of my slashed hand spread beyond the engine room."

"Sarge makes sense, as usual."

Pete slipped out of the cabin, heading for the engine room, where he interviewed the three witnesses separately.

Both white non-coms said once Rosetti got cut and had gone off to his cabin, they worried about him and decided they better tell somebody; they were short-handed now, after all. So they called the bridge and informed Mr. Connor of the accident. That meant Pete now had to interview everybody who'd been on the bridge, but first he wanted to get Big Brown's version.

"When Mr. Rosetti cut himself," Big Brown said, "Blake and Smith both froze. I've seen little girls react better to the sight of blood."

"But it doesn't bother you?"

Big Brown gave up a rare grin. "Mr. Maxwell, I worked at the Bucket of Blood back in Cleveland, remember? I've seen more red stuff than Dracula."

Pete smiled at that. "So you stepped in and helped Mr. Rosetti?"

"I did."

"*Some* white men might have objected to that, maybe even the one bleeding himself."

"I know. But he didn't. Neither did those squeamish white boys."

"Mr. Rosetti says he might have died if you hadn't been there."

Big Brown shrugged. "I doubt that. Sure, it was a bad cut, fairly deep, but nothing you die over. And, anyway, Mr. Rosetti didn't panic. Keeps his head, Mr. Rosetti. He'd have been fine, either way."

"After you helped him?"

"He headed back to his cabin."

"And after he did, what happened down here?"

"The two white sailors got to worrying about what would happen if Mr. Rosetti didn't get back to his cabin, you know, passed out or some such. I said Mr. Rosetti was fine on his own, but Blake called the bridge and explained what happened."

"Who did Blake talk to?"

"Mr. Connor."

This jibed with what Blake and Smith had told Pete earlier. "What then?"

A gentle shrug of massive shoulders. "Then we went back to work on the lube oil strainer."

"And nothing else happened?"

Big Brown mulled that a moment. "I believe Griffin came in, to see how we were doing. Then he left and we went back to work."

"Griffin came in?" Pete asked. Neither Blake nor Smith had mentioned Griffin; this was new information. "You 'believe' he did, or he *did?*"

Big Brown nodded with certainty. "He stopped by. He's not my favorite white boy on the ship, and I was sure to notice him. But he was only down here a minute or two."

"Who did he talk to, while he was?"

"Well, he didn't talk to me."

"But he did talk to Blake and Smith?"

"Sure. The white guys were standing together, talking. For some reason I wasn't invited."

"Did you hear what they were saying?"

"I caught parts."

"Did they tell Griffin about Rosetti?"

"Of course they did. Hell, there was blood on the deck."

"How long did that conversation last?"

Another shrug. "Maybe two minutes, like I said…then Griffin was gone."

"Any idea where?"

"Nope. Nor do I care. He's an unpleasant little man."

Pete had no argument with that. "Have either Blake or Smith been out of the engine room since Mr. Rosetti left?"

"Nope," Big Brown said. "And I been here the whole while, too—we about got this busted engine put back together, been workin' pretty hard to finish up."

"Good to hear."

"We get back up to full speed, maybe we can get ourselves to a port and the hell off of this tub, till you and Sarge or the Shore Patrol or whoever-the-goddamn-hell can *find* this damn murderer."

"We'll keep at it," Pete said. "We're working pretty hard to finish up, ourselves."

Then Pete headed back to sick bay to report to his partner; he'd just have to bull past that corpsman somehow. He considered Brown, Blake, and Smith off the suspect list, but taking their place were Griffin and the men on the bridge, Ben Connor included. Added to these names would be anyone Griffin might have told.

Dealing with Corpsman Jensen turned out a non-issue—the other corpsman, Jackson, was on duty, and the heavy-set sailor did not seem to have been told Pete was off the visitor's list.

Pete sat at Washington's cot and heard his own view confirmed by the bandaged detective. "Still plenty of suspects out there. Remember what I said, when we stood over what was left of your buddy, Driscoll?"

"That we have a smart killer."

"Don't never forget that. And he wouldn't be working up a last-second frame to fit Mr. Rosetti, if he didn't think...if he didn't *know*...we was closing in."

"Are we closing in?"

"I believe we are. He's smart, our killer, but he's also scared. We can benefit from that, if we don't get our own selves killed 'cause of it."

They agreed Pete's next step should be to interview the men on the bridge. There he found Connor with a helmsman and radarman Louis Frye.

Pete waved Connor over to the doorway of the chart room.

"Make up your mind, Pete—are you Dick Tracy or Hopalong Cassidy?"

"Huh?"

Connor gestured to the .45 in Pete's waistband.

"Oh," he said. "Yeah. Well, I'm not much for jokes right now, Ben. We have two men murdered, and one of them's Dick."

"Sorry. Bad habit, reverting to comedy. Jesus, we haven't even had time to pay our respects to Dick. It's sad and sickening, him in cold storage till this is sorted out. And now this kid Orville?"

"Yeah."

"At least it's not just white officers being targeted, small solace though that might be."

Pete glanced around the bridge. "Ben, has anybody up here left since you got the call from the engine room, about Rosetti?"

Connor frowned. "No. How'd you even know we got that call?"

Pete quietly filled Connor in—from Orville Monroe to the blood-drop trail, even a short version of his screwed-up accusation of Vince.

"Ben, if nobody left the bridge, my suspect list may have just got a whole lot shorter—down to that bigot Dale Griffin, and whoever he might've told about Vince getting cut."

Connor looked as if he might literally get sick. "Jesus," he muttered, and glanced about the bridge furtively.

"What?"

Very softly, Connor said, "I might... might have one suspect more for that list."

"Who?"

"There was one other person on the bridge when Blake called up from the engine room."

"Yeah?"

"The skipper."

Pete frowned.

Connor continued: "Not long after that engine room call, Captain Egan left. Told me to maintain course, said he would be back."

"*Has* he been?"

"No, but he's been on and off the bridge four or five times today. He comes and goes all the time. That's a Captain's prerogative."

"Right," Pete said.

The captain, more than anyone, had the run of the ship, and knew the *Liberty Hill* so very well, from fo'c'sle to shaft alley (and its escape tunnel), who of all the white officers had frightened skittish Orville Monroe the most. How nervous Orville had seemed around the captain, even on the bridge receiving praise for hitting that Jap Zero. An inherent fear of authority figures, especially white men in power?

Or something else?

FOURTEEN

SEPTEMBER 1, 1944

Considering how wrong he'd been about Vince Rosetti, Pete considered seeking Washington's counsel before taking any further action.

But the *Liberty Hill* had suffered two murders in a short time, and the officer in charge of the inquiry decided to press on and interrogate his two best suspects, starting with the very man who had given him the assignment: his captain.

Leaving Connor and the rest on the bridge, Pete went directly to Egan's door, where he knocked with a crisp confidence he did not feel. No answer. He rapped again, got no answer, then tried the knob—locked.

His hand went to the reassuring rough butt of the pistol, which he had returned to the back of his waistband. Then he tried the captain's office door—also locked. Next door was Driscoll's cabin, where the murderer had stowed Orville's body, and perhaps did not yet know of its discovery.

The door remained unlocked and, automatic in hand, Pete pushed it open and stepped into the cabin, lights off, porthole covered, merely a dim slant of illumination coming in from the passageway that highlighted the corpse of Orville Monroe.

Other than the deceased oiler, however, the cabin was empty. Pete checked the other cabins down the port side of the bridge deck—all unlocked, all unpopulated. Dropping down to the boat deck, he again went from cabin to cabin, starting with the officers' mess, moving forward to Rosetti's cabin, then around to the cabin he shared with Connor.

No Egan or, for that matter, Griffin.

Around the last corner of the boat deck, he checked the final cabin on the boat deck and dropped to the main deck. From the galley, through the enlisted men's mess, through the bosun's shack, the sick bay, and around the wheelhouse, he was still unable to find either man.

Finally, all that remained was the engine room. He entered and immediately found himself face to face with Dale Griffin. He fought an urge to pull the pistol, but Griffin was after all only a suspect ... and after his foul-up with Rosetti, Pete would act on reason not impulse.

"Mr. Maxwell," Griffin said, with what seemed to be a relieved grin on his boyish mug. "Boy, am I glad to see you."

"Why's that, Mr. Griffin?"

He gestured vaguely. "We can finally replace the lube oil strainer, but to do it, we're gonna have to shut down the engine."

"Understood," Pete managed.

The Texan Tom Whitford and the light-skinned oiler Lenny Wallace rolled up to listen in.

"That's all well and good," Griffin said, "only we can't find the CO to okay shutting down, and Mr. Connor won't do it without a say-so from either you or the captain."

Pete's mind raced with murder-inquiry questions for Griffin, but in front of him was another dilemma, actually two: the captain had gone missing and *somebody* had to run the damned ship.

The blond non-com gazed at him with wide-eyed expectancy. "Well, sir?"

"How long to make the repairs?"

Griffin winced in thought. "Now that we've got the strainer free and ready to remove ..." He turned to Whitford, then

Wallace. Neither man volunteered a word. Griffin took it upon himself: "...an hour tops?"

Pete let out a breath he'd been holding. "Shut 'em down—just let me call Mr. Connor first, and give him the heads-up."

"Right!"

"But we need to get more power out of those turbines. We're goddamn sitting ducks like this. Our Zero wasn't the only thing the Japs have sent into the sky lately."

"Understood, sir."

The engine-room trio moved out of Pete's way as he crossed to the desk and pushed the squawk-box button.

"Bridge," came a voice Pete recognized as radarman Frye.

"This is the XO—where's Mr. Connor?"

"Chart room, sir."

"Get him."

A moment later, a familiar voice came on: "Connor. What's up, Lieutenant?"

"We need to shut down the engine so these guys can repair it."

"I know all about it, but I can't find the CO."

"I can't find him, either, and I've been looking." He paused, but only briefly. "Ben, I'm taking full responsibility. We're shutting down the engine while they make the repairs. Meantime, I'll find the captain."

"Yes, sir," Connor said, his tone dubious.

Pete signed off and returned to Griffin, asking him, "Where did you go after you left the engine room, right after Mr. Rosetti got hurt?"

Griffin frowned. "Sir, shouldn't I be getting to the engine ...?"

"After this," Pete said, and repeated the question.

"Nowhere. Why?"

"Sailor, you better be more specific than 'nowhere.' Somebody's killed Orville Monroe..."

"What? Fuck, *another* killing?"

"Keep it down, will you? Orville got his throat slit, just like Mr. Driscoll…and whoever did it knew about Mr. Rosetti's injury."

Griffin's eyes flared. "What the hell you saying? Think *I* fuckin' did it? I wouldn't get close enough to that little faggot to breathe his air let alone slit his throat."

"Thank you for sharing such a touching display of sorrow for the death of a fellow sailor." Speaking of reason, not impulse, restraining himself and not punching this asshole was a major accomplishment. "Now, answer my goddamned question."

"I just went back to my cabin to get ready for the shift."

"Anybody see you?"

He gestured. "Tom, here."

Great, Abbott alibiing Costello. "You see anybody else? Talk to anybody else?"

"I don't think so."

"This is a murder inquiry, Mr. Griffin—someone on this ship is killing crew members, and he doesn't seem to discriminate between black and white. You want to try again?"

Somewhat agitated now, Griffin stood up for himself. "Nobody but Tom saw me, and I didn't even talk to him. Look, probably Mr. Driscoll caught Orville sucking off some other nigger, and got killed for his trouble. Then that other nigger bumped Orville off, you know, to cut his losses. So why don't you let me get to something *important,* sir, like the goddamn *engine?*"

Pete gave the sailor a smile that didn't have much to do with smiling. "If you killed Monroe and Mr. Driscoll, Mr. Griffin, you'll hang for it. You sure you want to play wise-ass with the man looking into it?"

Griffin said, "I ain't playin' at nothing, sir," bordering on insolence; but fear danced in his eyes.

Whitford shouldered over and growled, "Why don't you let the guy alone?"

Pete got nose to nose with the lanky Texan. "That's 'Why don't you leave the guy alone, *sir.*'"

Whitford swallowed and backed off. "Sorry, sir."

"Did your buddy here tell you about Mr. Rosetti cutting his hand?"

"Well, uh …"

"Did he or didn't he?"

"Well, yeah, I guess he did." Whitford's hands got busy with a shop rag. "News travels fast on a ship like this. So what?"

"So here's the latest scoop: you're a suspect, too."

Lenny Wallace stepped forward, his manner not at all confrontational. "Mr. Maxwell, sir—they didn't do it."

Mildly shocked by the Negro sticking up for the white noncoms, Pete turned to him with an appraising look. "How do you know?"

"I saw Orville, alive and well, and then I come down here and saw these two fellas. They *couldn'ta* done it."

"*When* did you see Orville?"

"Hell—I musta been with him, right before he got killed. I'm sorry to hear Orv's dead, sir. I actually *liked* the little guy.…"

Wondering if he'd found yet another suspect, Pete said, "Go on."

"We were talkin' in the mess, Orv and me, just shooting the breeze—I was tellin' him how proud we all was about what he done, shooting down that Jap? Then it was time for my shift and, well, I left the mess hall and just come down here. Griffin and Whitford, they already started their shift … and, honest, Mr. Maxwell, these two has not left since."

"That's right," Griffin piped up.

Wallace went on: "We all been working some odd hours, trying to get this engine problem fixed. Our regular shifts are all screwed up. Orville and me, we were in the mess, going over how the repair was comin' along? He been in here, workin'—now I was heading in."

Pete's eyes narrowed. "Do you know where Monroe was going, after he talked to you? He say anything?"

"Didn't say nothing, but he did leave the mess same time as me."

"What?"

"Didn't I say that? I saw Orv headin' up towards the bridge deck. Thought that was kinda odd, but I didn't say anything. Orville, he was in a funny mood—you'd thought him being a hero would make his damn day. To me, he seemed...spooked."

Griffin laughed "Spooked is right."

"Shut up," Pete snapped. To Wallace he said: "What was bothering him?"

"I got no idea. He didn't say nothing about anything. Spooked is just how he seemed to me."

Pete's eyes traveled from Wallace to Whitford. "Either of you talk to anybody beside each other?"

The sailors shook their heads; they seemed to Pete genuinely alarmed to be suspects.

The only way the killer was among these three was if they were in it together, and that seemed a ridiculous proposition.

Shifting gears, Pete said, "Shut down both sides of the turbine, get this son of a buck fixed and let's see if we can get the hell out of here."

"Aye aye, sir," Wallace said, and the other two chimed in the same.

Pete watched as the trio shut down the boilers and the turbines. The roar of the engine died slowly, which somehow only emphasized the customary ringing in Pete's ears after an engine-room visit. He looked across to the hatchway into shaft alley: he hadn't been in there since the captain assigned him the murder inquiry.

Not knowing exactly why, he found himself crossing the engine room and opening that hatch. After stepping inside, he was taken by the oppressive silence of the dimly, sporadically lit corridor. Without the engine running, the narrow space was a sort of endless coffin.

He edged forward until he reached the spot at the far end where he had last seen the body of Richard Driscoll. He stepped over the bloodstained deck and, as he neared the stern, someone dropped out of the escape tunnel and landed with a metallic *clomp,* maybe three feet from him.

Now Pete was staring into Captain Egan's rugged features, the presence of the captain almost as big a surprise as the pistol in Pete's grasp—he didn't even remember reaching for it.

Egan held up a single hand, like an Indian chief in the movies saying, "How."

But what the captain said was "We need a man-to-man talk." His hair a trifle mussed, Egan otherwise betrayed no signs of his climb down the tunnel. His uniform looked well-pressed, shipshape.

"I think we do," Pete said, "need to talk."

"Good. Put that pistol down."

"No. We'll talk all right, but I'll keep this where it is."

"That's an order, Mr. Maxwell. Lower that weapon!"

"No, sir. The Navy doesn't require me to take an order from a murderer."

Egan drew in air; the wild eyebrows wiggled and a rumpled smile formed on the weathered face. "Rather than argue that point with you, Mr. Maxwell, let's go ahead. Go ahead and talk."

"You expressed that desire first, Captain. You start."

"Ah, that much courtesy you'll pay your commanding officer? Kind of you." Egan shifted on his feet, not making a move toward Pete, just getting settled, looking for where to begin, perhaps. "No need at this point to mince words, son. You do know your friend Driscoll was making that little nigger suck his peter."

The words struck Pete like a slap; he felt his eyes tighten. "That's bullshit."

"No. It isn't. I put you in charge of this inquiry, knowing you were a smart college boy and knew how to think, and I'd be shocked if the possibility that Driscoll using that pansy as a catamite hadn't occurred to you."

And it did make sense to Pete, immediate, sudden sense: who was the "big, powerful" man that Orville had been too afraid not to accommodate? Driscoll must have been physically intimidating to the delicate sailor, but also Dick represented the white authority figure—cops in civilian life, officers in the service—that a Negro like Orv, with his terrible if ill-kept secret, feared instinctively.

Still, Pete heard himself say, "I don't believe it. Dick was a guy's guy."

"I'll say! Listen, don't tear yourself up, son—there's no doubt about this. Hell, I *caught* them at it."

"If you caught one of your officers doing … doing that," Pete said, gun in his hand leveled at Egan's chest, "why didn't you just place him under arrest?"

Egan shook his head. "Not good enough. Some sins deserve immediate punishment. There are things that *cannot* be allowed on a ship. What kind of jungle revolt would we have faced, if it became known among these niggers that a white officer was … hell, I can't even say it. Makes me sick. I did what *had* to be done. For the good of the ship. For the good of the Navy."

"What gave you that right?"

"The United States government. They put me in charge of the *Liberty Hill,* where *I* am the law. The captain is the ultimate adjudicator on *any* ship." He shook his head. "Goddamn it, Pete. You disappoint me."

"You have not fulfilled my every expectation either, sir."

Egan shook a massive fist. "Do you think I *wanted* to kill Driscoll? He was my XO! He could have made a fine officer. But what he was doing—that was unconscionable. And it was my duty, my right, to stop him. Command is about making the *hard* decisions."

"With all due respect, sir, you are out of your fucking mind."

He grinned and it was a face out of a Hieronymus Bosch painting. "That is the opinion of a hysterical, wet-behind-the-ears junior officer."

"But it will be backed up by the opinion of a court-martial. ..."

Egan shook his head. "Going down that path really isn't necessary, Mr. Maxwell. Not if you do the right thing."

"The right thing."

"Stand behind me when I report that Monroe murdered Driscoll and then killed himself out of remorse for his crime."

Pete goggled at the demented creature. "Do you really believe the ONI will accept that reading of the evidence?"

"What evidence? We'll bury these unfortunates at sea with full Naval honors—even the murderous Mr. Monroe, since an official verdict in the case will be pending."

Pete almost laughed, though crying would have been more like it. "And why would I even *think* about going along with this put-up job?"

"You should carefully consider it," Egan said with a kind of warped dignity, "because you have a career to think about, mister. Whether you remain in the Navy or seek your future in civilian life, how you handle yourself in this war will be key. And are you going to let a dead colored cocksucker and a nigger-loving traitor to the white race stand between you and becoming captain of your *own* ship, one day?"

Pete didn't respond right away. He stood in a kind of awe after hearing such a gloriously deranged speech.

Then he said, "No. Under Article 184, I am placing you under arrest."

"On what charge?"

"What charge? The murder of two men."

"Not two men," Egan said, and that hell-bound smile returned, and the eyebrows wiggled. "Two perverts—one a nigger! You would remove a veteran captain from this war for scum like that? You saw me save this ship in that storm!"

"Please be quiet, sir. Turn around—we're going up that escape hatch."

Teeth bared, Egan leaned forward. "Do you know what that little nigger had the audacity to say to me? That if I didn't give him his transfer, he would tell the world what I'd done to Driscoll, when we got to port."

"Sir…"

"There are a lot of things a man in my position of leadership must endure. But I was not about to put up with threats from a mincing little nigger. He was a problem, like Driscoll was a problem, and a transfer would only have passed on that problem to another ship. And where I come from, Mr. Maxwell, a captain does *not* pass his problems on to another ship. He solves them himself!"

"Fine," Pete said. "I'm the captain now, and I'm solving this problem. Turn around and march your ass to the brig."

Egan's hand went into his pocket so quickly it came out again before Pete even knew it, and the straight razor was in a tight fist, raised high with yellowish light from the nearest hanging bulb blinking off its keen edge. Pete had seen that razor before, when he watched the CO shave in his cabin; and he hadn't been enough of a detective to realize that razor was the very sort of narrow blade that matched the missing weapon in both murders.

"We have an expression back in Iowa, sir," Pete said and gave the captain a grin as awful as Egan's own. "Never bring a knife to a gun fight."

But that was when the engine started back up, the drive shaft spinning, the normal roar of shaft alley growing to fill their ears. And as the shaft started, Pete reacted with an involuntary glance its way, a movement that couldn't have taken more than half a second, but was enough for Egan to lash out.

The blade slashed through cloth and flesh, not deep, but searing, and Pete's hand loosened reflexively and the gun slipped from his grasp, *clunking* to the deck, while the two men wrested for control of the razor, Pete clutching the captain's wrist, twisting it, trying to shake the blade loose.

With his free hand Egan shoved Pete away, then tried to slice him again, but Pete backed up and the razor cut only air; quickly Pete stepped in and brought an elbow down on Egan's still-outstretched wrist, the captain's fist popping open and the knife tumbling from splayed fingers to clatter on the deck somewhere.

Razorless, Egan counterpunched, his right fist slamming into Pete's left eye. Rocked, Pete nonetheless managed to respond with a head-butt in the face, flattening a nose that had been broken many times before.

But the stocky older man seemed barely to notice, pummeling Pete in the torso, bending over bull-like, the cramped quarters no impediment to the captain's blows, his arms working like pistons from his sides.

Pete, a human punching bag now, felt his knees go weak but somehow he swung the side of his forearm up and into the captain's throat, and the man began to choke, the blows stopped, and by all means Egan should have tumbled and maybe would have, if there'd been room.

Instead the captain managed to shove Pete with both hands, sending the lieutenant staggering backward, and slipped past him, their bodies touching; then the captain was barreling down shaft alley toward the engine room. Pete gave chase, but his balance was off, and he was just catching up when Egan was through the hatch, locking it.

Pete knew at once how Egan would surely play this, coming through the hatchway and gathering fellow Negro-haters Griffin and Whitford to tell the pair a story they'd be glad to hear, namely that Pete was the killer of Driscoll and Monroe.

Alone in shaft alley, his mind turned to the only advisor he trusted.

I've done it, baby, I've screwed it all up—as a detective, I make a great choir director.

Stop it! Get a hold of yourself!

I could have spent the war in San Diego with my beautiful wife, but no, I had to be a hero.

You are a hero. Now act like one! You know who the killer is—now do something about it!

Kay was right: he still had one chance.

In the next thirty seconds, Egan would be on the squawk box, the escape tunnel blocked, and Pete would be trapped. When they reached shore, the bodies would be in Davy Jones's locker and the frame Pete had been fitted for would be nailed down tight. From shaft alley he would *really* get the shaft: the brig, then the gallows....

One chance left—he had to get up that tunnel ladder before anyone else could get there to block it. Charging back to the stern, he grabbed up the .45 on his way. On the run, he tucked it in his front waistband and soon was flying up the ladder into the tiny black cylinder, just big enough for one man, climbing completely by feel with no light in the tunnel—one hand on a steel rung and then the one above it and trusting that the next one would be there.

When he reached the top, he swallowed and his gulp might have been comic if his life had not depended on that round hatch not being locked...

...which it wasn't.

With a shoulder, Pete pushed up, the heavy steel hatch slowly squeaking on its hinges; then he jack-in-the-boxed out, eyes working to adjust to a sun peeking over the eastern horizon at about five o'clock.

That meant they were traveling northwest, and Connor had them back on course...and hopefully headed for Eniwetok.

On the main deck now—hidden from view of the wheelhouse by the aft five-inch gun platform and the winches for holds four and five—he stopped to get his bearings. The captain would no doubt be painting Pete the madman, poisoning the crew against him, maybe even Connor; right now, the only man he could still count on was Sarge Washington....

Pete had to get to sick bay not only to tell Washington what he'd learned, but to warn him—as the other investigator on the murders, Sarge was in as much danger as Pete.

He could sprint from his hiding spot, move up the starboard side past holds five and four, then could hide in the shadow of the fresh water tank while his pursuers went aft, to block the tunnel. He could then enter the wheelhouse, next to the galley, and make his way to sick bay. Egan would figure Pete was either trapped in shaft alley or doing his best to hide somewhere, till they reached port.

Time to move.

But he only traveled two steps before his path was cut off by steward's mate Willie Wilson.

The .45 was in his waistband, and Pete could have pulled it; but the last thing he wanted to do was aim that weapon at an innocent man again.

And Wilson showed no fear of Pete or the gun in his belt. The steward moved closer and whispered, "Mr. Maxwell, what the hell is going on?"

"It's bad, Willie—"

"Bad don't *cover* it! Captain's on the squawk box, sayin' you killed Mr. Driscoll and Orville."

"I didn't. The *captain* did. He's out of his goddamn mind."

Wilson nodded. "That's how I read it, but there's plenty who will buy whatever Egan sells 'em. Only way to work this out is get you to the brig, and put some reliable men on the door, so that bastard can't get to you."

"No, Willie—I need to talk to Sarge! I need—"

But a pistol report interrupted, and Willie's eyes widened; then Willie fell limply towards Pete, who caught the dead man in his arms.

Wilson's collapse gave him a view of Egan, nine or ten yards forward on deck, pistol in hand, planted and poised to squeeze off a second round.

Pete could only use the bulk of Wilson's body for cover, ducking, as above him the second shot hit the back of Wilson's head; in a haze of reddish mist, Pete felt the force of the shot and the literal dead weight of Wilson send him on his back, onto the hard deck. With the corpse on top of him, Pete could not get to his .45; so he pushed the body rudely off and rolled back under the gun platform, hoping for enough cover to circle around Egan, and go up the port side as the captain came aft, starboard.

That was when the horn for battle stations sounded—had Egan, losing control, sounded goddamn fucking *battle stations* over his fugitive? Pete had a surrealistic flash of himself zigzagging around the deck, as all the twenties, the fifty cal on the bow, and the five-inch gun over his head all turned their firepower his way. ...

Then the muffled mechanical purr of a not-too-distant Japanese Zero told Pete that a crazed captain was no longer the *Liberty Hill's* biggest problem. That plane Orville crippled must have made it back to its carrier, after all! And the Japs had searched for the wounded U.S. ship, and had now finally caught up with them.

They were close to full steam now, but their meager armaments would provide scant protection against a swarm of angry Zeroes, and any assistance was nowhere near at hand.

Alone on deck, Pete looked around him on all sides and saw no sign of Egan, though of course the gray rugged landscape of the ship gave the captain plenty of places to hide behind and sneak around, and Egan had his own .45, a powerful pistol that could blow your skull apart.

But the battle-stations bellow sent Negro sailors streaming on deck, heading for their positions in the gun tubs. Glad to be lost in a crowd, even a lone white face in a black one, Pete finally caught sight of Egan, loping for the wheelhouse. Was the psychopath on the run to take Washington out, while everybody else was on deck fighting the war? Or was the captain reverting to command mode, taking charge in the impending fight?

Either way, Pete had to pursue Egan; the crew would have to deal with the Japs—he had his own battle to wage. He sprinted up starboard, his pace punctuated by the overhead chatter of machine guns. Still running, he glanced back and winced at the orange blur of the rising sun from which emerged a Zero, diving.

Bullets chewed the deck as he leapt for cover. As the plane swooped past, Pete sprang from his hiding place and, staying low, jogged to the entrance of the wheelhouse.

Right before he caught sight of a Jap "Kate," the Imperial Navy's favorite bomber lining up at three o'clock, a torpedo hanging ominously from its belly, ready to give terrible birth. A frozen Pete watched agape as the torpedo detached and hit the water with a tiny splash, like a child off a pier, its wake marking the progress of the fish toward their exposed flank.

The Japs had no idea just how big an explosion their torpedoes could trigger with a hit on the *Liberty Hill*.

Snapping out of it, he dashed through the hatchway, not allowing his eyes time to adjust to the dark as he ran blindly for the stairs. Two flights later, he stood on the bridge wing, aware that Connor had seen the torpedo as well and turned the ship toward it.

The torpedo streaked toward the slowly turning *Liberty Hill Victory* and, for the briefest moment, Pete thought the fish might miss them.

Then the torpedo hit the propeller and rudder, exploding in a fireball that erupted over the stern. Pete knew instantly it was a mortal wound: death would not be instantaneous, but without power and steering, the ship Driscoll had called USS *Powderkeg* was now a sitting duck for the swarm of Jap planes.

And the first torpedo to hit one of the holds would send them up in a Port Chicago-style inglorious blaze.

Entering the bridge, Pete witnessed a remarkable tableau: Egan, eyes as wild as the brows above, waving a pistol at a helmsman no longer in control of the ship. The radioman and radarman stood motionless, hovering over Ben Connor, sprawled on deck, blood trickling from his forehead. Had Egan pistol-whipped him?

Not waiting for an answer, not even asking the question aloud, the XO of the *Liberty Hill*—ignoring the burn of pain in his right arm, where Egan had slashed him, blood still dripping and soaking his shirt—raised his .45 pistol and shot his captain in the back, the report in the confined space like another torpedo going off.

Egan tossed the gun as if to an invisible ally, and a scarlet flower blossomed between the captain's shoulder blades as the once-commanding figure took a weird bow on his way down, hitting with a *whump.*

Pushing up with one hand, Connor stared wide-eyed at the unconscious captain, who'd joined him on deck. "He was a goddamn *lunatic*! What the hell happened?"

"I'll explain in a lifeboat, if we're lucky," Pete said. "Right now we've got to abandon ship—that fucking fish knocked out the prop and rudder. Making us the biggest goddamn target in the Pacific."

"That's what I told Egan!" Connor said, Pete helping him up. "Tried to, anyway. He wouldn't listen!"

"Can you walk?"

"Won't be pretty, but yes."

"Sound abandon ship then, and get every man the hell off, before the next torpedo hits the jackpot."

"What about that sack of shit?" Connor asked, indicating the fallen Egan.

"Let him go down with his damn ship."

"Aye aye, sir." And Connor hit the abandon ship alarm. "Aren't you leading the way?"

"I'll be right behind you," Pete yelled. "I've still got business on this tub. Now go! Save the men!"

Then, through the starboard hatchway, the surreal image of a flaming Zero was coming straight at them. Everybody ducked, as if that would do a damn bit of good and, at the last moment, the Zero dove, crashing into the ship at about the waterline.

With this the *Liberty Hill* rocked to port, knocking all of them off their feet. Pete knew damn well the plane had hit the engine—Griffin, Whitford, and Wallace would almost certainly have been killed on impact. Ears ringing, he felt the ship immediately rock back to starboard, and start to list—seawater would be pouring through the gash in the ship's hull.

Connor was the first on his feet, this time. "Are you all right, Pete?"

"Yeah," Pete yelled, still on deck. "Go!"

Connor shoved the other three men out the port side hatch, then with a last glance, saluted Pete and said, "See you in the boats, sir!"

Pete nodded and, for several moments, just lay there on the deck, trying to catch a second wind but pulling in the stench of burning oil. If only he could go to sleep, maybe just for a few minutes... why did everything feel so heavy?

Get up, Kay said. **Get up!**

Tired... so tired....

You get up and get out of there! I could be expecting! Don't you want to know your son? Or your daughter?

I'm a father?

The tiredness faded and he looked down at himself and saw blood leaking through his pants leg. Piece of shrapnel. Leg felt cold, but there was surprisingly little pain. Struggling to his knees, he realized suddenly that Egan was staring at him.

"Help me," the captain said. "Don't let me die like this...."

Pete got to his feet. "I'm hurt myself. I couldn't carry you if I wanted. That wound'll kill you, anyway. I gave it to you, by the way."

"I can make it. Get some men. I can ... *make* it...."

"You taught me well, Captain. Command is about making the hard decisions. But the truth is—this one isn't all that hard."

As Pete left the bridge, even over the explosions and screams of the wounded and dying, he could still hear Egan shouting obscenities at him.

The wheelhouse was practically deserted now as Pete made his way back down the stairs, ending up in the sick bay. Cots and cabinets had been tossed around like a giant baby's toys. The wounded—no doubt including Sarge—had been cleared out, which was a good thing. The plane that crashed into the engine room had sent shrapnel flying everywhere and sick bay had a hole in its side you could drive a Jeep through, the ocean plainly visible, climbing ever closer to the hole as the ship did its best to sink before blowing up.

Topside, by now, Rosetti and Connor would be getting the lifeboats loaded. That would be Pete's next stop, making sure they got everybody off. He was on his way out when he heard a moan from the wreckage.

When the Zero struck the engine room, the generators must have been taken out as well—the only light in sick bay right now came from sun seeping through the gaping hole in the hull. Carefully moving wreckage aside, metal chunks (still hot) and assorted rubble, Pete searched for the source of the moans.

Pinned under a steel beam was a colored man's leg, still attached apparently. Working his way up from the foot, he yanked away sheets, pillows and chunks of mattress until, like a present he'd unwrapped, he found the face of Sarge Washington.

"What the hell are *you* still doing here?" Pete demanded.

"Just another lazy colored boy can't get his ass out of bed," Washington said. "I was helpin' out the corpsmen on deck—lots of wounded up there. Then I figured somebody oughta come back for Lassiter, but there was an explosion, over by where his cot was."

"No sign of him now."

"Not likely there'd be."

"Can you move?"

"You may not be the craziest white motherfucker I ever saw, but you are surely the dumbest. Sir."

"You mean—if you could move—"

"If I could move I would not be on this sinking son of a bitch, yes, sir."

"Then maybe I better lend you a hand."

"Start with gettin' this fuckin' beam off me."

Pete gripped the end of the beam and lifted, putting his back and legs into it as best he could at that angle. The beam budged, barely. When he let it back down, Washington shook his head and grinned without humor.

"Motherfucker's broken," Washington said, meaning his leg. "Never be able to move well enough, even if we get it out. . . . Get your white ass off this ship before it goes Fourth of July on you, son."

"Giving orders to a superior officer now?"

"Uppity, ain't I?"

Pete got up and moved through the shadows looking for a bar or chunk of wood strong enough to pry the beam up. Finally he found a shorter section of beam, which would have to do.

He stepped over and around assorted rubble, returned to Washington, and was about to wedge the smaller piece under the beam when the ship rolled, throwing Pete across the room, smacking him into a bulkhead.

Getting his breath, making sure he hadn't broken anything himself, Pete could see water flooding in now through the ragged cavity in the hull. Soon he was soaked, and the water was threatening to engulf the sad remains of sick bay. He threw a desperate glance toward Washington, still sitting, his shoulders barely above the lapping seawater.

"You okay?" Washington called.

"Haven't…haven't been hit that hard since Simpson lost homecoming."

"Ha! Listen, that roll knocked the beam off my leg."

"Can you get up? Can you hobble out of here?"

"I dunno. I don't think so."

"I knocked my knee. Not broken, but it's the same one I caught shrapnel in…I don't think I'm much better off." Pete got up and limped and sloshed over to Washington, the water to the sailor's neck now. Pete held out a hand and Sarge took it; together they pooled enough strength to get Sarge on his good leg, an arm slung around Pete's shoulder.

Sarge shook his head. "I dunno, man. Maybe you have a better shot at this on your steam."

"I don't think I can hack it alone, buddy. True what they say about colored guys?"

"That we dance good?"

"That you can't swim."

"Shit, I can learn. Even with one pin broke."

"Okay, then. Means all we got to do is get over to that door the Japs made for us.…"

Together, each with an arm around the other's shoulder, they waded over to the hole, pushing against the force of water rushing in.

They were next to the ragged-edged aperture when Washington said, "Captain done it, right?"

"Right."

"What happen to him?"

"I shot him in the back."

Washington grinned. "You're learning."

And Washington dove out onto the water, paddling against the current, and when the seaman had cleared the ragged teeth of the opening, Pete dove in after, and in seconds they were clear.

The two men swam alongside each other, both using mostly their arms, trying to put as much distance as they could between themselves and the dying *Liberty Hill Victory* before it could blow itself and them to heaven or hell, whichever the case might be.

But the USS *Powderkeg* never blew—true, her death could have been more dignified, as she slowly turned over and showed her belly to the sun, before slipping under. But the girl never lost her temper.

Thirty yards from where the ship slipped under, Pete—pausing with Sarge to tread the warm, bath-like water and catch some breath—spotted the lifeboat: Rosetti in the nose, Big Brown guiding the rudder. Weakly, Pete waved until Rosetti noticed him and they rowed over. While they waited, Pete slowly scanned the sky—the surviving Jap planes were gone, their work done.

The lifeboat was nearly full, but they would make room for two more. Big Brown came forward to help Rosetti while one of the others tended the rudder. Washington with his broken leg took some doing, but thank God for Big Brown, who lifted Sarge from the choppy water as if a child to set down gently within the boat.

Still in the water, Pete asked, "Connor make it?"

Rosetti nodded and grinned. "Got his own little command. He's trolling for stragglers, too. What about Egan? They say he went off his nut."

"Later," Pete begged off. "For now, just say... he didn't make it."

"Think we saved most of the crew," Rosetti said.

"Good work, Vince."

Big Brown hoisted Pete out of the water and into the boat and helped him over to where he could sit next to Rosetti, who saluted.

"Welcome aboard, Captain," Rosetti said.

FIFTEEN

AUGUST 27, 1989

On a beautiful sunny Sunday, just as morning was blurring into afternoon, a blue rental Pontiac Bonneville rolled to the curb in front of a small brick house with a well-tended lawn in a middle-class neighborhood on the South Side of Chicago. A concrete driveway to the left of the house led around to a two-car garage. Flowers accented areas under the windows and neatly trimmed evergreen bushes guarded either side of the walk.

Pete Maxwell had not been this nervous since that similar summer day in '44 when the Fantail Four had rolled up in a Jeep to goggle at a company of African Americans doing calisthenics on Treasure Island.

Kay squeezed his arm. "They could be eating lunch. Really kind of terrible just to drop in. You sure about this?"

Pete shrugged. "Number's unlisted. Must still be working as a cop."

"Honey, he has to be over seventy—he *couldn't* still be working."

"He might've made enemies. It'll be fine. We're friends."

But the friends hadn't seen each other since the war ended, and the Christmas cards had stopped maybe fifteen years ago and the friendly notes five years before that. Yet as with all men of his generation who served, the war, the experiences, good and bad, the friends he made, were ever with Pete. He often talked to Kay and their son about those days, but it was always funny stories, or things he was proud of, like going to bat for the crew and getting them food or shoes or comic books to learn from.

Never about the Zero and Kate attacks, or the murders, or the other nerve-rattling ordeals that he still dreamed about, at least once a month.

The inquiry into the murders aboard the *Liberty Hill Victory* was a behind-closed-doors affair at Tarawa, where various crew members had been recuperating; the surviving three of the Fantail Four, and a handful of others in the know, were questioned individually, advised that the matter was a confidential one, and told any further discussion of these events among the participants (much less the public) would result in serious ramifications. Pete had realized this was a cover-up, of course, but also understood what a wartime public relations nightmare revealing the truth would have been.

No official statement was made, although Orville Monroe and Willie Wilson received posthumous Silver Stars for their heroism in the Jap Zero attack. The captain's record was left unblemished, although the lack of any posthumous recognition may have left a question mark in the minds of some. Years later Richard Driscoll's family made a political fuss about Dick's lack of recognition, but—for reasons Pete never knew yet could guess—that had fizzled.

In a way Pete's war had just begun on the *Liberty Hill*. Pete was promoted to lieutenant commander and awarded the Navy Cross; Sarge Washington had made petty officer and won the Silver Star. They and the rest of the surviving crew were transferred to Logistic Support Company 507 and posted on an APL, a nameless hotel ship minus engines in the bay between Leyte and Samar. Again they'd been sitting ducks, and this time Pete, Vince Rosetti, and Ben Connor (both promoted to lieutenant, junior grade) were joined by a handful of other white officers and the contingent of colored sailors—actually stevedores—had swollen to six hundred.

Because the trio of officers had the respect of the core crew from the *Liberty Hill*—and thanks to Sarge for his help and leadership—the 507 achieved a number-one rating and never had a general or summary court-martial, which the other white-led Negro companies had all the time.

They got out of the car, Kay silver-haired but still petite and pretty in her yellow-and-red sundress, and Pete with salt-and-pepper hair and a paunch but crisply dressed in a dark blue golf shirt and lighter blue slacks and white patent-leather shoes. Arm in arm—Pete lugging the ancient battered cornet case by its frayed handle—the couple headed up the concrete walk toward the house.

Pete swallowed, gathered courage, and rang the bell. Five seconds passed.

Then the inside door swung open and a tall black woman with gray hair, beautiful features and a well-maintained figure peered at them through the screen. She wore the floral-patterned dress she'd probably worn to church that morning, an apron snugged around her waist.

And Pete could tell from her expression—a sort of stunned confusion—that not many white people came knocking at their door.

"Yes?" she asked, guarded but friendly.

"Mrs. Washington?"

"Hmm-hmmm."

"I'm not sure how you call your husband, but we called him Sarge. Any chance he's home?"

She tilted her head, studied Pete and Kay through the mesh, obviously puzzled by their presence. "May I say who's asking for him? We're just sitting down to eat—"

Kay gave her husband a nudge and a sideways look.

"Oh, I'm sorry," he blurted, flushing. "Would you just tell him that Pete Maxwell stopped by to pay his—"

"Lieutenant Maxwell?" she asked, eyes wide. "My lord, you *do* exist. I was beginning to think you were a figment of my husband's vivid imagination."

Behind her a deep voice, with a hint of irritation, called, "What *is* it, Dolores?"

She was smiling, a very lovely smile, and shaking her head; her eyes were curtained with tears. "I believe it's someone you'd like to see, Liss."

So that was what she called him: Liss, short for Ulysses. No wife could call her husband "Sarge," after all; what, and risk being outranked?

Sarge Washington, in a white short-sleeved shirt and dark slacks and maroon slippers, eased past his wife, opening the screen door to step out on the porch and face his past.

The two men both smiled, and the wives would later say the pair had seemed embarrassed; they would correct that: ashamed was the right word, that they'd let so many years slip by, as if their friendship hadn't been one of the most important parts of both their lives.

Sarge had a paunch, too, but age hadn't stooped him and he had his hair (steel-gray now) and still looked like he could handle anybody this side of Big Brown.

Pete said, "Sorry to just drop by," and held out his hand for Sarge to shake.

Sarge did, but then the two sailors hugged each other without shame, each clapping the other on the back and laughing so as not to cry.

Mrs. Washington was dabbing her eyes with a tissue, but Kay was just taking this in, fascinated, as if standing at an exhibit in a museum.

From within the house, another deep voice called: "Mom! Dad! Are we gonna eat or not?"

Despite the "Mom" and "Dad," this was no child, or at least was a fully grown one—a muscular black man about thirty-five, in white short-sleeved shirt and blue tie and black trousers, filling the doorway now. "Dad?"

"Meet Peter Maxwell," Sarge said, gesturing as if to the next act on the bill.

"Mr. Maxwell from the ship?" Sarge's son's expression indicated seeing Pete was about the same as having some other mythic figure, Davy Crockett or Paul Bunyan maybe, step from stories onto the Washington family doorstep.

"Yes, son. White boy who saved my life."

"Is *that* how he tells it?" Pete said. "Heck, he saved *my* life!"

Truth was, both men suddenly remembered the reality that they'd helped each other out of that ruptured sick bay; each, in the telling over the years, had turned the other into the hero of the piece.

Extending her hand to Sarge's wife with a smile, Kay said, "I'm Mrs. Maxwell—please call me Kay."

Pete, embarrassed, said, "I'm sorry, honey...."

"Pleased to meet you, Kay. I'm Dolores. Please, lovely as it is out here, you *must* come in."

Once inside, where chugging window air conditioners provided a near chill, Pete shook hands with Sarge's son.

"I'm Willie," the younger Washington said.

Pete and Sarge traded glances.

Dolores said, "He's our youngest. Named after a friend of—"

"Ours," Pete interrupted gently. "Great sax player, Willie Wilson."

"So I hear," Willie Washington said.

Dolores said, "You know, our other son should be along any moment now—in fact, when I heard the bell ring, I thought you were him."

Sarge said, "We're about to have Sunday dinner."

Quickly Kay said, "I told this husband of mine we should call first. I'm so sorry to intrude..."

"You're not intruding," Dolores said. "I hope you'll join us. I always make plenty—we're a family lives on leftovers."

"Sorry, Sarge," Pete said, as they trooped after Dolores and Kay into the dining room. "You were unlisted, and I couldn't find you."

"That's okay. I always was the detective on the team."

"Hey, I did all right."

Sarge grinned. "Yeah, you did."

They'd barely reached the dining room when the doorbell rang again, and Sarge went and got it. Moments later he was ushering in another formidable-looking black man, looking rather military in a policeman's uniform. His dark hair was cut close to the scalp, graying a little, and he greeted the strangers with his father's faintly mocking smile.

Sarge said, "This is our oldest son—Peter."

No more words were necessary. Pete crossed to shake the man's hand, meeting his forty-something namesake.

"Are the stories true?" Peter Washington asked.

"Probably not," Pete said, and smiled.

"I went into my pop's field because it was as close to a family business as we've got. Willie there's a cop, too, you know."

"I didn't."

"But for what it's worth, Pop seems prouder of his time in the Navy than anything he ever accomplished on the street. You know, he retired an inspector? Worked downtown, last ten or twelve years."

"Didn't know that, either."

"Why didn't you old boys keep in touch better?"

"Because I'm almost as dumb as your dad."

Peter Washington grinned. "Well, I guess that's possible."

They sat down at a table that fairly filled the room and ate a great big wonderful meal of roast beef and mashed potatoes and lima beans and (the only dish Kay might not have served) black-eyed peas. Everybody allowed Pete and Sarge to carry the conversation, but the two men did not reminisce, strictly catching up.

The Maxwells had one son, who somehow made a living writing mystery novels, and Sarge said with pride that his two "flatfoot" offspring also were "weekend warrior" musicians like their old man. They both played in a combo with their pop, Willie on drums and Peter on stand-up bass.

"Since I retired," Sarge said, spooning a second helping of mashed potatoes onto his plate, "I been booking bands. There's a big band we all play with, for that kinda gig, and a small combo for clubs and weddings. And my sons have a little soul act that their pop ain't hip enough to play in, but *is* hip enough to take 10 percent of."

Willie said, "Pop's making better money booking our bands than he did on the PD."

"The department never was about earning money, son," Sarge said.

"Tell me about it!" Dolores said, which got a nice laugh all around.

Sarge asked, "Are you still teaching school, Pete, in some little Iowa podunk? Last I heard you were."

"I did that for ten years," Pete said, "and loved it. Serenity High put on the first high school productions of *Oklahoma!* and *Carousel* in the nation—you'd've liked 'em."

"Some nice tunes in those shows. But what since?"

"Personnel manager in industry—office equipment. It's all right—make good money and work with people, and I *like* people ... mostly."

Sarge chuckled. "Yeah, there are exceptions. No music? Wasn't that a cornet case you set down inside my door?"

"Oh, I'm still active. I direct a church choir, and I've directed a men's choral group since right after the war. We've got a men's quartet, and I'm in it, that would put the Fantail Four to shame."

"I'm sure you're good, Pete," Sarge said, and sipped coffee. "But I doubt any four white boys could ever sing sweeter than the Fantail Four. You got no idea what that meant to us, you four fellas entertaining a bunch of lowdown colored sailors like us."

"We were afraid you'd be offended—spoofing the Mills Brothers, Ink Spots, and all."

"No. I think if there was any time in the war when I really felt that color wall come down, it was that night you guys sang and clowned around for us, like we were friends."

Pete shrugged. "Well... we were."

"Whatever happened to Ben? I know he stayed with Jack Benny."

"Yeah, Ben was lucky. I think Jack Benny must've been the only radio show to really carry over to TV. He wrote for all the big shows—staff writer on *McHale's Navy,* remember that? Did a bunch of *I Dream of Jeannie* and *Bewitched,* too."

"Is he... still with us?"

"No, he died a couple years ago. I, uh..." Pete risked a smile. "... I believe his fourth wife was a little too much for him. She was an actress about twenty years younger than him."

"So he died happy?"

Dolores slapped her husband's arm. "Ulysses Grant! Be respectful."

Pete laughed, and asked, "So whatever happened to Big Brown?"

"Would you believe it," Sarge said, "he turned up at a club gig here in town, maybe five years ago. Ol' Simon Brown went back to college! Got his master's."

"Well, he was smart enough."

"Sure was. Got his doctorate, became a professor of sociology at Cleveland State. Did a little volunteer football coaching on the side. What about Mr. Rosetti?"

"Why we're here," Pete said, and he smiled again but there was no joy in it. "Buried him Friday, out in Los Angeles. He stayed in law enforcement a while, then started up a security firm. Heart attack took him out."

"Kills more cops than gangbangers."

Pete nodded. "Our flight back to Iowa came through O'Hare. I talked Kay into us renting a car to drive home. I had something I had to do here, first."

"Yeah? What?"

"Well ... I'm doing it, Sarge."

The two men looked at each other, without expression, unless you noticed their eyes.

"Ever think about them days, Mr. Maxwell?"

For the first time today Sarge had lapsed into the colored street patois Pete had heard so often on the ship.

"Sure. Then maybe, after a few years, a little less. But lately ... little *more,* maybe. Can't help it, you know, when those names turn up in the obits."

Sarge nodded. "It was hell."

Dolores seemed about to scold her husband for language, but didn't.

Pete said, "Yeah, it was. But we looked out for each other."

Sarge chuckled. "Like that song you fellas sang—that Ink Spots tune. ... 'I'll Get By ... '"

Pete nodded.

"Summed it up," Sarge said. "Out of the whole damn war, that's the one time I *like* to think about. How we all ate together, officers, enlisted, black, white. All just workin' men that night. For some of those boys, that was the first night in their whole lives they got treated like real men. Fantail Four did that, you, Mr. Connor, Mr. Rosetti ... yeah, even poor Mr. Driscoll."

Dick Driscoll ... of all of them, the only one who remained young and vibrant, who had never had to suffer the indignities of aging. ...

"That cornet case," Sarge said, "carryin' it around ain't your idea of exercise, is it?"

Pete smiled faintly. "No. I played taps at Vince Rosetti's funeral. Kinda thought it might come in handy here, too."

"Hell, I feel fine," Sarge said.

Dolores slapped his arm again. "Liss! … You folks have room for pie? I got apple, and sweet potato."

"Too full right now," Pete said, and Kay agreed, adding, "But that does sound delicious."

"Well, can you stay and visit a while?" Dolores asked, getting up, starting to clear the table. "We can have coffee and pie a little later."

"Sure," Kay said, "and let me help you with that. …"

Sarge, Pete, and the two younger Washingtons helped clear the table, and then Sarge said, "Want to see where we make the magic?"

In the garage, Sarge flipped the wall switch on four overhead bulbs. No cars were in the garage, just a drum kit, upright piano, stand-up bass, a few amps and assorted electric instruments, as well as a master sound board and microphones for recording. Sarge moved to the piano, young Peter to the bass, and Willie to the drums.

Pete knelt and opened his cornet case, much as he had one distant night in a club called the Silver Slipper. As Sarge and his sons got settled behind their instruments, the two women came in and sat on folding chairs as if the four men were on stage.

Pete put the mute in his cornet. He began to play Taps, getting odd looks from the younger Washingtons but a knowing smile from Sarge. The somber funereal tribute ended on C and Pete transformed that C into the first note of an equally mournful "I'll Get By (As Long as I Have You)."

Willie kicked in with a drum pick-up after the first phrase, and the bass and piano fell right in, the tempo immediately accelerating to a nice bounce. They stayed with the melody two times through, then Pete took a solo, a lively, fluid, quick-fingered jazz variation that didn't entirely lose that nice melody, and Sarge followed with deft, perfectly chosen notes, little Basie-style tinkles that made Pete grin.

They took it home pretty big, almost Dixieland-style, and Pete thought about the Bix Festival back in Iowa, wondering if maybe he could get the Washington Combo to come out and play (and let him sit in).

Finally Pete landed, and they were doing a big finish when he turned the last C of "I'll Get By" back into the first note of Taps and played one more tribute to the men of the USS *Powderkeg*.

Then, after an hour or so of jamming, the musicians followed the two women into the house for coffee and pie—both apple *and* sweet potato. Room at the table for both.

A TIP OF THE CAP

On September 16, 1999, I sat down with my father—Max A. Collins, Sr.—to record his memories about life as a lieutenant (j.g.) in the U.S. Navy during World War II. The interview was lengthy and detailed. My father, who'd been suffering from lupus, died on February 23, 2000.

I had heard snippets of Dad's wartime experiences, and had decided perhaps as early as the 1980s that I would eventually base a book on his time as one of a handful of young white officers in charge of a large body of black sailors. My father had the usual prejudices of his generation, and I heard him tell a racially oriented joke now and then; but I also know he was extremely proud of how well he got along with the black sailors, including his efforts to teach them English and see to it that they were not treated as second-class citizens in any way.

Nonetheless, this is a work of fiction, and my father, unlike Pete Maxwell, was never involved in a murder inquiry. But his experiences in the Navy were significant—although the stateside Port Chicago disaster has been much written about, black sailors performing their dangerous work with munitions in the Pacific Theater has gone largely unrecorded.

My father's love and exceptional talent for music is reflected here, as well, though I must insist that he is not Pete Maxwell, and my mother (Patricia Collins) is not Kay, however much I may have plundered both their lives for details and color.

The several-hour interview with my dad was transcribed by Stephanie Keenan; thank you, Steph, for the hard work as well as the lovely comments about what a classy guy my father had been in those war years.

If my father deserves my biggest debt of thanks, my research associate, Matthew V. Clemens, comes in a close second. He helped flesh out the plot in brainstorming sessions, and put together a story treatment (incorporating his extensive research) from which I could work. Matt and I have co-written a dozen or so short stories (see our collection *The Lolita Complex and Other Tales of Sex and Violence,* published by Twilight Tales), and he has assisted me on numerous TV tie-in projects.

Matt's research efforts for this novel included a trip to Richmond, California, where he toured the *Red Oak Victory* and took hundreds of reference photos for our use. I wish to thank the Richmond Museum of History, owners of the real ship that serves as the setting for this book. The *Red Oak Victory* was originally constructed at Kaiser's Richmond Shipyard #1 in 1944. Back home again, she serves as a floating museum and is slowly being restored to her original specs by volunteers (at a cost of three million dollars still in the process of being raised).

We would also like to thank retired San Rafael police captain, Jerry Souza, who provided literature and diagrams and took Matthew to places in the ship that the general public never gets to see; Jeffrey Copeland, author of *Inman's War;* George Allen, OSM USN Ret.; Mark Ziegler EMCM (SW) USN Ret.; and documentary filmmaker Elaine Holliman.

From my earliest impulse to develop a suspense story from my father's experiences, I was guided by my love for two novels about the Navy in World War II: Thomas Heggen's *Mister Roberts* (1946) and Herman Wouk's *The Caine Mutiny* (1951). I noticed, very early on, that they were essentially the same story with parallel casts, the former a dark comedy, the latter a wonderful melodrama.

Tragically, Iowa-born Heggen wrote only that one novel (and co-authored the famous play adaptation) before his apparent suicide at thirty-one. Wouk adapted his novel for the stage, as well *(The Caine Mutiny Court-Martial)*, and has, of course, continued on as one of our most intelligent and strangely underrated authors of serious popular fiction. While I have no illusion that this work is in any way on their level, I acknowledge these novels and their authors as an inspiration.

Vital to this book were two volumes: *Better Than Good: A Black Sailor's War 1943–1945*, Adolph W. Newton with Winston Eldridge (1999); and *The Port Chicago Mutiny*, Robert L. Allen (1993). Also consulted were *The Divine Wind*, Captain Rikihei Inoguchi and Commander Tadashi Nakajima with Roger Pineau (1958); *Chicago's Two Gun Pete* (1988), Jerry Jones; *The Naval Officer's Guide* (1943), Arthur A. Ageton, Commander, USN; *Proudly We Served: The Men of the* USS *Mason* (1995), Mary Pat Kelly; *The Negro Handbook* (1947), edited by Florence Murray; and *Black Metropolis* (1945), St. Clair Drake and Horace R. Cayton. Also helpful were the WPA Guides for California and Illinois.

In addition, I screened both *Caine Mutiny* movies (the classic 1954 Edward Dmytryk-directed theatrical feature and the lesser-known but interesting 1988 Robert Altman–directed TV movie) as well as *Mutiny*, the 1999 NBC Port Chicago docudrama and a concurrent History Channel documentary, *The Port Chicago Mutiny*. John Ford, Joshua Logan, and Mervyn LeRoy's film *of Mister Roberts* (1955) was also screened.

Thanks to my longtime research associate, George Hagenauer, for taking a look at the manuscript; editor Sarah Durand, for her usual support; my friend and agent Dominick Abel, for his encouragement; and my wife (and in-house editor) Barbara Collins, whose numerous good suggestions for this novel included spotting a major omission. A captain never had a finer first mate.

ABOUT THE AUTHOR

Max Allan Collins has earned an unprecedented twenty-two Private Eye Writers of America "Shamus" Award nominations, winning for his Nathan Heller novels *True Detective* (1983) and *Stolen Away* (1991 as well as the PWA "Eye" award for Life Achievement (2006). In 2012, his Nathan Heller saga was honored with the PWA "Hammer" award for making a major contribution to the private-eye genre. In 2017 he was named a Grand Master by the Mystery Writers of America.

His graphic novel *Road to Perdition* (1998) is the basis of the Academy Award-winning Tom Hanks film, followed by two acclaimed prose sequels (also published by Brash Books) and several graphic novels. He has created a number of innovative suspense series, including Mallory, Quarry, Eliot Ness, and the "Disaster" novels. He is completing a number of "Mike Hammer" novels begun by the late Mickey Spillane; his full-cast audio novel Mike Hammer: *The Little Death*, with Stacy Keach, won a 2011 Audie for best original work.

His comics credits include the syndicated strip *Dick Tracy*, and his own *Ms. Tree*, and *Batman*.

For five years, he was the sole writer on the novel series based on the popular TV show *CSI: Crime Scene Investigation* (and its spin-off's), writing ten best-selling books, four graphic novels, and four award-winning video games. His tie-in books have appeared on the *USA Today* best-seller list nine times and the New York Times list three times, including *Saving Private Ryan, Air Force One, and American Gangster,* which won the Best Novel "Scribe" Award in 2008 from the International Association of Media Tie-In Writers.

As an independent filmmaker in the Midwest, Collins has written and directed four features, including the Lifetime movie *Mommy* (1996); and he scripted *The Expert,* a 1995 HBO World Premiere, as well as the film-festival favorite *The Last Lullaby* (2009). His documentary *Caveman: V.T. Hamlin & Alley Oop* (2008) has appeared on PBS and on DVD, and his documentary *Mike Hammer's Mickey Spillane* (1998) appears on the Criterion Collection DVD and Blu-ray of *Kiss Me Deadly.* His innovative Quarry novels are the basis of a Cinemax TV series, for which he provided the scripts.

His play *Eliot Ness: An Untouchable Life* was nominated for an Edgar Award in 2004 by the Mystery Writers of America; a film version, written and directed by Collins, was released on DVD and appeared on PBS stations in 2009.

Collins lives in Iowa with his wife, writer Barbara Collins; as "Barbara Allan," they have collaborated on nine novels, including the successful "Trash 'n' Treasures" mysteries, with *Antiques Flee Market* (2008) winning the *Romantic Times* Best Humorous Mystery Novel award of 2009.

Made in United States
North Haven, CT
13 October 2021

10299636R00166